Praise for Beth Cornelison

"Steady pacing and a solid plot, complete with a dramatic, passionate ending, are all hallmarks of one terrific romance."
—*RT Book Reviews* on *Colton Cowboy Protector*

"Cornelison has written a page turner that is truly enjoyable from beginning to end."
—*Fresh Fiction* on *Cowboy's Texas Rescue*

"A tough, protective hero is at the center of this suspenseful story. Good pacing, expert storytelling and sweet chemistry makes this story a page-turner."
—*RT Book Reviews* on *Protecting Her Royal Baby*

Praise for Colleen Thompson

"Sizzling chemistry and heartfelt love between Dylan and Hope make for one engaging story."
—*RT Book Reviews* on *The Colton Heir*

"RITA® Award finalist Thompson takes the reader on a roller-coaster ride full of surprising twists and turns in this exceptional novel of romantic suspense."
—*Publishers Weekly* (starred review)

"Equal parts suspense and romance, this fast-paced story is filled with plenty of action and intrigue. Vulnerable, genuine characters and an interesting mystery make for a thrilling read."
—*RT Book Reviews* on *Lone Star Redemption*

BETH CORNELISON

started writing stories as a child when she penned a tale about the adventures of her cat, Ajax. A Georgia native, she received her bachelor's degree in public relations from the University of Georgia. After working in public relations for a little more than a year, she moved with her husband to Louisiana, where she decided to pursue her love of writing fiction.

Since that first time, Beth has written many more stories of adventure and romantic suspense and has won numerous honors for her work, including a coveted Golden Heart Award in romantic suspense from Romance Writers of America. She is active on the board of directors for the North Louisiana Storytellers and Authors of Romance (NOLA STARS) and loves reading, traveling, *Peanuts'* Snoopy and spending downtime with her family.

She writes from her home in Louisiana, where she lives with her husband, one son and two cats who think they are people. Beth loves to hear from her readers. You can write to her at PO Box 5418, Bossier City, LA 71171, or visit her website, www.bethcornelison.com.

COLLEEN THOMPSON

After beginning her career writing historical romance novels, in 2004 Colleen Thompson turned to writing the contemporary romantic suspense she loves. Since then, her work has been honored with a Texas Gold Award, along with nominations for a RITA® Award, a Daphne du Maurier Award and multiple reviewers' choice honors. She has also received starred reviews from *RT Book Reviews* and *Publishers Weekly*. A former teacher living with her family in the Houston area, Colleen has a passion for reading, hiking and dog rescue. Visit her online at www.colleen-thompson.com.

COWBOY CHRISTMAS RESCUE

Beth Cornelison and Colleen Thompson

HARLEQUIN® ROMANTIC SUSPENSE

ISBN-13: 978-0-373-27942-5

Cowboy Christmas Rescue

Copyright © 2015 by Harlequin Books S.A.

The publisher acknowledges the copyright holders of the individual works as follows:

Rescuing the Witness
Copyright © 2015 by Beth Cornelison

Rescuing the Bride
Copyright © 2015 by Colleen Thompson

Recycling programs for this product may not exist in your area.

Printed in U.S.A.

www.Harlequin.com

CONTENTS

RESCUING THE WITNESS   7
Beth Cornelison

RESCUING THE BRIDE   143
Colleen Thompson

Dear Readers,

Cowboy Christmas Rescue is a story that was in the works for many months before it came to fruition. I was intrigued by the idea of working with another author to show two sides of one dramatic event, and Colleen Thompson's name was at the top of the list of authors to tackle this project with me. I'd met Colleen at writers' conferences and knew she had a great storytelling voice. More important, I knew from working with her on continuities in the past that we collaborated well and could share ideas and build on each other's creative energy.

Naturally, I was thrilled when she accepted my challenge to write a 2-in-1 story. We both had projects in the works that needed attention, but when our calendars cleared, we hit the ground running. I, for one, had a blast working out the intertwining details and parallel stories. *Cowboy Christmas Rescue* is the result, a story set in a place Colleen's fans will be familiar with: Rusted Spur, Texas.

Christmas nuptials, dicey winter weather bearing down on Rusted Spur and brokenhearted former lovers thrown together at the wedding ceremony. What could go wrong? In *Rescuing the Witness*, Kara Pearson and Brady McCall find themselves in the midst of a perfect storm of danger, intrigue...and a second chance at lasting love.

Enjoy!

Beth Cornelison

RESCUING THE WITNESS

Beth Cornelison

To Colleen Thompson—thanks for sharing
Rusted Spur and making this project so much fun!

Chapter 1

She'd known seeing Brady today was inevitable. He was, after all, one of the groomsmen. She'd also known seeing him would be difficult. One didn't fall out of love with a man like Brady McCall easily. She'd just never imagined it would be *this* hard.

Kara Pearson pressed a hand to her stomach, trying to calm the swirl of acid gnawing at her and hoping to avoid his detection as she wended her way through the crowd at the wedding. Despite reasons to be "jolly," like Christmas being a week away, and her good friends' nuptials, Kara was finding it hard to feel festive this year. Not only had Christmases been difficult for her since her parents had died, but this year she was mourning her broken relationship with the man she'd hoped to marry.

"There are a couple seats on the back row," she said to Hannah Winslow, her "plus one" and moral support for the wedding.

Hannah gave her a withering glance. "The back row? Really? How long are you going to hide from Brady?"

"Until I die or until it doesn't feel like I'm being gored by a bull when I talk to him. Whichever comes first." She tipped her head toward the back corner seats and tugged on Hannah's sleeve. "Come on. Before someone else takes them."

The Wheeler Ranch bustled with more activity than Santa's workshop on Christmas Eve, especially in light of the last-minute change of venue for the wedding festivities. The water pipes in the restroom for the ranch lodge, where the ceremony and reception had been set to take place, had sprung a massive leak that morning and flooded the building.

At first light today, Kara had responded to a frantic text from her friend April, the bride, to help relocate chairs, flowers and sound equipment as water gushed under the bathroom door and soaked the carpet of the lodge.

A few crazy hours later, the reception had been moved to Sal's Diner, the only place available at the last minute in tiny Rusted Spur, Texas, that could accommodate the caterer. The ceremony itself had simply been shifted outside to the ranch yard. Thankfully, the Texas Panhandle was enjoying one of the unseasonably warm December days that Southern states boasted on occasion.

But the balmy warmth came with a price. The pleasant temperature was the result of an encroaching cold front, compacting all the warm air in its path as it bulldozed into Texas. A line of violent thunderstorms was creeping in from the west, and the ceremony was on the clock. The groom's mother, in a dither to finish before the storms hit, waved her hands, hurrying people to take their seats.

Around the ranch yard, guests assembled, many of whom she recognized as clients of the large-animal veterinary clinic where she worked as a vet's assistant. Near the front, musicians tuned up, and behind her at the barn, ranch hands decked out a pair of first-class cutting horses with black-and-white ribbons and satin drapes in preparation for the bridal couple's departure from the ceremony.

"You okay?" Hannah asked.

"I've been better. The drama this morning didn't help my nervous stomach."

Hannah gave Kara's hand a quick squeeze. "You can do this. But…if you must toss your cookies, please remember these are new Kate Spade heels. Clearance sale or not, they still cost me my grocery money for the month."

Kara met her friend's crooked smile with her own. "I'll keep that in mind."

Hannah shoulder-bumped her. "Hey, you got this. And you look quite eye-catching, by the way."

Kara draped her coat and purse on the back of her chair, then tugged discreetly on the skirt of her red patterned maxi dress. It might be in the seventies now, but by the time the reception was over, the temperature was supposed to be closer to thirty-five. "Thanks. But eye-catching wasn't what I was going for. I was hoping for simple, trying to blend in. If April and Nate weren't such good friends, I'd probably be home now."

Closing her eyes, she mentally steeled herself and willed her queasy stomach to settle. She could have skipped the wedding, sure. But April Redding had been her friend since high school. More recently, Kara had grown close to the groom, Nate Wheeler, primarily because of the rodeo accident that had ended his bull-riding career. He claimed she'd saved his life—and maybe there was some truth to that—but she'd only been doing what rodeo clowns were supposed to do. She'd been well-trained for her weekend job as a bull-fighter. She'd distracted the seventeen-hundred-pound beast that had crushed Nate while the medics swooped in to help the injured rider.

Kara heaved an agitated sigh. She'd rather go up against that injured and angry bull again than face Brady today. And didn't that beat all? Being more intimidated by the man you'd once planned to marry than a raging Brahman?

"Everything looks so pretty," Hannah said, her tone as bright as the white ribbons, twinkling Christmas lights and red poinsettias that graced the trellis backdrop to the makeshift altar. "You'd never know the whole setup was moved here three hours ago."

"Mmm-hmm." God bless her, Hannah was trying to keep her calm and upbeat.

"I hope they start soon, though. I'm not sure how much longer that storm will hold off." Hannah cast a wary eye toward the black clouds bearing down on the ranch. "It'd be a shame to see the decorations ruined."

Kara wished they'd begin soon as well, but not because of the decorations. She simply wanted the service over before—

"Kara?" Brady's deep, powerful voice sent a bittersweet pang to her core.

—before Brady spotted her.

Rats! Of course he'd seen her. He had a sixth sense when it came to her. A homing beacon or internal Kara-GPS. It had been kinda nice when they were dating. But now, almost ten months after their breakup, his uncanny knack for tracking her down, whether around town or at a crowded ranch wedding, was becoming annoying. Okay, maybe not so uncanny. He *was* the new sheriff of Trencher County, Texas, so he probably had all sorts of gizmos and training he could use to track her.

How was a girl supposed to heal her broken heart and

move on when the object of her affection seemed to be everywhere she turned?

Taking a deep breath to quell the emotion that knotted in her throat, she faced the cowboy-turned-sheriff and tried not to let the sight of him in his tuxedo jacket, black Stetson and Tony Lama boots remind her of the wedding they'd never have.

"Hi, Brady." Damn the catch in her voice! She wanted him to believe she was fine in her new life without him, that she was moving on and had no regrets over what she'd thrown away when she left him. Kara squared her shoulders and pasted on a stiff grin. "Don't you look handsome!"

He tugged at the neck of his tuxedo shirt and gave her a lopsided smile that shot liquid heat to her core. "Glad you think so. This collar's choking me. I feel like a damn penguin." Lifting a shoulder in a dismissive shrug, he added, "Oh, well. Small price to pay to support Nate on his big day."

She nodded. "True. We can stand any discomfort for a short while when it means being there for our friends." *Like engaging in awkwardly polite conversation with your ex when he corners you.*

She introduced Hannah, her new neighbor, and he acknowledged her with a smile and a friendly greeting before shifting his gaze back to Kara and squatting beside her chair. "You look good. How have you been?"

"I'm fine." She grimaced internally at the inane and stilted conversation. Next they'd be talking about the weather.

"Good turnout today."

"Mmm-hmm. April and Nate are well-liked. I'm happy for them."

"Yeah. I'm glad people didn't let the change of location or threat of rain deter them." He nodded to the same ominous clouds Hannah had just remarked on.

Kara gave a wry laugh. *Called it.*

"Something funny?" he asked with a dented brow.

"We've resorted to talking about the weather?"

He opened his mouth as if to deny her claim, then clamped his lips shut with a scowl.

Ten months ago, this man had been half of her very being—her heart and soul and breath—and now they were reduced to banal formalities.

You have no one to blame but yourself. Breaking up with Brady was your choice. A fresh wave of guilt and remorse rolled through her belly. She knew her choice had been rooted in fear, but she couldn't see any way around the scars left by her father's death. Brady had made his choice—to take the appointment as sheriff—and she'd made hers. She couldn't, wouldn't bear the stress of knowing her boyfriend could be killed in the line of duty any day he reported to work.

"What I want to talk about is *us*. Later. Will you give me some time after the ceremony?" When she frowned, he added, "Please?"

"There's nothing to say. Nothing's changed."

"There's plenty to say, if you'll not shut me out."

"I—" The speakers screeched with feedback for a second, and the horses in a nearby pasture whinnied and tossed their manes.. Then soft music flowed over the assembled guests, indicating the ceremony was starting.

"That's my cue." Brady squeezed her arm as he stood. "Later, then?"

She flashed an uncommitted grin, which seemed to satisfy him, and watched with her heart in her throat as he strode down the center aisle to escort the mother of the groom to her chair.

"Wow. You didn't tell me how hot he was," Hannah said, fanning herself with her wedding program. "Black hair, blue eyes and a body straight out of a Hunks R Us catalog? Sweet."

Kara gave her friend a sidelong glance. "Not helping..."

"Sorry."

"I know he's gorgeous. And he's sweet and polite and witty—"

"The pig! No wonder you broke up with him!" Hannah gave her a teasing wink.

"Hannah!" she grated under her breath. "You're supposed to be supporting me today, not shoving me back into his arms. I told you why I left him. He took the interim sheriff position without any consideration of my feelings. And when I explained my concerns about the job, he dismissed my reasons as trivial. But my fears aren't trivial! My dad died in the line of duty."

She suppressed a shudder as the dark memories clawed at her. With a firm shake of her head, she shoved the bleak images down. "I don't want to live like my mother did, always wondering if her husband would come home safely at night, jumping every time the phone rang...and eventually having her worst fears realized." She swiped at the tears that bloomed in her eyes. "I can't do it."

Hannah rubbed her arm. "I'm sorry, sweetie. I didn't mean to minimize your pain. It just...seems like there should be a way for you two to work things out. If only—"

"Shh!" the lady behind them hissed.

Hannah scowled at the woman, but before she could retort, the processional music started. The first bridesmaids in their stunning red dresses started down the aisle. The assembled guests stood for the procession, and a pang of regret plucked her heart. April had given Kara the choice of being a bridesmaid or not, understanding her situation with Brady. Kara had declined, knowing that as part of the wedding party, she'd have been thrown together with

Brady time and again throughout the wedding activities. On top of her anxiety and heartache seeing Brady today, her chest clenched with disappointment and guilt, knowing she'd let her friend down.

But perhaps more important, she'd let herself down, allowing her emotions to control her life and sway her choices. She didn't want her decisions going forward to be guided by her heartache over Brady or her grief over her father.

She was roused from her morose musings as the bride glided gracefully past her. April's auburn hair was swept up in an attractive hairdo, and she was a vision in her wedding dress with Christmas-red trim. The dress was a perfect choice, adding a Christmassy feel to the ceremony while the A-line shape discreetly covered the secret April had only shared with her closest friends and family. She was having Nate's baby.

April looked beautiful, but a nervous tic tugged at the corner of her friend's lips. Had Kara not known her as well as she did, she might not have noticed the stiff discomfort in her smile. Earlier in the week, April had expressed her dismay over how the invitation list and reception plans had grown, but she'd granted her future in-laws their requests in a spirit of cooperation and good will. Add to that the last-minute crisis of burst pipes and a hasty relocation for the whole affair, and it was no wonder April looked stressed.

Kara turned her attention to the makeshift altar, to gauge the groom's reaction to his bride. But rather than Nate's expression, her gaze locked with Brady's. His eyes held hers with an unwavering, soul-piercing intensity that sent a tremor to her core. His face reflected not joy for the wedding couple, but a deep sadness and longing. His eyes told her exactly where his thoughts had gone. Their own canceled wedding. Had she not broken up with him, they would have been married this month in a similar Christmas wedding. She would have been wearing ivory silk and carrying poinsettia blossoms and baby's breath.

When April reached the front row and took her place beside her groom, Brady, standing beside the best man, blinked hard and discreetly wiped the corner of his eye. Kara's heart jolted. Dear God, was her tough and fearless lawman tearing up? She knew he had a soft heart under his alpha-dog demeanor, but seeing this display of emotion from him, knowing she'd caused his hurt, rattled her.

"Be seated," the minister said.

A rumble of distant thunder rolled across the pastures to the west, and a nervous twitter rose from the congregation as the people took their seats.

The minister tipped his head to look toward the sky and said, "Yes, Lord. We see the storm coming, but we want to give this blessed union the ceremony it calls for."

The people chuckled, and Kara was relieved to see April crack a brighter smile.

But like the encroaching storm, Kara's gut roiled darkly. She couldn't keep her eyes from straying over and again to Brady. To his square-jawed profile, to his ebony hair curling slightly around the stiff collar of his tuxedo, and to the devastated look in his piercing blue eyes.

He tried to hide it. And to the casual observer, he probably seemed fine. But she knew this man like her own reflection. She'd broken his heart along with her own when she'd left him, and her guilt gnawed inside her with vicious teeth.

"Marriage is a joyful and sacred institution, not to be entered into lightly, but with reverence and discretion..." the minister said, and Kara curled her fingers in her lap.

She hadn't taken her breakup with Brady lightly, but every day she had new regrets. She missed him deeply. A constriction like a fist squeezing her lungs clamped Kara's chest. She couldn't breathe. *A panic attack.*

Damn it! She'd been prone to them since witnessing her father's death as a teenager. She'd had several in recent weeks. It didn't take a genius to know why, but she hated them all the same. Hated the feeling of powerlessness.

"E-excuse me," she gasped to Hannah, who gave her a curious frown.

"Kara?"

Waving a hand for Hannah to stay put, she rose quickly from her seat. Kara hurried down the center aisle, fleeing the ceremony, fleeing Brady's penetrating and heartbreaking gaze. She just needed a moment alone to put her head between her knees, to catch her breath and center herself.

More thunder rumbled, and to Kara, it sounded like mocking laughter. *Foolish girl! You're a mess! Brady's better off without your drama and baggage.*

Hot tears pricked her eyes as she hurried toward the nearby barn, famous in the county for the giant Texas flag painted on the roof. She stopped just inside the barn door where the bride and groom's horses were tethered, awaiting the couple's departure for the reception.

She stroked the nose of the dapple gray mare, bridal ribbons woven through her mane and tail, and struggled for a calming breath. The soft snuffles of the gentle horse nuzzling her hand soothed her frayed nerves. "Good girl," she whispered to the mare, feeling her pulse settle and the tightness in her lungs loosen.

A tingle of awareness pricked her neck, a sense that she was being watched, and she turned to glance back at the wedding party. Sure enough, Brady's gaze was locked on her, a frown darkening his expression. Her heart kicked like a mule, and she spun away.

With a last pat to the mare's nose, she ducked deeper

into the shadows of the barn, out of his line of sight. Another grumble of thunder shook the walls as she sank down on a bale of hay to stew. She'd never get over Brady if she kept running into him in town. Was she better off selling the family home and leaving town, starting fresh somewhere else?

Brady's hands fisted in frustration. His every impulse was to go after Kara and find out what had upset her. She'd been pale and clearly struggling to breathe. If she was ill, someone should be with her. He'd seen her motion for Hannah to stay put, but regardless of Kara's instructions, her friend should have followed. He watched with a tight jaw as Kara disappeared into the barn. Something serious had upset her if she'd felt it necessary to leave Nate and April's wedding ceremony.

He tried to get Hannah's attention in order to signal her to check on Kara. But Hannah was watching the approaching storm clouds, as were many of the wedding guests. Rain-scented wind gusted through those assembled, stirring the decorative ribbons and whipping April's veil like the tail of an angry bronc. The encroaching storm clearly weighed on the minister's mind as he read through the liturgy with haste.

Good. The sooner the ceremony ended, the sooner he could find Kara. He intended to not only find out what had upset her just now, but to get overdue answers about why she'd left him. She'd skillfully dodged his questions and his attempts to talk privately for months. That ended today.

Give her a little space, his friends had advised. *She'll come around.*

She just needs time to realize how much she loves you, had been his grandmother's unsolicited take.

Well, Brady had given Kara time and space, and he was

tired of the passive approach. Kara and he were made for each other. She had to see that, and he *would* change her mind, starting today. At the reception. He'd find Kara and insist they talk candidly.

A murmur of discontent rumbled from the assembled guests, yanking him from his deliberations and concern over Kara's departure. He turned his attention back to the bridal couple and found them staring at each other with disturbing expressions.

"April? Don't do this," Nate whispered to his bride, his confusion and hurt clear in the furrow of his brow. "What's wrong?"

Brady's pulse tripped. What was happening? He'd been so focused on Kara, he'd missed the catalyst of this interruption to the wedding.

"I'm s-sorry, Nate." April's eyes sparkled with tears, and her face crumpled with guilt and regret. The bouquet she held trembled as much as her voice. "I'm so sorry. I can't do this."

Brady's gut soured with empathy for his friend. April was jilting him? Here? Now?

"Uh…do you need a moment?" the minister stammered.

"April, honey, what is it?" Nate's father rose from the front row.

Brady shared Nate's obvious shock and disappointment, but he kept his attention on April. She pressed a hand to her stomach, and her cheeks lost their color. Her knees seemed to buckle, and she crumpled as—

Crack!

Brady tensed as the unmistakable blast of gunfire rang through the ranch yard. Immediately, he shifted into lawman mode. Reaching instinctively for his sidearm, he grumbled a curse when he remembered he wasn't wearing his gun. He scanned the unfolding scene, taking in as much detail as possible. In the next second, a second shot was fired, a large vase of flowers behind the bride shattered, and the stunned crowd, realizing what was happening, erupted in panic.

Pulling his bride to safety, Nate rushed for the cover of a nearby pecan tree. Wedding guests screamed and either ducked or ran for cover.

Brady dropped low and scuttled over to the bridal couple. April had wrapped a protective arm across her baby bump.

"Is she hurt?" he asked Nate.

"No. But that was too close for comfort."

"Agreed." Brady glanced to the minister, who'd taken cover behind the portable altar. "Reverend?"

The minister nodded. "I'm fine."

Still crouched low, Brady spotted the bullet hole that pocked the trunk of the pecan tree and followed the trajectory of the gunfire to—his gut swooped—the barn. Where Kara had disappeared only moments ago.

His heart seizing, Brady sprinted toward the barn. He dodged fleeing wedding guests as another shot reverberated over the melee. When he spied one of his deputies directing guests to the safety of the main ranch house, he shouted, "Wilhite, the shooter's in the barn! Cover the back exit…" To another uniformed deputy, in attendance to direct traffic, he ordered, "Anderson, give me your gun and call for backup!"

Anderson handed Brady his sidearm and unclipped his radio. "Dispatch, 10-33! Shots fired at Wheeler Ranch."

"Someone, help!" Nate's mother cried from the first row of chairs. "George has been shot!"

Brady stumbled to a stop and spun back toward the wedding assembly. Though a bone-deep urgency pulled him toward the barn to find Kara, his sense of duty fought a tug-of-war. The shooter, the injured man, safety of the guests…this was his first real test as the interim sheriff.

Seeing several people scurry to aid the groom's father, Brady cast another glance to Deputy Anderson. Before he could shout his order, he heard Anderson tell dispatch, "10-52! Repeat, shots fired! Send backup and ambulance—"

Another shot fired inside the barn, and ice filled Brady's veins. His feet were moving again, toward the barn, toward the woman he couldn't bear to lose. "Kara!"

The crack of rifle fire jolted Kara from her brooding. At first she'd blamed a close lightning strike for the boom that had echoed through the barn. When the sound repeated, a bolt of alarm streaked through her. The bridal couple's horses were also unsettled by the loud noises. For an instant, she wondered if the gunfire was some part of the wedding ceremony, a military-esque salute of some sort. But the screams and sounds of chaos from the wedding guests disabused her of that idea. A deep chill settled over her. Something was very wrong.

Her heartbeat thundering in an anxious cadence, she rose from the hay bale to investigate, grabbing the reins of the dappled mare to settle her.

"Easy, girl," she crooned in a hushed tone.

The shots seemed to have come from inside the barn. She'd thought she was alone, but a low, grumbled curse dragged her attention to the hayloft. Kara took a couple steps back from the horses in order to have a better angle to see who was on the upper level.

Poised at the loft doors with a tripod and scope-equipped rifle, a man in a dark T-shirt and faded jeans took aim at the wedding party. And fired another shot. Toward the bridal couple. Toward Hannah and her friends from town. *Toward Brady.*

"No!" she gasped in horror.

Hearing her, the sniper snapped his head around and locked gazes with her.

A chill slithered through her as his menacing dark eyes narrowed. Something oddly familiar about him tickled her brain. She didn't know the man, but she knew she'd never forget his sharply angled face or the deadly intent that blazed in his glare.

He let a filthy curse word fly and groped for a pistol at his side. The shock that had rooted her for precious seconds morphed into action. As the sniper swung his weapon up and squeezed off a shot, she used her bullfighter-honed skills to leap and tumble behind a plastic barrel full of water. The bullet left a gaping hole in one side of the container, and water sprayed out. Plastic was no match for a high-speed projectile, a fact borne out when the man fired again.

Kara tucked into a tight ball, just as a bullet ripped through the barrel and pinged off the steel bar of a squeeze chute behind her. Her fright kicked into survival mode, an adrenaline-fueled instinct for flight. She'd seen the sniper's face. Could identify him. Clearly his intent was to silence the only eyewitness.

Shaking to her core, Kara got her feet under her and sprang from her huddle behind the now-shredded barrel. She sprinted toward the bridal couple's horses, which kicked the ground and tossed their heads, spooked by the noise and tumult. In one deft swipe, she unclipped the dapple gray mare, then launched into the decorated saddle. Slapping the reins, she urged the horse to run.

Chapter 2

As Brady neared the big barn with the Texas flag on its roof, a gray horse charged through the alley doors. He skidded to a stop and narrowly avoided being trampled. When the horse saw him, she reared up, almost throwing the rider. Brady stumbled back a step, dodging the flailing hooves. The panicked eyes of the rider met his for one heart-stopping second. Then in a blur of gray muscle, rippling white ribbons and red dress, the horse and rider galloped away.

Red dress. Brady's pulse skipped. He blinked against the dust kicked up by the departing mare and focused on the rider. Replayed the glimpse of wide, fearful brown eyes.

"Kara!" he shouted to her retreating back. "Stop! Kara, wait!"

But she didn't. He saw her kick the mare's flank as she raced out into the vast stretches of ranch property.

"Damn." Brady spit out the curse, and his gut kicked. He needed to go after her. Not only was he worried about

Kara galloping off into the coming storm, but she was also, almost certainly, his key witness to the shooting. *Or his key suspect.*

Even as his mind rebelled against the idea that Kara could have anything to do with the shooting, the logical side of his brain couldn't ignore the fact that she'd been in the barn at the time the shots rang out. And she'd fled the scene immediately after. Until he could question her and gather more facts, he couldn't write off the possibility she was involved. Which meant he had to stop her. Bring her back for questioning.

Just inside the alley doors, he spotted the roan gelding that had been saddled and gussied up for Nate to ride to the reception. An ATV made the most sense out on the open range, but Nate's horse was so handy…

Leading with his weapon, he entered the barn and did a visual sweep. Nate's horse, Rooster Cogburn, pawed the ground restlessly, and Brady grabbed the bridle and cooed under his breath, "Whoa, buddy."

A shadow moved on the back wall.

Weapon braced, he spun around. "Sheriff! Freeze!"

"It's me, boss." Wilhite stepped into the light, his own weapon still at the ready. "I haven't found anyone in here. The shooter must have escaped out the back during all the ruckus. His rifle and tripod are in the loft."

"Keep looking. Secure the scene and don't let anyone leave the ranch grounds until a full search can be completed." Brady unclipped Rooster and climbed into the saddle. "Anderson will assist until more backup arrives." He tugged the horse's reins to turn him. "You're in charge of the scene until I get back. I'm going in pursuit of a person of interest."

Brady flicked the reins and raced out of the barn. He'd have a hard time making up the lead Kara had on him, even if Rooster was faster than the mare she'd taken off on. He leaned low over Rooster's neck and charged across the ranch yard. When he reached the edge of the first grazing pasture, he jumped the fence and cut across the field at a full gallop. He knew Rooster wouldn't be able to keep up this pace for long, but he had to close enough distance to at least know which direction Kara had gone. Setting out on Rooster may have been the most immediate option, but Brady began to regret his hasty choice. An ATV would have been better in the long term.

As Rooster ate up distance, the first fat drops of rain splattered the earth and slapped his cheeks. Ahead of him, the gray veil of a downpour reduced visibility and promised misery as he searched for Kara. More important to Brady, though, was the danger the storm posed. Lightning strikes, flash floods and high winds were among the threats he and Kara faced out on the range, unprotected in this late spring storm. But whatever the risks, he would find Kara and bring her in. And not just because she was key to finding the shooter...but because she was key to finding his future happiness. Kara was the world to him, and her leaving had gored his heart like a raging bull's horns.

Kara rode across the wild landscape of the Texas Panhandle with no particular destination in mind other than getting *away*. Away from the sniper. Away from Brady. Away from the painful memories of what she'd lost. She gave the mare free rein, so long as the horse took her anywhere but the Wheeler Ranch and the many forms of danger there. A cocktail of emotions and shock held her in a semi-trance as she rode into the encroaching storm.

Images of Brady's hurt expression replayed in her turbulent thoughts, knotting her gut. When her brain shied from memories of Brady's penetrating gaze, the sniper's hateful glare crowded her mind's eye. In her dazed state, flickers of lightning became the muzzle flash as the gunman fired at her. The crack of thunder was the echoing concussion of each shot that rang through the barn.

She didn't even notice the rainfall until it swelled to a steady, heavy cadence. Juicy drops splashed on her face and dripped from her hair. The cool rain mingled with the tears already tracking down her cheeks and soaked her maxi dress so that it stuck to her skin. She stayed in her inattentive state until a particularly loud clap of thunder shook the earth and spooked the gray mare. Her horse reared up, shaking her mane with a whinny of distress.

Caught unaware, Kara had no chance to shift her weight or tighten her grip. She tumbled awkwardly from the saddle and into a shallow stream of muddy water. Her abrupt unseating jarred her from the grip of shock and heartache.

With pain and adrenaline blasting through her, Kara rolled to avoid the prancing hooves of the agitated mare. She tried to swipe the rain from her face, but her hands were just as sopping as her face, and she only smeared mud on her cheeks. When the dapple gray started to trot off without her, Kara sprang to her feet, slipping in the shallow stream of rain runoff. Her sodden sandals were less than useless in this weather and terrain, so she kicked them off and hurried, barefooted, to catch the reins on the mare.

"Easy, girl." Kara held her hands up and cooed soothing words to the horse as she approached. She was somewhat surprised the mare had stopped...until she paused long enough to cast a glance around her. Kara groaned as she realized where she was, what had happened while she'd had her head down against the wind and rain, her brain locked in tunnel vision, replaying the frightening events at the ranch.

The mare, given no guidance other than encouragement to keep moving, had taken the path of least resistance... and wandered up the bed of a dry creek at the bottom of an arroyo. She hadn't run any farther because they were surrounded by steep, striated walls of red clay stone, shale and gypsum. The way forward was rugged and rocky with rivulets of rainwater flowing down to fill the ravine.

Hell and damnation! The worst place to be during this kind of weather was at the bottom of an arroyo, where flash floods quickly turned dry creek beds into swift and deadly rivers. She shifted her panicked gaze to the cold water she stood in. Already the flow of runoff was ankle deep and rising rapidly. Her stomach pitched, and a low moan rumbled in her chest.

She watched helplessly from the bridge as Daddy battled the current, struggling to reach the woman's flailing arms. The wind lifted whitecaps in the river that splashed over Daddy's head. Every time his silver hair disappeared beneath the water, the fist squeezing her lungs choked her harder.

Kara's heart drummed at a rib-bruising pace, and her breath snagged in her throat. Memories of her father's final moments had been burned in her brain all those years ago, but most days, she managed to keep the ghosts locked away. But now, with the wind whipping stinging rain into her face and the damp chill soaking her skin, the images surged from the dark corners where she'd shoved them. A shudder raced through her that had nothing to do with the cold wind or icy water.

Another bright flash of lightning and nearby boom of thunder echoed through the canyon. With a shrill, frightened whinny, the mare bucked again and bolted away.

* * *

Brady paused at the fence line that marked the edge of the Wheeler Ranch property and strained to see any sign of gray horse or red dress through the curtain of rain.

Nothing. Not one damn sign of horse or rider in any direction. Only rain and black clouds. The vast Texas prairie stretched beneath the looming caprock escarpment, a line of towering rock which marked the abrupt shift from flat ranch lands to steep canyons, deep arroyos and dramatic hoodoos.

Brady clenched his jaw, frustration biting hard. Kara was out there somewhere. He couldn't just give up and go home. She had no protection from the rain and wind, and no means to defend herself from wild animals…or human predators.

Had the shooter managed to escape the ranch amid the chaos? Was the sniper, even now, hunting Kara as Brady was? That notion sent a tremor to his gut and gnawed at him with razor teeth. If, in fact, Kara was the only witness who could identify the shooter, it stood to reason the would-be killer would pursue her and try to silence her.

He bristled, his possessive and protective instincts roaring.

As he scanned the horizon, he noticed a shed farther down the fence line. His spirits lifted. Maybe, just maybe Kara had seen that shed and taken shelter from the storm inside. He tugged his reins and clicked his tongue, guiding Rooster toward the small building.

"Kara!" he called over the rumbling thunder and drumming rain. "Kara, are you there?" Reaching the shed, he dismounted and tied Rooster's reins to the fence. The shed door was secured with a padlock through a hasp. A quick circuit around the building showed no other entrance or window. Disappointment speared him, but another idea came to him. Did the Wheeler ranch hands keep an ATV or any other useful supplies in the shed that would help him find Kara?

Choosing a large rock from the ground, Brady cracked it against the padlock repeatedly until the screws holding the hasp in place jarred loose, and the lock fell free. He could repair the door for the Wheelers later. Right now, he had a mission.

Sure enough, two ATVs were parked inside, along with a small trailer stacked with fence posts and coiled wire. Shelves with tools, engine oil and first-aid supplies lined the walls. The keys for each ATV dangled from a peg by the door, and Brady helped himself. The first ATV chugged and whined but wouldn't start. Quickly he moved to the second vehicle and sent up a silent prayer as he turned the key. The engine roared to life and Brady released a relieved sigh. He pulled his cell phone out while he was in the protection of the shed and dialed Nate.

After several rings, a distracted-sounding voice came on the line. "Uh, yeah? What?"

"Nate? It's Brady. Sorry to take off like I did, but I think Kara saw the shooter. She got on April's horse and lit off toward kingdom come."

"What? Brady?" They had a bad connection. Reception was poor in many parts of the county, so this didn't surprise Brady as much as annoy him. Being incommunicado during a crisis was no way to run an investigation.

"Listen, what's happening at the ranch? Have my men found the shooter?" he said, talking louder as thunder rumbled outside.

"I don't know. I'm not at the ranch."

Brady knitted his brow. "Why not?" he barked. "I told Wilhite to keep everyone on premises until I got back."

"My…shot. Bleeding out, and…trauma cent— April… in my truck."

The snips of Nate's reply that Brady caught sent a chill through him. Had something happened to April after he'd left?

"Say that again, Nate? What about April?"

Then he recalled Nate's mother calling for help during the chaos.

"Gotta go…" Nate said.

"Wait!" Brady ran a hand over his face, wiping rain from his nose and brow. "I'm leaving Rooster tied to the fence by the equipment shed in the north pasture. Can you call and send someone to get him? I'm going after Kara, and I don't—"

He cut his sentence off as a crack of thunder rattled the shed and loud static crackled in his ear. "Nate?"

He checked his screen and read, *Call dropped.* Grumbling a curse word, he tried to phone Wilhite. He was painfully aware of how much time he was using, how much farther ahead of him Kara was getting. When Wilhite didn't answer his cell, he tapped out a rapid text, letting him know someone needed to get Rooster and asking him to let him know if Kara showed up back at the ranch.

Before heading out, he found a scrap of an old grocery sack, and wrapped it around his phone. Not much protection from the rain, but it was better than nothing. After stashing the cell phone in the breast pocket of his tuxedo jacket, he mounted the ATV and headed out.

Given that the rain had softened the ground, he searched the far perimeter of the pasture for hoof prints leading away from the ranch. Ten minutes later, he found what he'd been looking for. A definite set of tracks heading toward the rugged terrain of the Caprock escarpment. Nerves jangling, he wheeled the ATV around to follow the trail of prints. A few hundred yards out onto the plain, he found a sodden white ribbon, evidence he was on the right track. His pulse jacked higher.

He paused long enough to cup his hands around his mouth and shout, "Kara!"

Turning a full three hundred and sixty degrees, he scanned the area. Nothing. Just rain, more rain and an empty landscape.

"Damn it, Kara, where are you? What made you run?" He settled back on the ATV and squeezed the clutch, wondering if he meant what made her run from the barn today...or what made her run from their relationship?

Either. Both. He'd spent the past ten months asking himself what he'd done wrong, why she'd left him, how he could convince her they were made for each other. Sure, she'd been worried about him when he'd taken the interim position as sheriff—an unexpected direction for his career but one he was honored to accept—but her concern for his safety on the job seemed a trifling thing to break up over. It was ludicrous. When he'd told her as much, she'd twisted his words, and they'd had a pointless fight about him not respecting her or some such hogwash.

How could she think he didn't respect her? She was completely amazing. Her love for and rapport with animals, her quick wit and sharp mind...not to mention her unbelievable courage and skill as a bullfighter in the rodeo.

Calling bullfighters by the more popular term "rodeo clowns" was something of an injustice, in his view. There was nothing funny about what Kara and other bullfighters faced in the arena. Distracting an angry, bucking bull, protecting riders took guts, speed and lightning reflexes. He was proud beyond words that Kara was one of the few women bullfighters in the business. *Not respect her?* He scoffed at the notion. He respected the hell out of her. He just didn't understand her. He couldn't—

The ATV hydroplaned, spinning sideways and nearly tipping over as he crossed some standing water. Righting the vehicle, Brady shook his head and sucked in a cleansing breath. He needed to quit obsessing over his arguments with Kara and concentrate on finding her. He'd have a hard enough time navigating in this wretched weather and getting them both back to the Wheeler Ranch safely.

As he traveled deeper into the path of the thunderstorm, the pounding rain and whipping winds obscured visibility. The trail of hoof prints got harder and harder to follow as the storm washed the impressions away. But since Kara had seemed to be traveling a straight path, logic said his best bet was to forge ahead in the same direction the trail had been going.

Flat land gave way to sloping rock and ravines. Small streams of runoff filled every dip and crevice in the increasingly steep terrain. Surely Kara hadn't ventured into such dangerous terrain alone, especially not during a thunderstorm...

Within seconds of that thought, a movement to his right caught Brady's attention. The gray mare Kara had ridden away on trotted out from the shallow end of a ravine. Without a rider.

Okay, Kara thought as the mare disappeared down the arroyo, *so you lost the horse. You're stranded. The gully is filling with swift water. It looks bad, but you can't panic.*

Fruitlessly wiping water off her face, Kara drew a slow, deep breath and blew it out through pursed lips. *Stay calm and think.*

The first thing she had to do was get out of the arroyo. Seeing as how she didn't know how far the horse had come up the arroyo—damn it, why hadn't she paid attention where she was going?—and seeing as how her most immediate danger was the rapidly rising level of runoff water, her priority was getting *up*. The mare couldn't have climbed the steep rocky walls of the arroyo, but she had to try. Squinting against the sting of wind-driven rain, she eyed the ravine walls and picked a spot that seemed easiest to ascend.

Scrabbling to find toeholds and rocks or roots she could pull herself up with, she started the awkward climb. Her waterlogged dress clung to her legs, encumbering her movement, and the rough rocks scraped her hands and cut into her bare feet. But she struggled on, trying to ignore the pain. The wind made it difficult to keep her balance, and the rain left the rocks slick. The rapidly dropping temperature chilled her to the bone, and shudders of cold soon racked her muscles, hastening her fatigue. *Thank you, Texas crazy weather.*

She made it within a few feet of the top ledge, still too far to hoist herself up to level ground, before she knew she had to stop. She had to rest or risk losing her grip and falling. Glancing around her, she spotted an indentation in the wall of the arroyo. The space was too shallow to be called a cave but deep enough for her to sit and have limited protection from the howling wind and precipitation.

Mustering the last of her strength, she reached for the low-hanging branch of a cottonwood tree. The first limb she grabbed broke off in her hand. Losing that anchor shifted her balance, and with a gasp, she teetered precariously.

She grasped frantically for another branch. The new branch dipped and stretched from her weight...but held. The moment of panic fueled her muscles with a spurt of adrenaline. Heart racing, she used the new energy to edge toward the small outcropping of rock and dirt.

When she reached the narrow ledge beneath the protective rock angling out of the bluff, she sank tiredly to her bottom and leaned back against the wall of red clay stone. Shutting her eyes against the continuing rain and wind, she allowed her muscles to relax and her shoulders to droop. She'd take just a moment to catch her breath and regroup before she planned her next move.

Stranded. The word filled her with frustration and self-censure. She'd panicked when the sniper fired at her and allowed herself to get lost by indulging her shock and fright. She'd done exactly what her father had taught her not to, what went counter to her training as a bullfighter. Wrapping her arms around herself, struggling for a shred of warmth, she castigated herself for her gut-level, amateurish reaction. If she hadn't been so wrapped up in her misery over Brady, would she have had more rational wits about her? She gave herself a little shake. The question was moot. She was stuck here, and she had to deal with it.

Behind her closed eyes, the disturbing images of the sniper's glowering face returned and filled her with an odd sense of déjà vu. Dark eyes narrowed. Wide, flat nostrils flared. He'd had a birthmark or mole high on his cheek, just under his right eye. The man was the stuff of nightmares. He had the look of a man with no compunction about killing.

A shiver raced through her that had nothing to do with the growing chill ushered in by the storm. She blew out a shaky breath, knowing how close she'd come to being the man's latest victim. The idea was terrifying. Surreal.

A sniper. At April and Nate's wedding. Given a moment to reflect more calmly, she realized the significance. And the mystery.

It didn't make sense. Why would someone shoot into

a wedding party? Was this a random act of violence by a lunatic or had the man been a hired gun with a specific target? And if the gunman had been hired, who was the sniper trying to kill? And why couldn't she shake the idea she'd seen him before?

Her gut roiled. As the new sheriff of Trencher County, Brady would be in charge of the investigation. She bit her bottom lip and squeezed her eyes tighter, fighting the swell of anxiety that stirred deep inside her. She conjured her last sight of Brady, his arms raised, trying to flag her down as she charged out of the barn on the gray mare and galloped away from the ranch. The concern in his eyes, the questions in his furrowed brow hadn't stopped her then, but now they reverberated through her soul. After the shots rang out, had he been coming to look for her? Would he come out on the Texas plains, searching?

An ember of hope, a tiny warmth deep in her chilled body, flickered to life. She knew Brady could find her. Hadn't she been bemoaning his keen tracking skills, his uncanny ability to find her wherever she went in town? But with a gunman at the ranch and possible casualties—Lord, let her friends be all right!—where would Brady's sense of duty lie?

A crack of thunder jolted her from her thoughts and back to her current crisis. She angled a glance to the rushing runoff below her. The arroyo was already half full of swift water. Dread punched her in the gut. Determined not to become a statistic because of stupidity and her rash reaction, she gritted her teeth and forced herself back to her feet. Legs shaking from cold and fatigue, she willed herself enough strength to start her climb again.

After tying the reins of the mare to a scrub tree on high ground, Brady tugged the brim of his cowboy hat down against the brisk northern wind. If only the mare could talk. *Where's Kara*? he wanted to demand of the horse. *Why did you leave her?*

If Kara wasn't with the horse anymore, did that mean she was hurt? Or sick? Was she even now bleeding out, unable to breathe or lying unconscious in the harsh storm?

He huffed his frustration as he pulled out his phone again to text the horse's location to his deputies. He turned a disgusted look to the sky where black clouds still roiled, spitting frigid rain. As long as the storm produced battering gusts of wind and lightning, assistance from a helicopter search team was not an option.

Climbing back astride the ATV, he revved the engine and considered his path. He needed to check the arroyo where the horse had appeared, but he needed to do it from high ground. As if to remind him of the urgency of finding Kara quickly, lightning struck close enough to cause an almost simultaneous clap of thunder. Yes, the conditions were dangerous. Lightning was a worry, but he couldn't give up his search. The wandering mare was evidence that Kara was stranded out here in the storm. And she could easily be in more peril than he dared imagine.

Kara tried multiple times to pull herself off the small ledge and onto the safe ground at the top of the arroyo. But her feet slipped on the wet rock, and she couldn't find secure handholds along the inverted angle of rock above her. The same overhang that provided a modicum of shelter from the downpour also made ascending the last seven or so feet nearly impossible.

Shivering from cold and fatigue, Kara sank back onto the small outcropping and fought the dejection that tugged at her. She wasn't a quitter, and even though her circumstances seemed bleak, she couldn't give up. She had to find an alternative solution. Ever since she'd stood by and watched her father drown, she'd sworn she'd never be passive in a situation again. Maybe as a young teen she'd not seen a way to help him, but as an adult, she'd never submit to any problem or circumstance without a fight.

Except with Brady.

She scowled darkly. Where had that thought come from? Leaving might have been painful, but it had been necessary to save herself from certain problems later on.

That's a cop-out. You took the easy way out with Brady. You didn't fight for him or for a workable compromise.

Kara growled her frustration and slapped a scraped palm on the cold, wet clay stone. Was this how she was going to spend the long hours until the waters receded or she was rescued? Mentally beating herself up over decisions she'd made out of self-preservation?

Brady bore his share of the blame for their breakup. Though she'd never told him the full story about her father's death, he hadn't acted interested in her reasons for her fears. Had he listened to her concerns about his appointment as sheriff, had he respected her opinions and valued her input, she wouldn't have felt backed into a corner. She wouldn't have—

Kara coughed as she inhaled the rainwater that sluiced down her face and dripped from her hair. The wind blew the steady downpour against her chilled skin and caused turbulent waves in the river that cascaded below her. She didn't want to die like her father, sucked beneath the choppy waves of a fast-flowing current. *Help me, Daddy!*

The ache that had cleaved her heart for the past fifteen years swelled again and raked her soul. Seeing the rushing muddy water below her now brought all her worst fears from that night back to the fore of her mind.

"Stop it!" she scolded herself. She wouldn't dwell on

Brady or her father or the maniac sniper. She needed to stay positive, remain focused on the best way to stay alive and get back to town before she died of exposure.

Since the rain gave no indication of letting up anytime soon, and the water level of the flash flood in the arroyo kept rising, she knew she needed to find another way to the top of the cliff. Could she tear strips of her dress to make a rope and—

"Kara!" a male voice shouted in the distance.

Her heart stilled, and she held her breath until she heard the voice again.

"I'm here!" she yelled, "Help!" She pushed onto her feet, ignoring the sting of raw, chafed skin. The sound of an ATV grew louder, and tears of relief stung her eyes. But could she be seen here under the overhang?

Hastily she ripped a large piece of her red dress from the bottom hem and broke off a branch from a low-hanging cottonwood. After tying the scrap on the end of the stick, she waved her homemade flag and screamed louder. "Here! I'm down here! Help!"

Chapter 3

Brady divided his gaze between the rugged terrain in his path and the steep sides of the arroyo to his left. The driving rain obscured his vision, and the sight of the rushing water filled him with a queasy dread. Kara knew the dangers of flash flooding in the canyon areas, but knowing the danger and avoiding it were different matters. If she'd been hurt, she might not have been able to get out of the swift water's perilous path.

"Kara!" A bracing wind cut through his soaked tuxedo jacket, and an icy chill shook him to the core. The predicted cold front was settling in quickly. Hypothermia was a serious threat if he couldn't get her back to the ranch promptly. "Kara!"

Brady paused briefly and cut the engine in order to better listen for a response. But even without the rumbling ATV motor, the sounds of the storm and rushing water created a cacophony that drowned out nearly all other noises.

"Kara!" he shouted again hearing the growing desperation in his voice.

He was about to crank the engine again, when a flash of color just ahead of him snagged his attention through the veil of gray rain. Scrambling off the ATV, Brady jogged closer to the edge of the arroyo for a better look. Squinting against the water dripping in his eyes and craning his neck for a better view of the cliff below him, he glimpsed a scrap of red cloth at the end of a branch.

His heart squeezed. "Kara!"

The branch that held the limp, wet fabric wiggled harder.

"I'm here!" The voice was unmistakably Kara's.

He barely heard her response over nature's din, but the thin sound was the sweetest he'd ever heard. He barked a laugh that was half joy and half relief as he ran along the top of the arroyo to get closer. When he was more directly above her, he lay on his stomach and inched to the edge of the cliff. "Kara, it's Brady! I'm going to get you up from there, babe. Are you hurt?"

"Brady?" She sounded stunned, as if she'd had no faith that he would come for her. He shoved down the irritation and disappointment her lack of faith stirred in him. Right now, he had a job to do. There'd be time to debate his commitment to her and her lack of dedication to him after they were both safe and dry.

"Are you hurt?" he repeated more firmly.

"N-no. At least, nothing s-serious. Just c-cold."

Nothing serious. That could mean anything coming from Kara. She'd broken her ankle during a rodeo event once and not let anyone know until after she'd hobbled around on it facing down angry bulls all evening.

"Stay put. I'll be right back." He winced at the inanity of his order as he scrambled back to the ATV. He could picture Kara rolling her eyes at him. Stay put? Where was she going to go?

He prayed they'd have the chance to laugh at his goof later that evening—maybe by a warm fire while they sipped a brandy and talked out their differences?

Well, one could hope.

He opened the toolbox on the back of the ATV and grabbed out everything he thought could be useful. With a rope draped over his shoulder and the rest of the items clutched to his chest, he hurried back to the edge of the ravine.

"Kara, I'm going to lower a rope to you." But he needed an anchor to tie off to. Crud! What could he use? As he cast his gaze about, searching for a secure place to tie off, he called, "I want you to make a loop under your arms and knot it so it won't slip. Okay?"

"Got it. Hurry! The water is rising fast!"

He rejected the ATV as an option. It might be heavier than Kara, but the wet ground didn't provide solid traction. The nearest tree was several feet away, but he saw no better possibility.

Kara would have to climb out, away from her ledge, until she was in line with the tree. Risky, but if she was tied securely, he could pull her to safety even if she slipped.

He tied a wrench to the end of the rope to weight it and give it more direction when he tossed the end down. Lying on his stomach, he called to her again. "Kara, are you ready? Here's the plan…"

"Climb away from the ledge?" she cried when he explained his intentions. "But if I lose my grip or…"

She didn't finish, and her silence spoke volumes. Why didn't she trust him? Didn't she know he'd never suggest something that wasn't what he believed to be the best solution?

He gritted his teeth and swallowed the bitter discouragement her hesitation caused. "Kara, I'll get you up here, one way or another, but your climbing over toward the tree will make it easier and safer to pull you up."

"I...I see that. It's just—"

She paused, and he didn't waste time on further hedging or second-guessing. "Get ready. I'm lowering the rope now."

Kara bit her trembling bottom lip. She was immensely glad to have rescue from the icy cold and treacherous ledge, but having Brady as her white knight twisted bittersweet tendrils around her heart. The last thing she wanted was to be more vulnerable to Brady's numerous charms. Gratitude and respect for his valiant assistance warred inside her with anxiety. His selflessness and heroic side were two of the qualities that had made her fall for him... and were why she'd had to leave him. He was so like her father in that way. Always the rescuer, the protector, the one risking his own life to help another. But that selfless heroism had cost her father his life, and she couldn't bear the idea of losing another loved one to duty.

Still, she was eager to get out of her predicament and get home. Brady had seen fit to come to her aid, and she accepted that gift gratefully. Uncurling from her huddle against the cliff wall, she pushed onto her knees, shaking so hard from cold and fatigue she feared she might lose her balance and tumble into the swift water.

Pulse thundering in her ears, she eyed the rushing floodwater dubiously. One miscue could send her into that turbulent river. *Like Daddy.*

She swallowed the bitter taste that rose in the back of her throat and angled her gaze toward the top of the arroyo. When Brady tossed the rope down to her, she reached out to grab the end. She swiped a hand toward the dangling rope, but her groping hand came up empty. Even with the tool-weighed end swinging toward her, the overhang above her meant it hung just beyond her reach.

"I can't r-reach it!" she called up to him, her teeth chattering. The chill of the wind and rain, along with the cold air that had arrived with the storm, had numbed her muscles enough that her movements felt stiff and clumsy. She stretched as far as she dared, but her balance was off, thanks to lost finesse and chill-muddled dexterity.

"Keep trying. I'll swing it down again." And he did. But she still couldn't reach far enough to snare the dangling end.

Next, she tried using the branch she'd made her flag from to knock it closer. She had to hold the very end as she extended it out to the rope, but it was working…until her icy fingers fumbled her grip and the branch dropped into the roiling water below.

An anguished cry slipped from her throat, rife with both frustration and horror. The churning water swallowed the red scrap of fabric and whisked it away in seconds. She shuddered, knowing the same would happen to her if she fell. The violent current would toss and twist her body like a rag doll. Suck her under…*like Daddy.*

"Kara?" Brady's voice jerked her attention from the turbulent flash flood.

"It's t-too far out. I can't g-get it."

"You have to, Kara! Keep trying!" His voice sounded more frustrated than encouraging.

She hated the idea of admitting defeat. Disappointment plucked hard. "No d-dice, Brady. It's too f-far away."

She heard his muffled curse and shared his frustration. Dispirited, she flopped back on her bottom, and her shoulders drooped. Hugging herself and trying to chafe warmth into her arms, she pushed aside the failure and regrouped. *Think!* What else could they do?

"Fine. I'm coming down," he called.

She frowned and gave her head a little shake. Surely she'd heard him wrong. "Wh-what did you say?"

"I'm coming down to you. Just give me a minute to get tied on."

Kara's chest tightened, and her blood pressure spiked. "Brady, no! It's too dangerous. There must be another way!"

"You have a better idea? 'Cause I'm all ears. Meantime we're wasting daylight, and that water's getting higher."

She wished she could see him, could discuss their options face-to-face rather than shouting blindly, their voices drowned out by the wind, cascading runoff and pounding rain. But even more, she wished she had an idea that didn't involve Brady shimmying down a rope in these horrid conditions to save her. "Brady, wait. We can't—"

The scuffling sound of loose rock preceded a shower of gravel and mud, knocked loose from above. Her heartbeat scampered frantically. "Be careful! Brady, I—"

He grumbled and cursed, and the dangling rope shook and swayed. More loose red clay stone tumbled down near her, and she balled her hands in fists against her chest. Leaning out slightly, she craned her neck to glance up. She saw Brady's boots, his black tuxedo pants streaked with red mud as he rappelled down the sheer rock. The rope was twined around his leg and over his shoulder in a strange configuration of loops and knots. Though Brady was a champion bull rider and calf roper, rock climbing was not part of his resume.

Tension twisted inside her as he inched downward. "Brady, please!"

But she wasn't sure what her plea was. For him to be

careful? For him to abandon his idea and climb back up? For him to hurry and get her to safety? All of the above.

She held her breath as he eased closer. A few inches, then a few more. Letting out a length of rope, he slid down a foot, then another. His feet kicked at the rock wall, slipping and scrabbling for purchase. Each time he descended, she bit back a gasp, praying the rope would tighten and catch him.

Finally he was eye-level with her, and the sight of his black hair plastered to his head, the rain spiking the sooty eyelashes around his piecing blue eyes, burrowed deep in her soul. Here was the man she'd loved so dearly, braving the elements of this nasty storm and going to great lengths to bring her safely home. She wanted to cry for what she'd given up, for all he meant to her and for the desperate longing to throw caution to the wind in order to spend the rest of her life with him. "Oh, Brady, I'm sorry. I—"

A sob choked her, and he shook his head.

"There'll be time for that later." He canted toward her, and the rope creaked. "Grab on. Take my wrist, and I'll get yours."

"I—" She edged closer to him and held out her hand.

"Come on, Kara. A little closer."

She glanced down at the rushing water, at the sizeable gap from the edge of the outcropping to the rope. She wanted to trust him, but simply giving him her hand didn't solve the dilemma of the distance between them.

When she hesitated, he stretched toward her, putting himself at a precarious angle.

"No! Brady, be careful!" Even as she shouted the warning, her own foot slipped on the sodden red clay stone. Her foot shot out, and she landed hard on her backside. Stunned for a minute by the jarring fall, her second of the afternoon, she blinked back the rain that dripped in her eyes.

"Kara!" She heard the panic in his voice, and though

she'd had the breath knocked from her, she nodded to assure him she was unhurt...mostly.

"Stay there. Let me come to you." He shifted his position, pushing off the rocks with his feet to swing toward the drooping cottonwood tree branches. Grabbing one of the thick limbs, he used the tree as an anchor so that he could lean farther toward her. "When you take my hand, brace your feet. I'm coming onto the ledge with you."

She wasn't sure what his plan was, but she followed his directions. When he was safely to the small shelf of rock where she'd taken refuge, he drew her into a tight embrace.

"My God, Kara! Your skin is ice cold. What were you thinking, riding off into this weather like that?"

She tensed, not wanting to be lectured on her flight from the shooter. She pushed against his chest, struggling to free herself, but his arms were steel bands holding her close. "Obviously, if I'd been th-thinking clearly I w-wouldn't have ridden out here. The g-guy was shooting at m-me, and I panicked."

A twitch of surprise rolled through his muscles. "You saw the sniper?"

She nodded weakly, her head pressed against Brady's chest. His body radiated warmth, and she gave up her attempts to push him away. Instead she tucked herself closer to his heat and strength. "And when he saw me, he tried to kill me. When I rode off, I was in shock and scared. I j-just wanted to get out of there. Away from the shooter and...away from you."

His fingers dug into her arms, and he shoved her to arms' length. "Away from me? Why?"

She heaved a weary sigh. "I'd think that was obvious."

"Not to me, it's not!" He lowered his black brows and implored her with those damnably expressive eyes. "We were good together, Kara. Great together. What happened?"

Her gut wrenched, and she barked a humorless laugh. "Really? You want to have this discussion here? Now?"

His lips compressed in a scowl, and he swiped water from his face. "No. Not now. But we *will* have this talk! You owe me that much."

She shuddered. From the cold. From fatigue. And from dread of dredging up all that heartache.

"Geez, Kara." He slid out of his tuxedo jacket and put it around her shoulders. "We need to get you back to town before you suffer from hypothermia."

"T-too late." She gave him a weak wry grin, trying to lighten the mood, which he answered with another of his dark, scolding glares.

"All right. I'm going to retie the rope into a sling around you." He stepped back and started unwinding the rope from around his leg and looping it around her. "Then I'll tie on behind you, and we'll—"

It happened so fast, Kara had no time to react. Brady was there one minute and gone the next. And so was the front half of the ledge they'd been perched on. The loose shale under the outcropping had washed away, taking the red clay stone—and Brady—with it.

"Brady!" she screamed in terror. She searched the turbulent water, her heart in her throat. The seconds stretched out, miserable eons, before she spied the white of his tuxedo shirt where he was tossed in the powerful current. He bobbed up and swam as best he could in the fast water, but even the strongest swimmer had little chance against the power of swift water. A sob choked her.

Not again!

"Brady!"

Hitting the frigid water shocked his system, and Brady involuntarily gasped. A mouthful of muddy water rushed into his throat, choking him. He coughed and gagged, even as the turbulent water sucked him under. Adrenaline spiking, he fought to surface, but the pounding current rolled him and grabbed at him. He lost his orientation. Couldn't breathe. The icy cold stung him. His soaked clothes dragged at him. As his boots filled with water, he toed off the Tony Lamas, freeing his legs of their weighty encumbrance.

When he broke the surface, he sputtered out water and quickly gulped in air. But not enough. His lungs ached. His head throbbed. He moved his arms and legs, trying to paddle, to stay afloat. Something large and heavy crashed into his back. Debris, most likely.

Down he went. Beneath the water, all he saw was a blur of reddish brown. A flash of light. Shadows. Then suddenly he broke the surface, and he caught a snapshot of the terrain. Gray clouds. Rocky towers. A wind-whipped tree…

His pulse jumped, and instinctively he slapped at the water, flailing, grabbing for a branch. His fingers snagged leaves. His drifting slowed, but the foliage ripped free from his grasp. *Damn!*

Again he grabbed before the tree was gone. And found a small limb. The thin branch bowed and cracked.

No! He groped for another limb. Thicker, more solid. Coughing. Struggling for a breath as the flow of water tugged at him. His hand slipped, scraping his palm, but he clung to the branch of the cottonwood for all he was worth. He hauled himself in, using every ounce of strength in his shivering muscles. When the branch broke free of the trunk, he was washed downstream—all of eighteen inches. Pushed by the current, his body smacked into another thick branch of the tree. The impact slammed his diaphragm, forcing both air and water from his throat.

Pinned against the branch by the current, he blinked hard, fighting to stay conscious. The cold water sapped his strength, and his body ached from the battering of the debris and tree limbs. The struggle to draw air in his lungs left him dizzy. But losing his grip on the tree, giving in to the gray fuzziness at the edges of his vision, was not an option. Failure now meant both his death and Kara's.

A bone-deep tremor rocked Kara. She watched helplessly as the muddy water tossed Brady and slammed him against a cottonwood tree growing at a low angle from the arroyo wall. Her breath caught and held as she waited for some movement, some sound that told her he was alive. *Please, Brady! Move a hand. Call to me. Anything!*

Through her tears, past and present blurred and tangled.

The suicidal jumper. Her father's pleading with the woman. His heroic jump into the river to save her...and the heartbreaking image of his head disappearing below the water time and again as he tried to pull the woman to safety.

"You should be proud of your father. He died a hero. He gave himself in the line of duty," well-meaning people had told her.

But for Kara, her father's death was pointless. He'd cared more about a misplaced sense of duty than he had cared about her. She blamed his job, the inherent danger of law enforcement for stealing the man who'd been her lifeline when she was thirteen.

And now...would she lose Brady because he'd been trying to rescue her?

"Brady!" she shouted, her voice breaking.

She squeezed the rope in her hand, the rope Brady had been tying to her when the overhang gave way. The rope that—

Her pulse slowed…

The rope! With a sob of relief and revelation, she shot a glance to the coil she held. With a sobering breath, she shook herself from her self-pitying fog and panic. She had to act. She had the means to save both herself and Brady.

Giving the rope a hard tug, she reassured herself it was securely anchored at the top of the cliff. *Of course it was. Brady would have seen to that.*

"Brady, hold on!" she yelled as she knotted the rope around her waist. "I'm coming!"

To be sure she was tied fast, she threaded the rope between her legs to make a diaper sling, then back up under her dress. She prayed the rope was long enough to reach Brady. He'd washed a good way downstream. Once she felt she was lashed in, she faced the thundering water below her, and her stomach swooped.

Oh, dear God! Do I really have to go in that roiling maelstrom, that frigid death trap?

She did, if she was going to help Brady. She turned her gaze to the spot where Brady clung to the cottonwood, and her mind's eye saw her father's head sinking below the swirling water. *Daddy!*

The runoff rushing through the arroyo taunted her, and she sucked in a tremulous breath.

Was she destined to die the same way her father had? Adrenaline kicked her heart rate to a gallop.

Even if she died trying, she had to attempt to save Brady. Her life would be agony if she lost him on top of losing her father. Gathering her courage, she ran through logistics in her head. Not only did she have to swim to the cottonwood on the other side of the ravine, she had to account for the current washing her downstream. Timing was everything. She'd have to leap as far out across the water as she could. And upstream, buying herself a few more precious seconds to paddle to Brady.

As much as she hated losing the tuxedo jacket, she knew it would encumber her when she tried to swim. She shucked off the garment Brady had draped around her and groaned at the cold blast of wind on her arms. Glancing down at the soggy maxi dress stuck to her legs, she knew the yards of material had to go, as well. Its waterlogged weight and the impediment of a long skirt tangling around her legs would prove a liability she couldn't afford. Grimacing when she remembered how much she'd paid for the dress last week in Amarillo, she pulled at the seam and ripped off the bottom half of the skirt. Goose bumps rose on her bare legs, and her toes were already growing numb from the cold. Haste was of the essence. The temperature would only continue to drop, endangering her and Brady more with each passing minute.

Then steeling her nerves, she faced the rushing water.

"Daddy, help me!" she whispered to the heavens… and jumped.

Chapter 4

"**B**rady!" The sound of Kara's voice cut through the whoosh of water and the thudding in his head. His chest wrenched, knowing he'd failed her.

"Brady!" The branches of the tree shook, and a hand grasped at his belt.

Kara?

Fear for her life jolted him out of his reverie, and he cut a side glance to the woman battling the current and grasping for a hold on the cottonwood branch. Shifting his own grip to free a hand, he groped for her arm and hauled her closer to him.

Sputtering and shivering, she draped herself over the trunk of the tree and gasped for breath.

"What the hell are you doing?" he shouted, his tone sharpened by shock and concern for her.

Still panting for air, she angled an angry look at him. "Shopping...for prom!" she grated. "What...does it l-look...like?"

"It looks like you're trying to get yourself killed!"

She frowned and coughed. "Well…there's that, too."

Her sarcasm chafed his raw nerves. This was no time for jokes, no matter how snarky.

"Of all the—" He cut himself off, gritting his teeth as he tugged her onto the tree more securely. He didn't know whether to rant at her or kiss her. But when she raised her chin, facing him with muddy water streaming down her gorgeous face, her lush lips scowling at him and her golden-brown eyes flashing with fury, he chose the latter. He splayed a hand at the nape of her neck and captured her mouth with a kiss meant to claim her and calm his frustration with her recklessness.

She mewled a weak protest, then leaned into the kiss, her lips as eager and desperate as his. When he raised his mouth from hers, she met his gaze with haunted eyes. The emotion in them said what she refused to admit. She still wanted him, still needed him, still loved him.

But she quickly pulled her head away from his grip, and the tenderness in her expression was replaced with hard determination and pragmatism.

"Enough of that," she chastened. "Grab the rope. We g-gotta get out of this water before this branch g-gives way."

He jerked a nod, and clinging awkwardly to the tree trunk with one arm, he began tugging at the knots in the rope. "That was a foolish risk to take, babe—" he huffed a sigh "—but thanks."

Her brow furrowed. "Like I'd stand by and watch you drown? I had no choice!"

He cut a wry glance at her. "You're killing me with your sentimentality."

Growling under her breath, she said, "I just meant—"

She shook her head and batted his hands away from the knot at her waist. "Can we save the argument for later?"

"I have no desire to argue with you, Kara." Undeterred by her swat, he slid his fingers along the rope, feeling for the configuration she'd devised to secure it around her.

She gasped as his hand moved between her legs.

"Brady, stop it!" She pushed again at his arm, sputtering when the wind blew a wave into her face.

"Used to be, you'd say, 'Don't stop.' Remember those days, babe?" He sure did, and the memory stirred a heat low in his belly. "Tangled up in the sheets rather than some old rope?"

Her answering glare said she wasn't amused. "Not the time, Sheriff."

He pressed his mouth in a grim line. He missed the sense of humor she used to share freely with him. The easy camaraderie that helped them through difficult times and filled their quiet moments alone with laughter. Resigned to her all-business mode, he addressed the situation with a similar efficiency. "You did a great job with the sling you made. No point untying it." He fumbled one-handed to unfasten his belt buckle, and her eyes widened and grew smoky. *So she wasn't immune to him, after all.*

"Brady…" Her tone held a warning.

"Settle down, babe. You've made your point. But rather than undo your sling, I'm going to fasten my belt through the loop at your waist."

Her tense expression eased, and she bobbed a nod. With shaking hands, Kara helped him poke the leather belt under the rope. When he cinched it more tightly, her hips were tugged more snugly against his.

Kara gave a breathy little gasp as he settled into the intimate position and wrapped an arm around her to bring her chest against his.

"You're enjoying this, aren't you?" Her eyes narrowed with accusation, but he didn't miss the ragged flutter of her breath against his cheek. Or the throbbing pulse in her neck. Or the widening of her pupils. She was as aroused by the contact of their bodies as he was.

"So sue me. I won't apologize for the fact that you turn me on, even in the worst of circumstances." He arched an eyebrow, adding, "At least I'm honest with myself about what I'm feeling and what I want."

Her jaw dropped in affront, but muddy water splashed in her face, making her cough and gasp for a breath.

"Okay, babe, hold on to me. Tight. This could get dicey." Without waiting for her to follow his instruction, he shifted his free hand's grip to the rope. They dipped lower in the water, and she threw her arms around him, curling her fingers into his shirt.

Before releasing his hold on the tree branch that had saved him, he smacked another quick kiss on Kara's lips. "For luck! Now hang on!"

With a silent prayer, he let go of the cottonwood and seized the rope with both hands.

Kara clenched her teeth, both to keep them from chattering in the desperately cold water and to keep from getting more of the muddy runoff in her mouth. Tense with fear, she clung to Brady and repeated a silent chant in her head. *Please, please, please, pleasepleasepleaseplease!*

At first she fixed her eyes on the opposite side of the arroyo, to the rocky incline they'd have to scale after crossing the water. If they got across the water…

No! No negative thoughts! They could do this. *Brady* could do this. He was strong and capable and determined…

She shifted her attention to his slow hand-over-hand progress as he pulled them against the current. His biceps and shoulder muscles flexed and bulged as he fought the swift water. She tried to help by scissor-kicking, but the chill had seeped deep into her muscles, leaving her legs numb and weak. Seeing how far they had to go to reach safety discouraged her, so after a few minutes, she focused only on what was right in front of her—the next few inches of rope they needed to travel. Brady's heroic efforts to pull them through the water. His rugged face, scrunched in exertion. The fire of dogged determination bright in his eyes.

She curled her lips in, still feeling the warm tingle of his kiss there…and dancing in her veins like sparks rising from a campfire and swirling in the night sky.

He'd come out in this horrible storm to look for her. And as she'd predicted, he'd found her. She didn't try to name the warm feeling that swelled inside her.

When Brady grunted with effort, she glanced again to his grip on the rope, the slow hand-over-hand progress as he pulled them against the waves. Sympathy twisted in her chest. His palms had to be raw from the wet hemp rope. Under the best of circumstances, ranchers wore gloves when working. She needed to help him, had to lend him whatever strength she could muster.

She reached for the rope, just below his grip and pulled for all she was worth.

"Kara! D—" He choked on a mouthful of water, but the anxiety in his tone spoke for him.

She answered with a defiant look and continued to squeeze the rope, tugging and inching hand-over-hand with him. Her muscles quivered, but pulling together, they moved more quickly toward the far side of the ravine. Soon they were hoisting themselves up, out of the water, feet scrabbling to climb the clay stone wall.

When at last she heaved herself over the top edge of

the ravine wall, Kara flopped on the muddy ground, completely spent.

But Brady had other ideas. Still attached to the rope at the waist, he fumbled to undo his belt. When he was unhooked from her, he rose on his hands and knees beside her, and he tugged at her arm. "Come on. Get up. You're losing body heat, lying in those puddles."

"I'm…s-so tired." She used every bit of restraint left in her not to sound whiny when she voiced her objection. The simple truth was, her energy was sapped, and hypothermia was settling in…quickly.

Brady staggered to his feet, and with strength he found God knew where, he lifted her in his trembling arms. Carrying her, he stumbled to the ATV and sat on the ground with her on his lap. He chafed her aching arms, though his hands were as cold as hers. Covering one of his hands with hers, she turned his palm up to examine it. As she'd expected, his skin was red and blistered, scraped by the rough rope. Her hands were raw, too, but Brady's were much worse.

"Oh, Brady…" She touched the abraded skin gently with her fingers.

"I'm fine." He tugged his hand from her grasp and wrapped his arms around her again.

She curled against him, savoring the security of being out of the water, safe on high ground. Brady had saved her life.

Gratitude tugged at her, deep in her core. No…more than gratitude. A deeply poignant sense of reassurance and affection that brought tears to her eyes and stole her breath. "Y-you came after m-me."

Brady's hands stilled for a moment. "Of course I did. Why would that even be a question for you?"

"I—"

He cut her off with a kiss that burrowed deep into her,

warming her from the inside and reviving feelings she'd worked hard to bury in the past several months. A bittersweet pang wrenched in her chest. Good Lord, she'd missed him, missed his kiss.

The brush with death, the biting cold and her staggering fatigue conspired to strip away pretenses and protective intentions. She was emotionally raw and vulnerable, and she needed what only Brady had ever given her. Lifting her arms to circle his neck, she angled her head to deepen the kiss, greedy for more. But even as she clung to him and took refuge in the caress of his mouth on hers, a stubborn voice in her head warned her of the danger she would be in if she opened her heart to him again.

With his hands splayed on either side of her face, Brady nudged her head back and looked deep into her eyes. "Babe, when you bolted out of that barn and took off, you were my highest priority. When I heard the gunfire, I'd thought you'd been shot, and when you rode off like that, hell for leather—"

"The sh-shooter…" She paused as a chill sent a shudder through her. "Has he been c-caught?"

Brady's chest heaved as he sighed. "Not last I heard. But I'm guessing my phone is dead, thanks to our swim." He coughed and shook from the cold, too. "We'll have to wait until we get back for an update."

She tipped her head to gaze up at him in confusion. "You didn't s-stay to l-look for him? B-but you're the sheriff. Wh-why—"

"Well, I could hardly be two places at once, could I?"

"But…"

"I left Wilhite in charge of securing the scene and tracking down the shooter. He and Anderson are more than competent in handling things until we get back."

"B-but…"

"Hey—" He cupped the side of her face and pinned her with his gaze. "I made my choice. You'll always be my first priority." He pressed warm lips to her forehead. "So… don't make me regret my choice by badgering me about it. Okay?" He flashed her a crooked grin, and she scoffed a soft laugh.

Despite his current teasing, she hadn't missed what he'd said. His first priority? The sentiment touched her. And yet…

Brady's earlier choices contradicted his claims about her place in his life. She squeezed her eyes shut as she burrowed closer to his body heat. Wherever she truly stood with him, he was here now. He had rescued her. And she wouldn't take that for granted.

"Th-thank you…for coming. For finding me…"

He hugged her more tightly and chuckled. "Just doing my job. You are my key witness, after all. I need you to identify the shooter when we get back to town."

She raised her chin again and scowled. "*That's* why you came after me? Because it was your job?"

He looked startled by her tone. "It was a factor. Not the only factor, or even the main one, but part of the reason. Yes."

She hunched her shoulders and glared at him.

He shook his head and dragged her close again, wrapping his arms around her. "What? You scold me for not doing my job by staying to look for the sniper, and when I say finding you was part of my job, that's wrong, too?"

She groaned, and her teeth chattered as another blast of chilly wind buffeted them. "I didn't say that. I just… I d-don't want to fight." She was too cold, too tired to think straight.

He sighed. "I don't want to fight either." A tremor rolled through him as well, and he bit out a curse. "We have to get warm somehow."

"Any ideas?"

He scooted her off his lap and moved to the back of the ATV. "I think I saw a first-aid kit in here. Maybe there's an emergency blanket in it."

She rose to her feet and watched him rummage in the cargo box and extract a red kit. He cracked open the seal and rifled the contents.

"Bingo!" he said, his face brightening. Tossing the remaining first-aid items back in the cargo box, he opened the tightly folded emergency blanket and wrapped it around her shoulders.

The thin metallic-looking plastic sheet was cold at first, but as designed, it trapped what little body heat she created. Soon she felt a pocket of warmth growing around her.

"Is this the only one in there?"

Brady nodded. "Yeah. But you need it more than I do."

"We can share." She wobbled closer to him, raising the corner of the blanket to pull him in with her.

He huddled under the silver sheeting for a moment, holding her close, then edged back. "You take it. I need my arms free to drive the ATV. We have to get back before the temperature drops any more."

"Yes! Please. I'd kill for dry clothes and a cup of hot coffee right now."

Brady swung a leg over the ATV and turned the ignition key. The engine whined and sputtered. "Come on! Start, damn it!"

Kara's chest tightened with dread. If the engine didn't start...

She cast a wary eye to the sky. Though the rain had slowed considerably, the low-hanging silver clouds moving in promised sharply colder air. Already her breath formed a white cloud when she exhaled. Her exposed toes were red and numb, and she knew she was in danger of getting frostbite if they were still here when darkness fell.

She clenched her teeth to keep them from chattering. *Please, God. Let the engine s—* Before she finished her silent plea, the ATV roared to life, and Brady revved the engine to warm it up. Finally something had gone right!

Brady jerked his head toward the ATV seat, hurrying her. "Climb on. Let's get outta here."

She didn't need to be told twice. Straddling the seat behind him, she clutched the emergency blanket in her fists and put her arms around Brady's chest, below his arms. He drew the loose ends of the blanket over his lap and tucked them under his legs.

With her chest nestled against his back and the blanket providing a barrier at her back, they set out. Despite the wind created as they sped across the rugged terrain, Kara savored a pocket of warmth under the emergency blanket. The cold air stung her eyes, so she buried her face in Brady's neck. She couldn't wait to get home and fix a fire in her fireplace. She'd drink a giant mug of peppermint hot chocolate with marshmallows, calories be damned, and cocoon herself in her grandmother's old Christmas quilt. A grin tugged the corners of her mouth, her frozen cheeks twitching at the prospect of warmth and the sweet treat.

Several minutes into the ride home, she peeked up to gauge how far they had to go. She could see the red barn of the Wheeler Ranch still a good distance away, and when she scanned the surrounding terrain, she spotted something else that tugged her conscience. She squinted to make sure she was seeing what she thought. The gray mare was standing across the rolling plains about a mile from them.

"Brady!" She jostled him and aimed a finger in the opposite direction of the ranch. Shouting to be heard over the engine, she said, "I have to bring her back. Take me to her."

He slowed to a stop so that they could talk over the noise of the ATV. "We can send someone out after her when we get back."

"No." She tightened her grip on him. "I took her. I need to bring her back."

Brady glanced over his shoulder at her. "While I respect your sense of honor and responsibility, our priority needs to be getting to the sheriff's department."

"Brady—"

"Do you even have the strength to ride? You could barely stand a few minutes ago."

"I've had time to rest, and I've warmed up a little bit." She paused, considering the reality of his question. "If you help me get on her, I can ride her back to the ranch. It's not that far."

"Kara, we need to—"

"I can do it, Brady! I need to make this right. It's my fault…" She sucked in a shuddering breath. "Please, just take me to her."

He turned his gaze back to the mare and huffed a sigh. "All right. But I'm following you back to the ranch. As soon as we can turn her over to one of the Wheelers' hands, you're coming with me to the station to make a statement and give a description of the shooter."

Brady turned the ATV and headed toward the horse. Once they'd untied the restless mare's reins, Kara positioned herself beside the horse, one hand on the saddle horn. "Can I get a boost?"

Brady moved up behind her, stooping to lift her as she swung onto the saddle. Tired though she was, having his hands splayed on her, his intimate grip on her thighs and bottom, sent a prickle of lust to her core. Her leg muscles quivered as she mounted the mare, and not entirely because of fatigue and cold.

He frowned at her exposed legs and rubbed his palms briskly over her red, chapped skin. "Damn, Kara. Look at you! What happened to the rest of your dress? I could've sworn it was longer."

"I made alterations before I swam over to get you. I didn't want my legs getting tangled up in all that extra material."

His face darkened, and he opened his mouth as if to comment on her alterations or her rescue but snapped his mouth closed. Instead he said, "I'll be right behind you if you change your mind."

With a nod, she snapped the reins and set off, guiding the mare back toward the Wheeler Ranch. She focused on the bright red barn with its Texas flag. The barn's roof had been trimmed with white Christmas lights that glowed like a beacon in the gloomy weather.

But as she rode nearer the barn, a chest-constricting dread swamped her. Had they found the shooter? Would the man be lying in wait for her? She inhaled a shallow breath trying to calm the skittering of nerves. Brady said he'd left his deputies in charge of securing the scene. Even if the sniper hadn't been caught, the man would have to be crazy to stick around the crime scene. Surely the shooter was long gone. Though that made her feel better about returning to the Wheeler Ranch, a suspect in the wind was bad for Brady as sheriff…and the community. A sniper loose in Rusted Spur? Her gut roiled. She hated the idea of Brady leading the search for a killer.

And as Brady's only eyewitness, she would be his best shot at identifying the man.

She gripped the reins tighter and whispered a prayer. "Please, let the man be in custody already. Please, let this be over!"

Chapter 5

"No dice, boss. We've questioned everyone that was at the wedding. No one saw anybody suspicious, and after the shots were fired, everyone was just trying to get to safety," Wilhite said.

Brady muttered an expletive and shifted the cell phone he'd borrowed from a ranch hand from one ear to the other. "Casualties?"

"One. George Wheeler was hit and got airlifted to the trauma center in Lubbock. Nate and April have driven to over to be with him." Brady recalled the garbled call he'd made to Nate earlier.

While he was relieved to hear April was all right, he hated knowing that George Wheeler's condition was grave enough to need an airlift to a trauma center. "So April and Nate have gone to the hospital?"

Hearing half the conversation, Kara gasped and whirled toward him. "What? Were they shot? Is it April's baby? What—"

He held up a hand and gave a quick head shake to calm her while Wilhite said, "A few other folks had minor injuries as they scurried for cover."

Kara continued to stare anxiously, waiting for answers.

"And you have no leads yet on who the shooter was or where he is?" Having turned the mare over to the hands and given them directions where to find Rooster, Brady placed a hand at the small of Kara's back to escort her out of the Wheelers' stable. They each had a blanket draped around their shoulders, but horse blankets were a poor substitute for dry clothes and a hot meal. Food and a shower would have to wait until he'd found the shooter.

"We're working a few leads," Wilhite said. "I'll fill you in when you get here."

"I'm on my way. Meantime, tell area agencies to be on the lookout for a white male in his forties, about five foot ten, military haircut, brown eyes, dark hair, wide flat nose and a mole or birthmark..." He sent Kara a querying glance, and she tapped her right cheekbone. "Under his right eye."

Wilhite read the description back to him for confirmation.

"Oh, and I need you to send someone to Kara Pearson's house. Make sure nothing's out of order there. Have the officer bring dry clothes for her. The key is under the flowerpot at the end of her porch." He heard Wilhite grunt in disapproval and arched an eyebrow at Kara when she scowled at him. "And, yes, I've told her such a clichéd hiding place is asking to be robbed, but she contends Rusted Spur is a safe town, and she needs a hidden key for emergencies."

"I have a better idea. Take me home to change before we go to the sheriff's department," Kara said. "Besides getting dry clothes, I have to feed Jerry."

He arched an eyebrow in query.

"My new cat. A rescue."

Of course. Kara and her animals…

He held up a hand to quiet her as he continued instructing Wilhite. "I also need a replacement phone. Mine is somewhere in a washed-out arroyo a few miles from the Wheeler Ranch. The department should have one I can use until I can get a personal replacement."

Exiting the main alley of the stable, Kara stopped walking and crossed her arms over her chest as she glared at him.

Ignoring her pout, he finished his business with Wilhite, adding, "And have the officer that goes to Kara's check on her cat." He shot her a look that asked, *Satisfied?* "We should be there in five minutes. Get an artist in ASAP. I want Kara to help us create a composite of the shooter when we get there." He handed the borrowed phone back to the hand, who'd followed them to the stable door, and met Kara's gaze. "What's that look for?"

"I can't even go home for a hot shower and change of clothes?"

"Not when we have a violent criminal in the area. Finding the sniper trumps everything else, including our personal comfort. Time is of the essence in locating this guy, and he already has a four-hour lead on us." He paused and looked her up and down with a dent in his brow. "Unless you need to see a doctor. Do you have any injuries you haven't mentioned? Any lasting effects from our dunk in the water or the cold?"

She shook her head. "I'm okay now. A warm building, hot coffee and dry clothes are all I need." When he gave her a skeptical look, she added with a sassy grin, "You can trust me on this. After all, I work for a doctor."

"A doctor for horses and cows."

"Close enough."

"In that case, we're going to the station." He took her by the arm, tugging her forward as he marched across the muddy ranch yard toward his F-250.

She jerked her arm from his grasp. "And who died and made you the boss of me?"

Brady faced her, his jaw tight and his hands balled at his sides. "I'm the boss of you, because I'm the sheriff of this town, and you are my key witness to a felony crime. Do I need to take you into custody or are you going to come willingly?"

Kara snorted and shook her head. "Of course, you don't care what I want. Your job is all that matters. It was ten months ago, and it is now."

Needles of irritation prodded him. "What are you talking about? I care about what you want."

"Unless it conflicts with what *you* want. Namely, your position as sheriff. Right?"

Brady goggled at her. "Really? For months I've been trying to talk to you about us and what you want, and you've avoided me. But *now*—when there's a sniper to track down, when we are both freezing cold, hungry and exhausted—now you want to argue about your issues with my job?"

"My issues?" she hissed. "You make it sound like it's all my fault! That I'm being a whining prima donna or something!"

"I didn't say—" Brady cut himself off as a biting gust of wind cut through his wet clothes and sent a chill to his core. He sucked in a deep, calming breath. "Look, I want to have this conversation. Really, I do. But not now. Right now, we need to get to the sheriff's department and do all we can to catch the guy that shot at our friends and put Nate's father in the hospital."

Contrition and grief washed over her face, and her shoulders sagged.

"So are you coming willingly, or do I have to take you into custody?"

Holding her blanket closed with one hand, Kara blew warm breath on her free hand and sent him a disgruntled look. "I'm coming." As she strode past him, she grumbled quietly, "Your Majesty."

Gray dusky light filled the sky as they pulled into the sheriff's department parking lot, and Kara experienced an unsettling sense of déjà vu. She'd arrived at the sheriff's department about this same time of evening on the day her father drowned, and she'd been forced to give her account of what happened for the official report. The small beige brick building that housed the sheriff's department hadn't changed much in the sixteen years since her father's death. Nor had the sense of dread and grief knotting her gut. Being back here revived all her memories and emotions from that day, as if the intervening years had never happened.

Only the man sitting beside her was different. Yet having nearly lost Brady today in the same manner in which she'd lost her father added another layer to the eerie and upsetting familiarity of her return to the utilitarian one-story building and cracked pavement parking lot.

Brady grabbed his gym bag from the back seat, then escorted her inside. He held the front door for her and signaled to the first deputy he saw. "Anderson, we need two large cups of hot coffee ASAP and bring Kara whatever she wants to eat."

His side glance asked her to fill in that blank.

"Uh, just a hamburger is fine."

Returning his attention to the deputy, he said, "Make

it two…no, three burgers from Tumbleweeds. No onions, extra mustard and sweet potato fries."

Kara blinked her surprise as Brady reeled off her usual customized order. Remembering how she liked her hamburger wasn't a difficult thing, yet she was moved by his thoughtfulness all the same.

An older woman with her gray hair in a bun walked into the reception area from a back room. "Afternoon, sheriff. Heard you had a rough time today." She handed him a cell phone. "You asked for a new phone?"

"Yes. Thank you, Earlene." He took the phone and swiped the screen. The battery needed charging, but it was functional.

"You got lucky. The week before Christmas, this was the last one on the shelf at E-Mart."

Earlene turned to Kara and smiled. "Hi, Kara, dear. Are you all right, honey?"

"I'll live."

Earlene had worked in the department when Kara's father had been a deputy, and as the wife to a rancher, the older woman was a frequent customer at the large animal veterinary clinic where Kara was an assistant.

Brady waggled the new phone. "Make sure everyone in the department has this new number." He gave the older woman a wink of appreciation as he ushered Kara down the hall to an interrogation room, and she took a seat at the small scarred table. "I'm going to change and see if Wilhite's found you dry clothes. I'll be right back."

Before he left, he turned up the thermostat, and she grinned, remembering her father telling her how he used to hike up the temperature in the interrogation room to make suspects sweat—literally. Just being inside, out of the cold, damp air, was blissful, and she salivated, thinking about the coffee and burger on the way.

"Somebody round up some towels or a blanket for Kara," she heard Brady shout down the hall. "And where's the sketch artist I asked for?"

Kara closed her eyes and gathered her thoughts. As horrid as the memory was, she needed to conjure up the face of the shooter, search her recollection for distinguishing marks, eye color, clothing...anything that could help Brady and his deputies track down the man who'd opened fire at the wedding.

Her mind drifted to Nate and April. She knew they were safe, but Brady had said Nate's father had been shot and was critical. Such a dark stain on what should have been their happiest day!

Deputy Anderson entered the interrogation room and set a large Styrofoam cup and a few sugar packets in front of her. "I'm afraid we're out of creamer."

She shook her head in dismissal, even though she typically liked a generous amount of milk in her coffee. "This is fine. Thanks."

"Sheriff McCall asked me to get started taking your statement. He'll join us in a minute."

"Sheriff McCall? So formal, Burt. Have you forgotten I nearly married the man?"

The deputy smiled. "I haven't forgotten. But the boss likes everything by the book and professional, so there's no trouble down the line with the prosecution."

She grunted. By the book. That was *so* Brady. "I understand."

"The artist will be here in about twenty minutes, but for now, can you give me an account of what happened today at the Wheeler Ranch? You were attending the wedding, correct?"

"That's right."

"Did you see anything or anyone that seemed out of place or suspicious as you arrived?"

"No." She shook her head. "Honestly, I was looking for Brady. I really didn't notice much else."

Anderson arched an eyebrow as if her admission was an intriguing bit of gossip.

He led her through questions about what she remembered from the start of the ceremony up to the point where she left for the barn.

Brady came in before she could answer, wearing a clean, long-sleeved Mavericks T-shirt and blue jeans. Before he took a seat across from her, he placed four half-and-half creamers next to her coffee.

She raised a startled glance to him. "I thought y'all were out of creamer."

He smiled and put a finger over his lips. "Shh. Those are from my private stash. Don't tell anyone, or I'll be forced to share."

Deputy Anderson scoffed and gave Brady a disgruntled look. "Private stash, huh?"

"You heard nothing. Carry on." He nodded toward the notepad where Anderson wrote her answers.

While the deputy glanced down to find his place, Kara ripped open the first of the four creamers. *Exactly four. Just as she liked.*

"So you left the ceremony and entered the barn. Why?"

"Because... I thought it would be quiet. Private."

"No," Deputy Anderson said, "I mean why did you leave the ceremony before it was over?"

Kara paused in the act of dumping her last creamer in her coffee. Her gaze flew to Brady, and her hand trembled. "Because I...needed air. I...was upset."

"What had upset you?" Anderson pushed.

Her mouth dried as she held Brady's intense blue stare.

His eyes echoed Anderson's question, and her throat, her voice felt paralyzed. How did she admit to Brady that he still held her heart in his hands? That leaving him was the most difficult thing she'd ever done, and not a day went by that she didn't question her sanity for having given him up?

When she didn't answer for several moments, Brady tilted his head and narrowed his eyes in query. "Kara, do you need him to repeat the question?"

With a sigh, she dropped her gaze to the table, to her hands, still red and chapped from the cold. "I was upset over seeing Brady again," she said with a glance to the deputy. "It was painful to be at a wedding, to have him watching me from beside the groom with so much hurt and accusation and challenge in his eyes."

"Accusation? I d—" Brady bit down on his words and visibly reined in his response, fisting his hands on the table and tightening his jaw.

After a tense second of silence, Deputy Anderson said, "Sheriff?"

Brady shook his head. "Sorry. Please, continue."

Kara pinched the bridge of her nose and groaned. "Look, this is difficult for me to talk about, but there's really no point dancing around the issue. We all know the situation between us." She drew on the steel nerves that helped her climb in the rodeo arena with bucking bulls and broncs and turned on her seat to face Brady fully. "I still have feelings for you, and it hurt like hell to see you standing up there in your tux, hearing the liturgy read and knowing that we'd never have the wedding we planned."

Brady's expression changed. Not dramatically, but she knew him well enough to detect the slight lift of his brow, widening of his eyes and softening of his mouth. He sat straighter, and bittersweet emotion lit his eyes.

"So, yeah, I was upset," she plowed on, ignoring the

squeezing ache in her chest. "I was having a panic attack or something and needed space. Someplace quiet to regain my composure. The barn was the closest and easiest place to go. I saw the horses waiting just inside, and...well—" she flapped a hand toward Brady "—you know that animals help center me. How working with animals helped get me through losing my father."

He bobbed his head in a quick nod of agreement.

People had teased her about her menagerie of animals, but rescuing dogs and cats—and turtles, chickens and goats—had been therapeutic. She'd found purpose, unconditional love and a career path as she took care of the strays she adopted. Because of her work schedule at the veterinarian clinic and frequent trips out of town for rodeo events, she'd winnowed her animal population down to one cat and a red-eared slider turtle.

Deputy Anderson shifted in his chair, clearly uneasy with the maudlin emotion and personal nature of what passed between her and Brady. Had the situation not been so serious, she'd have laughed at the lawman's deer-in-the-headlights look. *Men!* Why did sentimentality put them off?

A knock broke the tense silence, and Brady called, "Yeah?"

A female deputy poked her head in. "I have Ms. Pearson's clothes. And Deputy Wilhite asked me to tell you Lillian Scruggs, the forensic artist from Amarillo, has arrived."

"Thank you, Smith. Send her in." Brady stood and took the grocery sack the deputy held out to him.

"Oh, and I fed your cat some dry food while I was there," Deputy Smith said, looking to Kara. "He was meowing a lot and seemed pretty hungry."

She cracked a smile. "He's Siamese. They're a loud,

talkative breed. But, thanks. I'm sure Jerry appreciated getting some supper."

Brady passed the bag to Kara. "Why don't you go change before you start with the artist?"

"Thank you! I think I will," she said more sharply than she intended, but her nerves were frayed, and fatigue, hunger and stress were doing a number on her patience.

In the ladies' room, she stripped out of her wet clothes and eagerly donned the dry ones. Thank goodness a female officer had been sent to her house. She hated to think of one of Brady's men pawing through her underwear drawer and bras. By the time she'd changed into the clean jeans and thick fleece sweatshirt, her food had arrived as well, and she dived into the burger and fries as if she hadn't eaten in a week.

Thus began a multitasking fest as she gobbled her dinner, worked with the artist between bites, and answered additional questions for Brady.

"Based on the trajectory and location of the bullets recovered at the scene, we have reason to believe April was the shooter's target," Brady said.

Kara paused with a sweet potato fry halfway to her mouth. The food in her stomach rebelled at the notion of someone hurting her sweet friend.

"Can you think of any reason someone would want April killed?" Brady asked, tapping his pen against his notepad.

She scowled. "Of course not! April's a kind, generous, warm-hearted person. Why would anyone want to hurt her?"

Brady drew an impatient breath and, puffing his cheeks, blew it out with a groan. "Your personal opinion of her is not what I asked. Now think!"

She tensed at his scolding tone and swatted at his hand when he snitched one of her fries.

"Has she mentioned any harassing phone calls or trouble with a client? Maybe a disagreement from high school that has blown up again on Facebook?"

She wiped her greasy fingers on a napkin and dug through her memory for anything April could have mentioned. April was a paralegal for the Texas Justice Project, a nonprofit foundation that worked to get wrongly convicted inmates out of prison. She acknowledged with a wince that her friend's job was fodder for any number of disgruntled people's wrath.

"How's this? Is the nose right, now?" the artist asked, turning the sketch toward her. Her head throbbed as her attention was pulled in a different direction. The artist had, in fact, done a remarkably good job rendering the shooter's odd combination of sharply angled cheeks, chin and jaw with his flat nose. So good, in fact, that a tingle of recognition became a flash of memory.

She gasped and, without thinking about the action, she reached for Brady's hand. Squeezing his fingers, she stared at the drawing and focused on bringing the memory to the fore.

"Yes," she rasped.

Brady leaned toward her and covered her clutching hand with his. "That's him? The man you saw today?"

She nodded. "Something about the eyes is still off, but… it's close." She cleared her throat and squeezed her eyes shut, trying to grasp on to the memory that taunted her. "But I…saw him before today, too."

Brady stiffened. "What?"

"I…" Kara searched her memory, her heart thudding. "He…he was at the funeral!"

Brady frowned. "What funeral?"

She opened her eyes to blink at Brady. "For April's boss, Martin Villareal."

Brady sat straighter, and his eyebrows shot up. "The lead attorney for the Texas Justice Project?"

"The same. He was killed in a hit-and-run accident in Austin while jogging, and I went with her to the funeral because Nate was busy with something he couldn't get out of."

Brady tugged his hand loose from hers, so he could write. "When was this?"

"A couple weeks ago."

"And you're sure the guy you saw today is the same man you remember from the funeral?"

"Pretty sure. I remember he looked out of place. He didn't fit in with the suits and other lawyer types that were there." She leaned toward Brady and chewed her bottom lip. "Brady, April was really upset about her boss's death. And not just for the obvious reasons—the suddenness, the lack of a suspect, the tragedy of it all. She said that last summer the office had received lots of threats. Back in June, they won a big case, getting this guy exonerated for murder." She bit her lip as she thought. "What was his name? Champion? Campbell?"

"Chambers?" Brady suggested, a knowing look on his face.

She replayed the name in her head. "Yeah. Chambers."

"Ross—"

"—Allen Chambers," she finished with him. "You've heard of him."

"His trial and exoneration have crossed my news feed more than a few times. Now that you mention it, I remember Nate saying April was involved with Chambers's case."

"Driving home from the funeral, she told me the evidence for exoneration was clear-cut, but there were still plenty of people who were none too pleased with her team from the Texas Justice Project for leading the movement to have Chambers cleared. The office received hate mail, bomb threats…"

"Any specific to April?"

"Well…yeah. She did that TV interview about the case, and it called attention to her, where she'd normally be working in the background. She hated the attention. You know how private April is. I guess when she got hate mail directed to her, she dismissed it, along with the other crazies blasting the office."

Brady pinched his nose. "So there *are* people out there with a beef against April, even if indirectly, because of her work with the Texas Justice Project."

Kara bit back the impulse to defend herself and her naive, gut-reaction protests earlier. Yes, it was unfathomable that anyone would want to hurt the April she knew. But clearly April could have earned enemies through her legal work.

That was, after all, what April had suspected about her boss. "Yes. Someone could have a beef with her because of the Chambers exoneration or any other case she worked. In fact—" Kara's gut soured as the full extent of her conversation with April came back to her "—she said she had reason to believe there was more to Villareal's death than simple hit-and-run."

Brady's laser gaze shot back to her, his eyebrows lifting. "Go on."

"When we were driving home from Austin, she told me she feared the hit-and-run was a planned attack. April suspected that her boss could have been murdered."

Chapter 6

Kara's face drained of color as she gaped at him, the ramifications of what she'd remembered clearly crystalizing for her. "If April's boss was murdered, if she was the target of the sniper...and this guy is still out there..." Kara released a ragged breath. "Brady, April is still in danger! That guy could go after her again. He could—"

"I'm way ahead of you, babe." Hitting the intercom button on the phone by the door, he said, "Earlene, get Nate Wheeler on the phone for me, and send Wilhite back in here."

"Roger that, sheriff," his dispatch operator/front desk officer answered.

When he faced Kara again, her brow was furrowed.

"What?"

"Don't call me *babe*."

He blinked and tightened his jaw. "You used to like it."

"Past tense. We're not a couple anymore, so... I'm not your 'babe.'"

He huffed a sigh and squeezed his pen so tight he was surprised it didn't snap. "Whatever." With everything else coming down today, she was worried about him using his old endearment for her?

Wilhite opened the door. "You wanted to see me?"

"Yeah. What have you heard back on the fingerprints recovered from the abandoned car?" To cover his irritation with Kara's bluntness, he scratched a note on his pad to look into the threats made to the Texas Justice Project last summer and any information the Austin police had on Villareal's accident.

"Nothing yet. Lab's backed up, as usual, but they thought they'd have something by morning."

Brady clenched his teeth and shook his head. "Not good enough. We need to find this guy before he disappears in the wind...if he hasn't already." He pounded the arm of his chair with his fist. "Call the lab back and tell them this is high priority."

Wilhite lifted a corner of his mouth. "Already did, but I'll call again and give 'em another push. But it's the weekend before Christmas, boss. Folks are on vacation, and the lab is working a skeleton crew."

Brady muttered a pithy curse in response. "Call the Austin PD and ask them to send us mug shots of anyone even close to the description *Miss Pearson* has given us." He spoke the formal address with emphasis. "Especially anyone who might be considered a gun for hire."

Kara frowned at him, then lifted her cup, looked inside and set it back down without drinking.

"Austin? Why Austin?" Wilhite asked.

"Miss Pearson thinks she saw the shooter in Austin a couple weeks ago at a funeral. Bring the mug shots in here as soon as you get them for her to review."

Deputy Wilhite nodded. "Will do."

Anything else?"

"Yeah. Bring Miss Pearson more coffee and four creamers from my bottom left desk drawer." He cut his glance to the forensic artist. "Ms. Scruggs, coffee?"

The artist smiled and shook her head. "No, thanks."

"What abandoned car?" Kara asked after Wilhite left.

"The one my men found a short distance down the road from the Wheeler Ranch while we were swimming in icy floodwaters." He heard the off-putting tone in his reply and immediately regretted it. He wanted to rebuild his relationship with Kara, not fight with her. But her comment about not being his "babe" had stung more than he cared to admit. To him, Kara would always be his. She would always be part of his soul.

She shifted in her chair and wet her chapped lips. "Why didn't you tell me about the car before now?"

"Because you're not one of my deputies. You're here only because you're a material witness to the shooting," he replied, his tone matter-of-fact.

A flicker of hurt flashed in her eyes before she dropped her gaze to her plate of fries. She'd been eating with gusto moments ago, but since recognizing the man in the artist's drawing and making the connection to April, Kara had only played with the food. Knowing her soft heart, her compassion and love for her friends, he knew how hard she must be taking the theory that April could be in danger.

"Sheriff, ringing Nate Wheeler on line two," Earlene said via the intercom.

"Thanks." He lifted the receiver in time to hear his friend answer the call. "Hey, man, it's Brady."

"Thank God it's you," Nate said. "We've been worried as hell you might have been ambushed out there or frozen or something in that storm—"

"I'm fine. Kara, too, but—"

"So Kara was the missing guest?"

Impatient to get to the point, Brady said, "Just listen to me, Nate. Do you still have April with you?"

"Yeah, why?" Nate's voice was strung with tension. Understandable, since his wedding had been disrupted by gunfire, and his father was fighting for his life. Not to mention the whole issue of April's apparent cold feet just before the shots rang out.

"I have reason to believe she was the target of the shooting. Kara has remembered seeing the shooter at Villareal's funeral, and based on that and the trajectory of the bullets, I believe April's still in very real danger. We haven't found the shooter yet, so keep April close and your eyes open for anything suspicious."

Nate heaved a weary-sounding sigh. "We'd drawn the same conclusion, but your confirmation only strengthens my arguments."

"Arguments? Everything okay, man?"

He grunted. "Long story. Thanks for the warning. I won't let her out of my sight."

"Should I send one of my deputies up there for added protection?"

"I've got this, Brady. You're shorthanded as it is, and I want every man available looking for the scum that shot my dad. God only knows where that guy is and what his next move might be. The sooner April and the baby are safe, the better."

After assuring Nate that he and Kara were unhurt from their ordeal and receiving a "no change" status update on Nate's father, Brady promised to keep Nate informed on the progress of the case and hung up. As he turned back toward Kara, Nate's words replayed in his head. *God only knows where that guy is and what his next move might be.*

A chill raced down his spine. Kara had seen the sniper... *and he'd seen her. He'd shot at her.*

April's life wasn't the only one in danger. The shooter could easily come after Kara and try to silence the only witness to his crime.

Chapter 7

Kara worked for another hour with the artist, getting the sketch of the man's eyes closer to what she remembered and fine-tuning aspects of the drawing that were still off a bit.

Brady sat across from her, watching and listening...and making her nervous. Something in his countenance had changed after his call to Nate. He assured her Nate, April and the baby were fine, if stressed out by the day's events, but she could sense something had changed.

"How close to right is the drawing now?" Brady interrupted after tapping his fingers restlessly for several minutes. "If we're down to tweaking the length of his earlobes, I'd like to get copies made and sent out to local businesses and law enforcement around the state."

The artist glanced from Brady to Kara with a question in her expression. "Ma'am?"

Kara sent him a disgruntled frown, then studied the picture one more time. "There's still something nagging me about it that's not right but…I can't put my finger on it. I'm sorry. Maybe if we finished in the morning after I've gotten some sleep—"

"No." Brady swiped a hand down his jaw and groaned. "We need to send the picture out tonight. Like hours ago. Is it close enough?"

Kara flopped back in the chair and plowed her fingers into her hair. Mud from the floodwater had dried in her hair, despite the mini-wash she'd done in the sheriff's department bathroom. She wanted the picture to be exactly right, but she also longed for a hot shower and her own bed.

"It's…ninety-five or ninety-eight percent right, but—"

Brady grunted and slapped a hand to his forehead. Shoving his chair back, he took the sketch pad from the artist. "Thank you, Ms. Scruggs. We're done here. If you'll stop by the front desk and sign out, Earlene will see to your payment."

Brady headed to the door with the drawing.

"So I'm done?" Kara asked, pushing her chair back, as well.

"No." He aimed a finger at her. "I'll be right back. Stay put."

"But—"

He disappeared without listening to her protest.

She growled under her breath and dropped in the chair.

"Cut him a little slack, honey," Ms. Scruggs said as she gathered her purse and coat.

Kara blinked at the woman. "Pardon?"

"The sheriff." She smiled sweetly and laid a hand on Kara's shoulder. "He's tired, too, and working hard to deal with this mess."

Flashing a polite smile, Kara said, "I know. It's just…"

"Even though he's been kinda tough on you tonight, it's obvious how much he cares."

Kara's pulse kicked. "I, uh—yeah. He cares about his job—" *More than he cares about me*, she thought gloomily. "And he's good at it."

"Well, yes." Ms. Scruggs tucked her purse close to her body and stepped out from behind the table. "But I meant how much he cares for *you*."

The comment so closely contradicted her last thought that Kara goggled, stunned for a moment. "Um, wh-why do you say that?"

Ms. Scruggs chuckled lightly. "Oh, honey. It's so obvious. Have you not seen the way he looks at you?"

"Uh…" She'd felt Brady's gaze even when she couldn't meet his eyes, but—

"And from what I overheard at the front desk when I arrived, he took off into the storm this afternoon to look for you. Is that right?"

Kara gave a small, stiff nod.

The artist flipped a hand up. "See, there. He could have delegated that to a deputy or another agency or any number of guests from the wedding who know that property like the back of their hand. But Deputy Wilhite said the sheriff didn't think twice about going after you himself."

She shifted in the chair. "Well, we do have some history…"

"History?" Ms. Scruggs marched over to the door, sliding her arms into her coat. "History implies everything is over, in the past. And there's nothing 'over' about how that man feels for you." She gave a wink as she pulled the door open and backed out of the room. "And I'd wager, if you were honest, your feelings for him aren't in the past either."

Kara opened her mouth to argue, but a lump clogged her throat.

"Good night, honey." Ms. Scruggs waggled her fingers. "And good luck with the sheriff. You're a lucky girl to have a man like that."

A squeak of dismay wheezed from Kara's throat, but only after the door had swung closed. Burying her face in her hands, she dropped weakly back into her chair.

Lucky to have Brady? Yeah, that's how she'd felt…once.

Okay, if she were honest with herself, she still had feelings for Brady. Of course she did. That's why it was so hard to be around him. It hurt to think about what she'd lost when she walked away from him. A damnable little voice in her heart said she'd made the most foolish mistake of her life letting him go. The easiest way to shout down that little nagging voice was to simply avoid him. Out of sight, out of mind, right? She snorted indelicately. If only it were so easy.

And, as if on cue, Brady waltzed back into the interrogation room and closed the door behind him. She eyed him through the gaps between her fingers.

"All right. Earlene and Anderson are getting copies of the composite of the sniper sent out all around town, and Wilhite should have those mug shots for you to look at shortly. I have to do a bunch of paperwork." He said the last with a groan of resignation in his tone. Then with a deep fortifying breath, he shook his head and squared his shoulders. Sir Galahad readying for battle. "Do you need anything before I go dig into reports and requisition forms?"

She moved her hands to the top of the table and let her back hunch, her head loll back. Fatigue had settled deep in her bones, and keeping her eyes open was a bigger challenge by the minute. "My bed."

When Brady didn't reply for several seconds, she raised her head and met his gaze. Though she'd answered honestly and meant nothing provocative with her reply, she saw heat and longing in his eyes. Her mouth dried as her mind conjured the same memories that she guessed, based on his hooded gaze, he was mentally replaying. Nights spent in her bed, wrapped in each other's arms, sheets twisted and quilts thrown off.

Tired though she was, a spark of lust zinged through her and fueled her pulse to a needy, expectant rhythm. After the day she'd had, the roller coaster her emotions had been on, the beating her body had taken, she'd love nothing more than to curl up naked under her covers with Brady and lose herself in his kiss, his caress, the heat of his body against hers.

"Brady..." she whispered, her voice a husky rasp.

"I'm afraid we're not quite finished with you, Miss Pearson."

His formal address speared her heart. She'd been snippy about his use of his endearment earlier, but the stiff formality cut at her even more than the intimate nickname had. She wished she could take back her defensive bickering, the testy tone and sharp words born out of her fatigue and pain. An apology rose to her tongue, but before she could find the right words, he said, "We'll try to make you comfortable until your services are no longer needed."

Again with the stiff formality. As if she were some Jane Doe and not someone with whom he'd shared a toothbrush, made love and dreamed of the future.

Defeat punctured the bubble of emotion filling her chest. Clearly they'd get nowhere laying their past to rest tonight. Not while he was in full-on sheriff mode. Kara sighed and raked fingers through her messy hair. "Why can't I go home now? You have your sketch, and I've told you all I remember about the shooting and seeing the guy at the funeral."

"Soon. Once you've looked at the mug shots Wilhite is pulling together and I finish a bit of paperwork, I'll take you home."

"I don't remember inviting you."

"Cute," he said with a wry grin. "But I'm not letting you go back to your house alone. Whoever the shooter was, he hasn't been caught."

A fresh spurt of alarm shot through her. "You think he'll come after me? But how? He doesn't know who I am, where I live—"

"Maybe." Brady flipped up a palm. "Maybe not." His eyebrows lowered into a V as his gaze darkened and drilled into her. "If this guy is a professional, a gun for hire, as we suspect he might be, he'll find a way to identify you. He won't leave a loose end."

Acid puddled in her gut, and despite the quiver of fear shimmying through her, she scoffed a laugh. "You're not making me feel better."

Her humor, her default defense, did nothing to crack the grave look on Brady's face. "My job's not to give you a false sense of security. It's to keep you safe, and that's what I intend to do."

Heart thundering, she gaped at Brady, stunned speechless. This ordeal wasn't over. She could have a killer tracking her at this moment.

After a tense moment of silence, he blew out a breath and shuffled back to the door. "You can sleep on the couch in my office until we get the mug shots in for you to look at. Or you can wait in here. Your choice."

Still in shock, her tired brain slow to process this latest bombshell, Kara made no move to get up and follow him to his office. He apparently took that as a refusal of his offer and slipped into the hall without a backward glance. The click of the closing door rattled her nerves as if it were the clank of a jail cell slamming shut. She cast a glance around the sterile, aged interrogation room, and a shudder rolled through her.

She didn't want to be alone. Though she'd prided herself

on her independence since her mother had died of cancer
a few years after her father's drowning, she'd never truly
liked being on her own. Her pets and her friends helped
fill some of the void in her life, but nothing really filled
the empty part of her soul that longed for a companion.
Until she'd started dating Brady.

Her capable and headstrong side chafed at the notion of
needing anyone. Counting on anyone, investing herself in
anyone only set herself up for heartache and disappointment later, the cynical voice inside her said. But at night,
when she couldn't sleep, when the dark revealed her deepest hurts and desires, she longed for someone in her life.

"Nothing wrong with that," her friend Hannah had told
her when Kara had confessed to being lonely.

"Wanting love, wanting to find someone to share your
life with—*a soul mate*—doesn't make you weak," Hannah had said as they shared a bottle of wine on a recent
Friday night. "It makes you human."

Kara slumped in the interrogation room's hard chair,
achy, frightened and dejected as she recalled that conversation. For a while, she'd thought that someone special would
be Brady. But his new career path—or more precisely, his
disregard for her wishes—had forced her to make the hard
choice to leave him.

Not knowing how long it might take for Deputy Wilhite
to obtain the mug shots, Kara shoved back her chair and
dragged herself to her feet. Stepping into the corridor, she
glanced down the empty hall. She knew which office was
Brady's. The sheriff had used the same one since before
the days when her father had been a deputy.

She headed toward Brady's door, taking in the shiny
Christmas garland and pictures of Santa and his reindeer
decorating the walls. Earlene's doing, she felt sure. A pang
of sadness twisted in her chest at the thought of spending

another Christmas without her parents. Sure, she'd made plans to have dinner with Dr. Rutledge, her boss at the vet clinic, and his family, but she knew it had been a pity invite. Poor Kara, no family to spend Christmas with. Hannah would be in Dallas with her sister. April and Nate were supposed to be on their honeymoon.

Another twinge of worry tugged at her. She prayed Nate, April and the baby were safe. At least they had each other. Now husband and wife.

She frowned. Or were they? Had they finished their vows before the sniper opened fire? She hadn't thought before now to ask.

When she reached Brady's door, she paused on the threshold. He looked up from the spread of documents on his desk. He nodded a head toward the worn and aged couch across from him, then bent back over his work. "Help yourself."

"Are April and Nate married?" she blurted.

He glanced up again, clearly startled by her question. "Uh…no."

Her heart sank, disappointed for her friends. "No? The sniper stopped the wedding before they got that far?"

Brady's desk chair creaked as he leaned back, his expression somber. "Actually, April stopped it."

She blinked and scowled. "What?"

"Right before the shots were fired, she told Nate she'd changed her mind. That she couldn't go through with it."

Dismay rolled through her, and Kara grabbed the door frame for support. "Oh, my God. Why?"

"Good question. All hell broke loose before she could explain herself."

She stumbled to the couch and sank onto the thin cushions. "Poor April."

"Poor April?" He gave a humorless chuckle. "What

about poor Nate? He's the one who got dumped. I'm sure he feels pretty rotten." He shook his head, then muttered, "I know how that goes."

She sent him a peeved look for his side comment, then shook it off. Still not the time to get into their relationship... or rather, their former relationship. "I just meant, April must be hurting and so confused to have changed her mind."

"I guess. I—" Brady's desk phone rang, interrupting whatever he'd planned to say. Reaching for the receiver he said, "Excuse me."

Kara considered the thin, lumpy couch for a moment while Brady listened to the caller, adding the occasional "mmm-hmm" or "okay." While the sofa didn't look especially comfortable, it beat the chair in the interrogation room, hands down. She lay down on the couch, using her stacked hands as a pillow, and closed her eyes.

Soon, the drone of Brady's voice and squeak of his chair faded into oblivion, and she drifted into a restless sleep.

When Brady finished his call with the Austin PD sergeant who was sending the mug shots, he turned his chair back to his desk and surveyed the stacks of paperwork that had piled up just since he'd left the office the day before. The shooting incident and manhunt for the sniper meant he was buried with a whole new mountain of documents, forms and reports. The paperwork was tedious and boring for guy like him, who thrived on the mystery and science behind catching criminals. On days like today, he missed forensics. He itched to get in the field and dissect a crime scene, to study the physical evidence in a lab and assemble the puzzle of what happened. Instead, he was trapped in his office signing requests for information, typing up incident reports from others who'd done the interesting work.

He'd taken a job as interim sheriff because he thought it

was a career move he couldn't pass up. But more and more, he regretted his decision, especially since it seemed to be the crux of the issue behind Kara leaving him.

He really didn't understand her objection to his job. After all, her father had been in law enforcement. She'd given him some reason along the lines of how dangerous the work was, but Brady had easily dismissed that excuse. Rusted Spur was hardly a hotbed of criminal activity. With the exception of today's shooting, the biggest danger he encountered on the job was generally a paper cut from all the stupid forms he had to complete.

No, he was certain there was more behind Kara's breakup than him taking the interim sheriff position. He just wished he could pin her down for more than five minutes to get some real answers from her. Maybe today, once he had all of the law enforcement responsibilities behind him, he could wrangle the truth from her. She owed him that much after what they'd shared.

He shifted his gaze to where she slept, curled on his sofa, and something deep inside him quickened at the sight. She'd hate to be called vulnerable. She would, no doubt, lift her chin in that irreverent, stubborn way she had and scoff in his face if she heard him use that term about her. She was, after all, the same woman who climbed in the ring with bucking bulls. She was the woman who'd risked her life in the flash flood today to save his neck. She was the woman who'd picked up the pieces after losing both parents in a few short years and worked her way through college. But she wasn't immune to bullets, and when he thought of how close the sniper had come to shooting her today, his stomach filled with acid.

He also could have lost her to exposure if he hadn't seen the wandering mare and tracked Kara down. Or she could have died in the swift water, trying to rescue him.

Yeah, his Kara was brave and capable—sometimes a little reckless—but she was human. And the traumas of the day had taken their toll on her.

Even in sleep, her brow bore a dent of worry. With her hands tucked under her head, she reminded him of his five-year-old niece when she napped at his house during his sister's visits. Kara's cheeks were still red and raw-looking from weathering the cold front, and her chapped lips were parted slightly as she slept. He thought of days past when he'd watched Kara sleep early in the morning before he'd kiss those same lips and head out to work.

His possessive and protective instincts surged inside him, tensing his muscles. If the sniper was looking for Kara, he'd have to come through Brady to get her.

Shifting his attention back to his paperwork, he groaned aloud when he found a purchase order from Earlene for toilet paper and office supplies that needed his approval. Clearly his predecessor had been a control freak.

His desk phone buzzed, and he punched the speaker button so he could continue signing forms while he talked. "Yes, Earlene?"

"I've got Harold Bunch from down at the Stop-N-Shop on line two. He says he thinks he saw the guy in the sketch you released a couple hours ago."

Brady paused mid-signature, his pulse kicking. "Put him through."

"Yes, sir."

"Oh, and, Earlene, the next time you have to buy toilet paper or any other supplies for the office, just buy the damn stuff and don't fill up my inbox with more paperwork. All right?"

"I... Yes, sir, sheriff."

He scrubbed a palm over the stubble on his cheek and

jabbed the button for line two. "Mr. Bunch? You say you saw the man in the sketch we sent out earlier?"

"That's right, sheriff. He came in 'bout ten o'clock, I'd say, bought some cigarettes and a sandwich outta the deli case. He had one of them knit hats on—you know, like the teenagers wear even when it's a hundred degrees outside. I don't understand why kids today think they need a winter hat on all the time. This is Texas, after all. I mean, I can see it today, now that it's turned cold—"

Brady drummed his fingers on the desk, trying to be patient with the store clerk. "Mr. Bunch, the man who came in...you're sure it's the same guy in the sketch?"

"I reckon so. That hat was pulled low, but I saw his face plain enough. It's the same guy."

Brady processed that information. So the sniper had stayed in the area. A dangerous move. Maybe he thought April was still in town and wanted another shot at her.

"Mr. Bunch, did anyone else see him? Do you have security cameras in the store?"

"Well, Jim and Mabel Greer was in here at the same time, and we was talkin' about the wedding down at the Wheeler Ranch today. The guy seemed like he was in a real big hurry to get outta there after he paid for his cigarettes, but then he slowed up all of a sudden and acted mighty interested in the candy aisle. When I asked him if I could help him find anything, he shook his head and took off. I think he was eavesdroppin' on Mabel and Jim."

A prickle of apprehension crept up Brady's neck. "Can you remember, specifically, what you were discussing that might have caught his attention?"

"Well, let's see..."

Brady shoved the paperwork aside and leaned toward the phone as if he could hurry the store clerk's recollection with his anxious body position.

"We'd talked about how it looked like the bride was changing her mind right before everything went to hell. Then Mabel was sayin' how the Pearson gal lit out of the barn on the bride's horse and...well..."

When the man hesitated, Brady gritted his teeth. "Go on."

"She said she saw how you took off after her like maybe you thought Miss Kara'd done the shooting."

A sick feeling churned in Brady's gut. "Mr. Bunch, think carefully. Did you mention Kara Pearson by name in this discussion?"

"Well..."

Brady waited through another nerve-scraping hesitation.

"I believe so. Mabel said something 'bout how you and Kara were a couple once, and weren't it a shame that y'all hadn't made it work out."

Brady shoved down the frustration of having his love life discussed by the town, and focused on the more important detail. The sniper could have learned Kara's identity, could know the name of the one person who'd seen him at the scene of the crime.

"Did the guy, by any chance, pay with a credit card?"

"Naw. Cash."

Brady had expected as much, but it was worth a shot. "Thank you for calling, Mr. Bunch. I'll send a deputy by to take an official statement."

He disconnected the call and rocked back in his desk chair with a deep exhale of dread. Suddenly it seemed far less likely that the sniper had left town to look for April and more likely he'd stayed to find Kara. And keep her quiet.

Chapter 8

"Kara?" A quiet voice she knew well nudged her out of sleep, while a warm hand gently shook her shoulder. For the briefest moment, she could pretend she was at home in her bed, that this familiar routine was just another day like she'd shared with Brady so many times before. He was leaving for work and telling her goodbye…

"The mug shots from Austin are here. We need you to look at them."

And just like that, the sweet sense of familiarity, that all was right with the world once more, shattered. Mug shots. Of the shooter. Who'd tried to kill her.

Adrenaline and a renewed disquiet shot through her, and the cobwebs of sleep were banished. She sat up quickly, blinking against the light in Brady's office. "How long was I asleep?"

"About an hour." He put a hand under her arm to help her rise to her feet, but she batted him away. "Sorry to wake you, but the sooner we get an ID on this cretin, the better."

She scrubbed a hand over her face and pushed her unkempt hair back from her face. Her muscles were stiff, and she moaned as she pushed to her feet and stretched the kink from her back. "Lead on."

Wilhite was waiting on them in the interrogation room, a laptop set up with a screen full of mug shots already on display. With a wave of his hand, Brady motioned her to the chair in front of the computer, then took a seat beside her.

"So how does this work? I just look at all these pictures and tell you if I see the guy?" Her stomach fluttered a bit at the thought of the shooter's dark glare.

"Pretty much." Brady angled the computer so they could both see the screen. "Just remember, he could have facial hair or a different hairstyle, even a different hair color. So look at the things that don't change. Nose shape, spacing of eyes, moles and so forth."

She leaned forward and narrowed her gaze on the faces staring back at her. "None of those."

"Take your time. Look carefully," Brady said, but clicked to the next screen.

She studied the next set of mug shots, all too aware of the brush of Brady's arm against hers as he leaned in to look, as well. Wasn't this task hard enough without the distraction of Brady's hard muscles and warm body next to her? The scent of his aftershave clung to the clothes he'd changed into and tickled her senses.

She steeled herself to his effect on her and tried hard to concentrate on the pictures that flashed on the screen. "No. No. No," she said again and again as the parade of faces yielded nothing.

After several minutes with no success, Brady sighed.

"Are you sure, Kara? Concentrate. None of these guys look even remotely familiar?"

She cast him a disgruntled side glance. "Don't you think I'm trying? I want to catch this guy as much as you do. Maybe more. After all, he shot at me. He tried to kill me."

Brady held up a hand to silence her. "I know. But I also know you're tired and want to be sure you're really focusing. This is important."

A snarky retort formed on her tongue, but she swallowed it. Bickering with Brady served no purpose. Rubbing her fingers against her temple, Kara studied the screen again. "No, none of these."

Brady clicked the next screen, and she shook her head at the unfamiliar faces. But when the next screen came up, one face jumped out at her. Her pulse spiked, and she grabbed Brady's wrist. "Wait!"

She leaned closer and squinted at the screen. Pointing, she asked, "Can you make that picture bigger?"

With the roll of the wireless mouse and a few clicks, Brady made the mug shot that had caught her attention full screen. A chill seeped to her bones, and she said in a raspy voice, "That's him."

Brady gave her a hard look. "You're sure?"

She studied the picture and knew right away why she'd not been able to get the eyes just right with the sketch artist. The mark under his eye wasn't a mole.

"It's a tattoo," she mumbled, more to herself than anyone else. A teardrop tattoo, she realized, and shuddered.

She remembered watching a movie with Brady months ago, in which one of the characters had a teardrop tattoo. Brady had explained to her that the tattoo had two meanings. Originally, such a mark signified the wearer had been raped in prison. More recently, the body art had been adopted by those who wanted to tell the world they'd committed a murder. She'd wager the sniper's tattoo meant the latter.

"Kara?" Brady prompted.

She wrapped her arms around herself, recalling the moments of terror in the Wheeler barn, the crack of gunfire ringing in her ears and this man's lethal glare boring into her. "Yes. I'm sure that's him. That's the guy who shot at me at the Wheeler barn today." She frowned and looked at the clock. "Or yesterday, rather."

"And Villareal's funeral in Austin. Same guy you saw there?"

She stared at the man's craggy face and nodded. "It is."

Brady turned to Deputy Wilhite. "Get me everything you can find about Dennis Cobb. And have the lab compare the fingerprints from the abandoned car with the ones in the system for Cobb."

Wilhite jerked a nod as he left the room. "I'm on it."

Brady put his hand at her nape and his fingers massaged the tense muscles of her neck. "Good work, ba—" He paused, sighing, then finished, "Kara."

She savored the bone-melting bliss of the deep rubs and tried not to think about how much she missed his touch. Brady's fingers were as talented with a foot or shoulder rub as they were in bringing her to climax.

Don't go there...

Kara cleared her throat and glanced back at him. "So can I go home now?"

He dropped his hand from her back and moved to the door. "Soon. I don't want you going alone, and I have a thing or two to finish up before we go."

Pivoting on the chair, she angled a dubious look at him. "We? You're going home with me?"

"That was the plan."

"Why? Haven't I cooperated? I've answered all your questions, told you everything I remember—"

"Kara, I have a report that a guy that looked like your sketch was seen at the Stop-N-Shop earlier tonight." Brady squared his shoulders. "I don't think it's safe for you to be home alone. He could be looking for you. I'm going to stay with you until he's caught."

Her heart thumped harder, but she couldn't be sure whether it was because of the news that the shooter was still in the area...or because Brady was volunteering his protection. Both scenarios were cause for alarm.

On one hand, she had a man gunning for her life. On the other hand, she had Brady, poised to break her heart. Again.

"We got a match!" Wilhite announced as he strode through Brady's office door without knocking. He waved a sheet of paper, then slapped it on Brady's desk. "The prints from the abandoned car match the ones that belong to the repeat offender outta Austin that Kara identified as the shooter."

"Dennis Cobb?" Brady asked for confirmation.

"Dennis Cobb."

Kara sat up from where she'd been slumped on Brady's couch again, waiting for him to take her home. He could tell she was disgruntled with him over his plan to guard her, but...too bad. Not only was it his job to protect her, he cared about her. She needed to get used to the idea that he was going to stick to her like fly paper until Cobb was arrested. Longer, if he had his say. He couldn't help believing fate had thrown them together for a reason. He intended to take full advantage of the opportunity to hash things out with her.

Wilhite tapped the top of the page where Cobb's name

and mug shot stared back at Brady. "The guy's got a rap sheet a mile long. Car theft, assault, parole violations and drugs, to name a few."

Kara grunted her disgust. "So why is the guy on the street instead of locked up?"

Brady thought of his earlier conversation with Nate and Kara's assertion that she'd seen Cobb at the funeral she'd attended two weeks prior with April.

"Cross-check Dennis Cobb and any known associates with anything related to Martin Villareal's death earlier this month." Then, after a moment's thought he added, "Or any connection to Ross Allen Chambers's exoneration."

"Chambers?" Wilhite sounded stunned.

"You heard me. And call Nate Wheeler and find out if he or April know the name. If he was gunning for April, as we suspect, there's got to be a connection somewhere."

His deputy gave a low whistle. "All right. I'll let you know what I find."

As his deputy turned to leave the office, Brady frowned. "Wilhite? When did you come in today?"

The deputy shrugged. "8:00 a.m."

Brady stood and put on his duty belt and coat. "That's what I thought. Get some sleep. Give all this to Deputy Smith to work on tonight, and we'll pick it up in the morning."

Wilhite opened his mouth, and before he could argue, Brady added, "That's an order. I'm taking Kara home and will work from there until further notice."

Wilhite divided a knowing look between Brady and Kara. "Okay. Good night…and good luck."

"Finally." Kara pushed to her feet and stretched, eager to get home to her own bed. She followed Brady to the front of the sheriff's department, determined not to think about what it would mean to have Brady in her home again.

As they passed the front desk, Earlene called to Kara. "Wait a minute, honey. I forgot to give this to ya earlier." She reached under her desk and slid out a cardboard box with a variety of items, from cardigan sweaters to wrapped gifts. "This is all stuff left behind by folks at the wedding when they scattered after the shots were fired. The deputies brought it all here for safekeeping until the owners claim it." Earlene pulled out Kara's small dress purse and held it up. "This is yours, right? I checked the ID in the wallet."

A sense of gratitude washed through Kara, and a giddy joy raised a smile on her face. "Oh, my gosh, yes! Thank you." She took the purse and opened it, checking that her phone, her wallet, her keys were all still there. "I was afraid I was going to have to replace all this, cancel credit cards, change the locks on my house… You've just saved me major hassles! I could kiss you."

Earlene chuckled. "Save your kisses for the sheriff, honey. I'm just glad I could get it back to ya."

The older woman winked at her, and a sting of heat flushed Kara's cheeks as the kisses she'd shared with Brady at the arroyo flashed in her memory. She cut an awkward side glance to Brady, and the heat in his eyes said he was remembering those stolen moments, too.

Normally she'd be quick to correct anyone who suggested she still had any relationship with Brady. Why couldn't the town just let the idea of them together go? But she was so happy to have her belongings back, she let the comment slide. Tucking the purse under her arm, she turned to follow Brady out to his truck.

Finally something had gone right today. She allowed herself to exhale a breath she'd not realized she'd been holding.

The moment of relief was short-lived, however. As soon as she climbed in Brady's truck, she pulled out her phone and checked her messages. She had four missed calls and a dozen texts. Most were from Hannah, frantic to know where she was and if she was all right. But several texts were from Nate's phone. April had used her fiancé's phone to text:

Nate's dad shot. Following airlift to Lubbock. Where are you? Are you safe? Love u, A.

The messages that followed grew increasingly urgent-sounding, asking for assurances that Kara was safe and begging for word of her whereabouts. Updates on Nate's father were not encouraging either. But the most recent message April had sent was the most ominous, echoing Brady's theory about Cobb.

Nate says u saw the shooter. Please b careful. The creep may come looking for u. Let me know u r ok!! A.

Kara rubbed her weary eyes and quickly typed texts to both April and Hannah, reassuring them she was safe and apologizing for worrying them. After sticking her mobile phone back in her purse, she leaned her head back and closed her eyes.

Today had been so long, so traumatic...and if Brady and April were right about Cobb's intentions, the worst was yet to come.

Brady's thoughts went in a hundred directions as he drove Kara back to her house. The manhunt for Cobb, the possible connections to Martin Villareal's death...and

Kara. Always Kara. His thoughts hadn't been far from her since the day he met her.

Deep inside, he knew the events of today and the hours he'd spend with her until Cobb was arrested could make or break their relationship. Kara might argue that they had no relationship anymore, but he wouldn't give up on her without one last chance to understand her reasons for leaving. Her response to his kisses earlier this afternoon told him she still had feelings for him. They still shared a physical chemistry that sizzled and smoldered just under the surface of her pretenses to the contrary.

Gravel crunched under his tires as he turned onto her driveway and eased toward the front of her house. As his headlights swept the yard, he searched the property for signs of an intruder. Her house was dark except for a string of twinkling Christmas lights strung across the front porch roofline.

Kara had the passenger door open and was stumbling out of the front seat before he even had the truck in park. He hustled to catch up with her as she dug her keys out of her purse.

"Kara, wait!" he said in a low tone, wrapping his hand around hers before she could put the key in the lock.

"What now?" she grumbled, and her shoulders drooped. Her fatigue rolled off her in waves, and he knew how eager she was for a shower and sleep. But her comfort didn't preempt her safety.

"We have no idea where Cobb is." He took the key from her with surprising ease, which spoke to the extent of her weariness. "Let me go first, check things out, before you go in."

Her eyes widened as his meaning registered, and she cut an anxious gaze to her dark house. "You think he could be in there waiting for me?"

"I think it's better to be safe than sorry." He pushed her back from the door with a firm nudge. "Stay away from the door until I give the all clear. Got it?"

She gave him a dazed stare and a small nod.

Standing to the side himself, he unlocked the door and pushed it open. Taking his service weapon from his holster, he led with his gun as he eased inside, sweeping his gaze around one room, then the next. He moved deeper into the house, turning on lights and checking behind doors and furniture. He actually hoped Cobb was hiding somewhere in Kara's house. He'd love nothing more than to take the bastard down tonight and free April and Kara from the menace that hung over them all like a black cloud.

When he entered the laundry room, he reached for the switch for the overhead light. A rustling noise and movement by the large sink caught his attention, and he whipped his weapon toward the spot.

"Me-row!"

The loud meow jolted his heightened senses. Flicking on the light, he frowned at the large Siamese cat with dark brown markings that sat up in a laundry basket and blinked sleepily. "Hello, beastie." He huffed out a breath as his pulse settled back into a normal rhythm. "So you're the latest critter in her collection, huh?"

"Me-row!" the cat answered, and eyed Brady warily.

When he moved closer to pat the cat's head, the tom jumped out of the basket and skittered out of the room for cover.

From the kitchen, he heard Kara's voice cooing, "It's okay, Jerry. He won't hurt you. Come here, sweetie."

He found her crouching in the middle of the kitchen floor, rubbing the cat's neck. "I thought I told you to wait for the all clear."

"I did wait. When I didn't hear gunshots, shouting or

a scuffle, I figured it was safe to come in." She glanced up at him with a confident look. "And it is clear, right?"

He reholstered his gun. "Yeah," he grumbled. "You got lucky this time. But next time, do what I tell you."

She rolled her eyes and walked away from him, which irritated him all the more.

"Where are you going?" he asked as he followed her, his tone frosty.

"To get a hot shower and go to bed." She paused in the hall and faced him. "Do I have your permission, *sheriff*?"

She glared at him for a few seconds before continuing down the hall and disappearing into the bathroom.

Brady stared at the closed door, a hollowness in his chest. What had happened to them? He stayed where he stood, as if rooted to the spot, and took in all the familiar sights of her home. Not much had changed since the last time he'd been here. For that matter, not much had changed since her parents had lived in this house. She'd preserved her childhood home, from the ancient appliances in the kitchen to the worn furniture filling the living room, as if changing anything meant losing her parents again.

Family pictures featuring Kara in pigtails, her parents' wedding pictures and her father in uniform hung in angled lines on the walls. A ratty old afghan was draped on the back of a rocking chair, both hand-me-downs from her grandmother, and a soft light glowed above an aquarium tank, where a small turtle paddled happily in the water.

He noticed Kara's Christmas tree in the corner of the living room and strolled over to plug in the lights. He admired the shimmer of colored lights and shiny baubles for a moment. He'd spent so much time at the office since taking the interim position as sheriff, he hadn't seen any point in putting up any kind of holiday decor.

He heard the shower turn on, and he went back out to

his truck to get his laptop. As much as he wanted a nap, he had a job to do, and he knew he wouldn't sleep until he put a few more pieces of the case together. After returning with his computer, he sat on her couch and turned the laptop on. His mind drifted while he waited for the start-up to complete and all his programs to load.

His gaze returned to the closed bathroom door, and his conscience tweaked him. For someone who wanted to smooth things over with his ex-girlfriend, he sure had been testy with her at times today. Shaking his head, he opened a file to read but only made it a few pages into the document before the sound of quiet sobs filtered down the hall from the shower.

Brady's heart clenched, and he shoved off the sofa. He reached the bathroom in a few long strides and didn't bother knocking as he charged in.

"Kara?" He heard a gasp and a loud sniff.

"I'm okay."

"Can I do anything?"

"No."

He sighed and dropped his chin to his chest. "Look… we've both been under stress today. With everything that's happened and being tired and cold and hungry… I know I've said some things I shouldn't have. I was rude at times and…"

The water cut off, and the only sound in the room was the slow drip from the bathtub spigot.

"Well, I…just wanted to say I'm sorry," he finished, compunction squeezing his chest.

She said nothing for a few seconds, then pulled the edge of the shower curtain back enough to peek around it. "Will you hand me the towel on the hook behind you?"

Brady turned and found the fluffy blue towel she meant and handed it to her. She let go of the shower curtain in order to take it, and he caught a tantalizing glimpse of her, naked, before she wrapped the towel around her.

His libido kicked in hard, and he felt the hot rush of blood to his groin. She looked just the way he remembered—the mole by her navel, the lush curves of her hips and breasts. And the small white line of a healed gash above her collarbone where she'd cut herself on a sharp edge of a pen gate at a rodeo as she'd escaped a charging bull last year.

He shuddered, remembering the icy fear that had filled him when he saw her lying on the ambulance stretcher, bleeding. He'd thought the worst, pictured a goring, until he'd reached her, and she'd laughed at his grave expression. *"I just need a few stitches and a tetanus shot, tough guy."*

She stepped out of the shower, one hand propped on the wall for balance. Hands trembling, she tucked the corner of her towel in over her breast to secure the wrap before raising her eyes to him. Her expression was weary and sad, and Brady's chest contracted in protectiveness and sympathy.

"I'm sorry, too. I've been difficult today, and my only defense is that…" She closed her eyes and bit her bottom lip as if trying not to cry again. Which wasn't working. The bridge of her nose crumpled and fat tears leaked out the sides of her eyes.

Without hesitation, he stepped closer and pulled her against him, hugging her firmly to his chest. The delicate scent of her shampoo teased his senses, and the throb of desire pumping through him beat harder.

"I'm sorry, babe," he whispered, pressing a kiss to the golden hair slicked to her scalp.

"You said that already," Kara muttered. Her face was buried in the hollow beneath his throat, her breath warming him through the thin fabric of his T-shirt.

"I know." He pushed her to arm's length and met her gaze. "But an apology is something that should be said face-to-face, not through a shower curtain." He stared into the whiskey-brown eyes he'd missed so much and couldn't stand the thought that she was no longer in his life.

Bowing his head, he slanted his mouth over hers and drew deeply on her lips. Her body tensed slightly at first, but soon she'd relaxed against him, her lips moving in rhythm with his. Heat filled him, along with a spark of hope that he'd finally chipped through the wall she'd erected between them. If the disaster today led to a reconciliation between them, he'd have the best Christmas present he could have ever asked for.

But all too soon, Kara's gripped shifted, and she pushed against him, shaking her head. "No…stop. I can't…do this." She bowed her head, and her shoulders shook gently as she started to cry again. "Nothing's changed, Brady. We can't—"

Her voice cracked, and when she tried to pull away, he firmed his grip and groaned. "Kara, I'm sorry. Not just for today, but for whatever I did that drove you away. I don't understand what I did, but I want to make up for it. Give me a second chance."

When she didn't respond, he tipped her chin back up and swiped the moisture from her cheeks with thumbs. Ducking his head, he kissed her again, softly, once. Twice. "We still have something special, something worth fighting for. Can't we at least talk?"

She lifted one eyebrow. "Will you listen to me?"

Her request seemed odd…and kind of redundant. Wasn't listening implied when one talked things out with a lover? He knitted his brow and cocked his head, trying to guess what was behind her request.

Immediately she gave an exasperated sigh and rolled her eyes.

"Of course I'll listen," he promised before she could turn away.

She stilled and narrowed a dubious look on him. "Promise?"

"I promise."

Her expression brightened, and he took this as a good sign. A very good sign. More progress than he'd made with her in almost a year.

She lifted a corner of her mouth and gave a small nod. "'Kay."

He gave her a broad grin and hauled her back into his arms for a hug. She swayed a bit as he sealed the deal with a kiss. "But first…"

Bending, he scooped her up, cradling her against his chest.

Though she wilted against him, she grunted a protest. "Brady—"

"At ease, babe. Just taking you to your bed. You're about to drop." He pivoted in the small bathroom, angling his body sideways to get out the door. But as he navigated the turn to her room, he heard a thump.

"Ow," she muttered. "Foot, meet door frame."

He winced. "Sorry. Guess you're not the only one who's a little too tired for their own good."

She patted his chest and chuckled. "I'll live."

"Still…" He set her down on her unmade bed and lifted a foot to examine. "Let me see it."

She flopped back on the pillows and giggled harder. "I said, I'll live." She mumbled something about surviving a sniper and floodwater, and her laughter swelled. The sound was sweet music to his ears. She truly had a joyous, infectious laugh, one of many things he'd missed about her.

He smiled at her but persisted in checking her foot. And still she laughed.

"What's so funny?" he asked, unable to contain his own chuckle in light of her chortling fit.

She wiped at her eyes and shook her head. "I have no idea!" Which only made her laugh harder.

He joined her in peals of laughter, enjoying the stress release after the tragic and trying day. Savoring the moment of levity with her. God, he'd missed this. Missed her sense of humor, her warmth, the optimistic way she made him feel even after a bad day.

He pulled the covers over her and kissed her forehead. "Good night, Princess Punchy."

She sobered a little as he started for the door and patted the other side of the bed. "You're not staying?"

"Naw. I've got work to do."

She pushed up on her elbows. "But you're bound to be as tired as I am."

He shrugged and stretched. "Little bit, yeah. But duty calls. If you need anything, I'll be in the living room."

With that he backed out of her room, flipping off the light. He had a sniper to catch.

Chapter 9

Kara padded into her living room late the next morning, rolling her shoulders and finger combing her hair from her face. Even though she expected to find Brady there, her heartbeat stumbled a bit when she found him asleep on her couch.

He sat with his head lolled at a slight angle against the cushioned back of the sofa, his laptop open on his legs. One hand rested on the edge of the keyboard, and one hand had slipped to the couch at his side. The computer screen had gone to screen saver mode and had rolling images of colorful ribbons parading at random across black.

Kara tiptoed over to him and carefully lifted the computer from his lap.

Brady jerked awake as soon as the weight left his legs. He gave her a startled and somewhat confused look before rubbing his eyes and sitting up straighter.

"Good morning." She gave him a smile.

With a grunt, Brady rubbed his face and cast a look around the room. "What time is it?"

She glanced behind her to her parents' grandfather clock, which stood sentinel near the end of the hallway. "About ten forty-five."

His eyes widened, and he shot a glance to the clock himself. "Crud."

"Didn't mean to sleep that long?"

He pulled his laptop back onto his legs and tapped a key to wake the screen. "I didn't mean to fall asleep at all."

Kara snorted and headed for the kitchen. "You're not superhuman, Brady. Everyone needs sleep. Even sheriffs. Can I tempt you with some coffee?"

"Definitely." He continued tapping at his computer and called to her without looking up from the screen. "How did you sleep?"

"You have to ask? I was all but unconscious until ten minutes ago." Kara walked into her laundry room and turned on the light.

Jerry sat up in his laundry basket bed and yawned.

"Morning, fella. You hungry?"

He meowed his loud Siamese yowl and hopped out of his bed and to the floor.

Kara reached down to scratch his head, and Jerry rubbed against her shin. "Sorry I'm late this morning," she told the cat. "You wouldn't believe the night I had."

"Meow!"

"I know, right?" She took the bag of cat food from her pantry shelf and went to his bowl. The dish was already mostly full. She shot a look toward the living room. "Brady, did you feed Jerry this morning?"

"Yeah. He was hollering about it at sunrise, and I was afraid he'd wake you, so…"

She looked at Jerry who sat at her feet, blinking at her

groggily. "Well, then, Jerry. I hope you told Brady thank you."

"Meow!"

"You're welcome, Jerry," Brady called.

Jerry followed her as she made her way to the kitchen cabinet to start the coffee. He started up a litany of discordant meows and yowls as he wove around her legs and paced the floor.

"Any news on the case?" She pulled out a coffee filter and began setting up her brewer. "They find Cobb yet?"

In the next room, Brady muttered another curse word, drawing her attention. He was staring at his cell phone, swiping through screens. If Brady was cussing, the news couldn't be good. "What is it? What happened?"

He glanced up and shook his head. "Nothing. I slept through a text from Nate, but apparently he reached Wilhite, so…"

Her gut clenched. "Nate? About what? His father? April? The baby?"

Brady waved her off. "Nothing for you to worry about."

With that, he bent his head over his phone again, texting someone. Dismissing her.

Anger spiked from deep inside her. She slapped the counter so hard her whole arm ached, and a startled Jerry skittered out of the kitchen for his bed.

"Damn it, Brady! Don't do that!"

Frowning, he looked up from his phone. "Don't do what?"

She stomped back into the living room and aimed a finger at him. "Don't brush me off like I don't matter! Nate and April are my friends, too. If something has happened to them, I want to know about it."

He leveled his shoulders. "You were asleep, and it's nothing you needed added to your plate of concerns."

She tensed her fists and growled. "That's not the point! If we're going to have any kind of future, you can't keep blowing me off and ignoring my feelings like they don't matter!"

He jerked backward as if she'd shoved him, blinking, his expression stunned.

For a few seconds he said nothing. Then his cheek twitched in a half smile.

A smile? He thought this was *funny*?

Irritated even further, she was about to launch into him again, when he said, "Then you have considered us having a future. That's progress."

She scoffed her incredulity. "*That's* what you heard me say?"

He rubbed a hand over his face. "Oh, I heard the nonsense about me ignoring your feelings, but I chose to focus on the positive. If you see even the possibility of a future for us—"

"Not if you think my feelings are nonsense!" She felt her body shaking from the inside out. Hurt and frustration and fury knotted in her core and pounded in her veins.

He shoved to his feet and squared off with her. "I didn't say your feelings were nonsense. You're twisting my words!" He took a breath, and in a calmer tone, he said, "I love you, Kara. Deeply. How can you question that? Especially after yesterday."

She plowed both hands through her hair. Tears pricked her eyes. "I know you love me. That's not the issue. It's not about how *you* feel. It's about how *I* feel."

His brow furrowed. "Are you saying you don't love me?"

"Still not the point, Brady! Listen to me! The issue is you don't *respect* my feelings."

"What? That's craz—" He cut himself off, his expression saying he'd finally heard himself.

Her whole body wilted, and she gave him a sad smile. "I need you to *hear* me. Really hear me. My feelings and opinions and fears are what they are, whether you agree with them or not. I need to know that you have heard me when I tell you what's in my heart and soul, and that even if you don't share my view, that you've valued my thoughts. That you've considered my feelings and that we have a true partnership. That's the only way we can ever build a future, Brady. With respect for each other. With openness and honesty and consideration of each other's opinions and fears and feelings."

He reached for her, his eyes softening. "I thought we had that. I—" With the back of his hand, he stroked her cheek, then cupped her chin. "Tell me what you need. What can I do to fix this?"

She drew a slow breath in. "Hear me out. Let me talk, and try to understand where I am, who I am."

He nodded, his grip tightening on her and his gaze bright and eager. "All right. I'm listening."

After their coffee had brewed and they'd each had a bite of breakfast at Kara's request—empty stomachs didn't lend themselves to productive conversations, she claimed—they settled on her couch with steaming mugs and the whole day before them. Nothing, barring murder and colossal mayhem, was more important today than figuring out what had sent Kara running months ago. Working out their differences and getting their relationship back on the right path was job one, Priority A for Brady.

Listen, she'd said. Okay. He could do that.

"All right." He turned up a palm, inviting her to speak first. "The floor is yours."

She threaded her fingers through her hair and exhaled. "Wow. Where do I begin?"

"You could start with why you left me. Why did my taking the job as sheriff send you running?"

"Because of my dad. My mom and I lived with the constant fear of him not coming back from work. Any day could be the day that he was injured or killed in the line of duty. Do you have any idea how exhausting, how stressful that kind of worry is?"

"So this is about your worry that I'll be injured in the line of duty?"

She hesitated. "Well, yes…"

He caught himself before he groaned his dismissal of that concern. *Listen to her*, he reminded himself. *There has to be more to it than that.*

Kara was winding the tassels from a throw quilt around her fingers. "And no."

With effort, Brady swallowed the impulse to direct the conversation. This wasn't an interrogation of a suspect. He had to give Kara the space, the time and the freedom to explain things in her own time and her own way.

Dropping the quilt fringe, she reached for her coffee and took a fortifying gulp. Then, clinging to the mug with a white-knuckle grip, she began quietly, "The day my father died, we had been in town picking up a few groceries for Mom. She'd wanted to make apple fritters for our Sunday breakfast, but needed fresh apples and cinnamon. I remember it was a rainy day, one of many we'd had in recent weeks. The river through town was full and flowing fast. When we got to the river bridge, Dad spotted the lady right away. She was standing on the railing looking out over the water. Dad stopped the car and got out. He told me to stay put, which was easy enough to do because I didn't want to get wet in the rain."

Brady tensed, and a wave of dread washed through

him. "Wait a minute. You mean, you were with your dad when he died?"

She met his eyes and nodded. The stark grief in her eyes sucker punched him. How had he not known this? He knew her father had drowned, but she'd never told him she was there. "Kara—"

"As he walked toward the lady, she yelled at him to stay back. He tried to calm her down, to talk her out of jumping, but she was really worked up, screaming and crying and not making sense. When he made a move toward her, she climbed over the railing. This was before everyone had cell phones, or I would've been calling 911 right then and there. Next thing I know she was gone, and Dad was running to the railing, looking down. At that point, I couldn't stay in the car any longer. I knew what he meant to do, and I knew how dangerous it was."

Tears sparkled in her eyes, and acid puddled in Brady's gut. He knew what was coming and was helpless to stop it. He knew the pain it had cost Kara and was at a loss how to heal it.

He slid closer to her on the couch and stroked her cheek. She shivered when he touched her, then closed her eyes and continued.

"I yelled for him to stop, but he just ordered me back to the car, took off his shoes and dove in after her. I think I screamed. I'm not really sure. I just remember feeling kinda numb and completely terrified."

Her teary eyes had a faraway look, and she stared at the wall where her father's picture hung. She swallowed hard and whispered, "I ran to the railing and looked for him. The water was dark and muddy. Swirling with eddies and full of debris. I saw him swimming, fighting the current, and for a while, it looked like he was going to save her.

But when he reached her, she fought him. They both went under, and…I remember feeling my heart sink with them."

A tear broke free from her lashes, and the sight of that lone drop on her cheek squeezed his heart like a fist.

"He came up again a couple times, but every time he went back under. And every time he went under, a little piece of me died with him. I've never felt so helpless in my whole life. I thought about jumping in after him, the way he had to try to save the lady…"

Brady winced, hearing this. Even though he could understand a young Kara's inclination to help her father, had she gone in the water, her fate would likely have been the same as her dad's. He inched closer to her, coaxing her into his arms. His embrace seemed to break the dam holding back the full flood of her grief. She buried her face in his shirt, and her shoulders shook as she quietly sobbed.

"I couldn't drive yet and… I h-had no way to call anyone," she said and sniffed, "so I just stood there in the rain, in shock, shouting for my dad to answer me, but…"

"Oh, babe, how awful." He squeezed her more tightly, at a loss for words. He couldn't imagine the heartache and trauma she'd suffered, watching her father drown. A twinge of something—guilt, disappointment, frustration—wound through him, boring a hole in his soul. How had he not known the terrible secret she'd been keeping all these years? Had she not trusted him?

"I don't know how long it took before a car came along and helped me. Maybe twenty minutes? An hour? It felt like forever." She raised damp eyes to him, and his heart wrenched for her.

If he could absorb her pain, obliterate the dark shadows haunting her expression, he would in a heartbeat, no matter the cost. He framed her face between his hands and kissed her forehead. "That's terrible, Kara. I'm sorry. I—" He furrowed his brow and shook his head in disbelief. "Why did you never tell me this before?"

She laughed without humor. "I've never told anyone before. Not since that night. I told Mom and the police, then never spoke of it again."

He cocked an eyebrow, surprised at this revelation. "Not even to a trauma counselor? Didn't your mother—"

Her scoff cut him off. "My mother had enough to deal with being a single parent, handling her own grief and going back to work to support us. I wasn't going to burden her with what I was dealing with."

"So you suffered in silence?"

"So to speak."

"And…what were you dealing with?"

She sighed and leaned into his chest again. "Nightmares. An irrational fear of water. Occasional flashbacks thanks to triggers like rainstorms. Or the smell of cinnamon and apple."

Brady's chest froze, and he saw the day's events in a new light. "Or flash floods when your ex-boyfriend gets swept up against a cottonwood?"

Her fingers curled into the flesh of his arms, and he felt the shiver that raced through her.

"Yeah," she whispered, her voice a mere breath. "That was hard. I—I was…terrified."

"But you came in after me, just like your dad went in after that woman." He hugged her more tightly, pride and gratitude and awe swelling in his heart. "You saved me. You were understandably scared, but you saved me." Brady kissed the top of her head, his own eyes burning with tears. "You are the bravest woman I know, Kara. What you did—"

"Brave?" She snorted her disagreement. "I just said I

was terrified. If it hadn't been you, I don't know if I could have done what I did."

"Yes, you would have. Because you are your father's daughter. Fear doesn't negate the courage behind the action. In fact, it makes it all the more impressive. You'd have been crazy not to have been scared."

Another indelicate snort and wry chuckle. "And here I thought it was going in the flash flood that made me crazy."

He stroked her sleep-mussed hair, and thought again about her reply. "What do you mean, if it hadn't been me?"

She tensed in his arms and didn't answer for a moment.

"Kara?"

"Of course I went in after you. You're...*you*. I..." She hiccupped a sob. "I couldn't imagine life without you. I've already lost so much. If you died—"

His heart warmed, while sympathy for her losses twisted in his gut. But she'd all but said she still wanted him in her life, and that gave him hope.

Kara levered back from Brady's embrace and met his eyes. Reliving the day her father had died and the harrowing experience of going into the water to save Brady had left her mentally exhausted. "So back to your original question...why did I leave you?"

His gaze sharpened, and the muscles in his jaw flexed as he clenched his teeth.

"I've lived the horror of losing someone I love to the duty that comes with the badge. I've seen my mother live under the strain of waiting for *that call* in the middle of the night and then grieving when *that call* did come. My dad was just going to the grocery store that day in June, but he had a duty because of his badge that got him killed. Mom went through hell, and that's not a life I want, Brady."

"So you're saying I have to choose? My job or you?" His tone told her how unjust he saw that ultimatum. And she agreed.

"No, Brady. As hard as it would be to live like that, I would never put you in that position. That wouldn't be fair."

He tilted his head, the bridge of his nose denting in confusion. "Then what is the reason?"

She sucked in a cleansing breath. Blew it out from puffed cheeks. "When I tried to explain all this to you before, how hard it would be for me, how painful the memory of my dad's death was, you dismissed my feelings as 'unwarranted.' 'This is Rusted Spur,' you said, 'not Dallas.'"

She pitched her voice lower as she quoted his arguments from months earlier. "'Being sheriff here means stolen chickens and parking tickets, not murder and mayhem.'" She sent him a level gaze. "I could point out that today proved that theory wrong—a sniper showed up in Rusted Spur, and you were in the thick of it—but that's not my point either. It's not about who's right or wrong about the inherent danger of the job."

"Okaaay…" The furrow in his brow deepened. "So why—"

"Because you didn't listen to me." She clapped a hand to her chest to emphasize her point. "I was hurting because of my dad and scared for you, and when I tried to tell you, when you had the chance to weigh my feelings in the decision whether to take the interim sheriff position or not, you made me feel unimportant. You dismissed my worry as baseless without knowing the whole story. We should have had *this* conversation—" she jabbed a finger in her palm "—back then. But anytime I tried, I got the same eye roll and 'Don't be silly. You don't need to worry' brush-off."

He opened his mouth as if to deny it, then frowned and scrubbed a hand over his jaw.

"My feelings are what they are, Brady. They are real, they are important, and they should matter to you."

His face fell. "They do, babe."

"Even if you don't agree with my opinions, even if you think my fears are unwarranted, I need to know that you can at least respect how I feel and will listen to me, will consider my feelings, when I tell you what's in my heart. I need to know I matter to you. In all ways."

Brady stared at her, looking a bit stunned.

"I left because too often I felt my thoughts and feelings and opinions were being dismissed. Trivialized."

With an exhale that seemed to deflate him, Brady closed his eyes and shook his head. "I had no idea I was doing that. I'm so sorry, Kara. I never meant…geez." When he raised his gaze to her again, guilt and apology filled his eyes. "Can you forgive me?"

She took his hand in hers and laced her fingers with his. "You promise to listen to me, like you are now, from now on? I'm not saying I'll always get my way, but I want to know I've been heard."

He narrowed a stern look on her. "I'll make that promise if you'll promise me something in return."

Surprise kicked her pulse up a notch. A conditional promise? Kara cocked her head, curious and a bit leery. "Promise you what?"

Chapter 10

Brady took both of her hands in his, his gaze hard and piercing. "No more running away."

She drew her head back, her spine stiffening. "Pardon?"

"We were apart, almost lost what we have together, because you ran from me. Rather than sit down and force me to have this conversation, you avoided me."

Kara wished she could deny his claim, but he spoke the truth. After a brief hesitation, a moment of self-recrimination, she nodded. "You're right. I avoided you because being around you hurt. I missed you so much."

His face crumpled in confusion. "And all those months, I just wanted to talk to you, to understand what happened between us. If you missed me, why not talk to me?"

She pulled her hands from his and rose from the couch. She walked a few steps away, then turned back to him. "I guess I didn't believe you'd listen. Experience had told me you wouldn't."

"You didn't trust me."

She frowned. "I didn't say that."

"And yet yesterday, knowing I was at the wedding, knowing I was just steps away when Cobb shot at you, you ran then, too. I would have protected you with my life, Kara. But you took off on that horse and almost died out in that storm!"

She raked her hair back, stunned that he was bringing up yesterday's events. "I was scared! I was…in shock. I—"

"You saw me. Right outside the barn. I was coming for you, and you blew right past me and took off. You didn't even give me a chance to help you!"

"I went to the barn to get away from you! I was hurting."

Her admission seemed to slap him. A crestfallen look shadowed his face.

She spun away and paced the floor, burning off the nervous energy that revved in her blood when she remembered the terrifying moments in the barn. "And then that…that *cretin* shot at me, and I was just trying to save myself. I panicked."

She faced Brady again. "Okay?" She raised her hands as if surrendering. "I panicked! Not smart for a bullfighter, I know. I'm not proud of it, but that's what happened. I was in shock and scared, and I ran. As simple as that."

"But you ran. You didn't trust me to help you, to be there."

She opened her mouth. Closed it. Maybe he was right, at least partially.

"Kara, listen to me, now. *Hear* me." He pushed off the sofa, holding her gaze with eyes dark with passion and conviction. Taking her shoulders in his hands, he said, "I will always be there for you. You will always be my first priority. Nothing is more important to me than you are."

She stared back at him, her heart pounding. As desperately as she wanted to believe him, shards of doubt still pricked her. "What about your job? Your duty to your position as sheriff?"

His jaw tightened, his lips thinned as he frowned in frustration. "I've made a commitment to the people of this county. I can't just drop everything and walk away, if that's what you're asking me to do."

"I'm not asking anything, Brady. But now you know how I feel about living with a lawman…and why." She backed out of his grip and marched back to her bedroom.

As much as she wanted to believe they'd made progress working out their differences, in some ways, nothing had changed.

"He's there? Now?" Hannah asked, her voice vibrating through the phone with intrigue and excitement.

"Yeah." Kara stroked Jerry's head. The tom, who'd followed her down the hall and settled on her bed, ate up the attention. "He brought me home last night, and he's still here."

"Then what are you doing talking to me? Get on with the make-up sex."

Kara closed her eyes, and her body hummed at the images Hannah's assumption brought to mind. "It's not like that. We still have things to work out."

"Like?" Hannah prompted.

She chewed her bottom lip and thought about it. "He says I ran away. When he didn't hear me, instead of pressing the issue, having the heart-to-heart that we needed to…I ran."

"And didn't you?"

Her stomach rolled, guilt stirring inside her. "I guess I did. I was hurt and…dang it, Hannah. I'm just so tired of hurting. Of grieving."

"Are you…maybe…using your pain as a shield? Keeping the old wounds alive as an excuse not to trust him with a second chance?"

Kara scowled. "Have you been talking to Brady? He accused me of not trusting him, too."

Hannah laughed lightly. "Great minds think alike?" Then more soberly, "So...do you trust him? Will you give him a second chance?"

"I want to, but..."

"But nothing. Stop talking to me and get out there with him. Talk to him, spend time with him, make love to him. Put a little elbow grease into patching things up with him." Hannah chuckled. "If I had a hot cowboy like him, Lord knows I'd be working hard to get things straightened out and on the right path!"

Deep down, Kara knew her friend was right. She couldn't let old wounds, old fears and worries be an excuse for keeping Brady at arm's length. If they were going to have a future, that future needed to start now. Her happiness was hers for the taking, if she had the courage to reach out and grab it.

Over the next few hours, Kara puttered around her house, doing a little straightening, some gift wrapping, and some baking. She made a pot of soup that they ate throughout the day. Though she sat in the living room with him, reading while Brady worked, she gave Brady the quiet and space he needed as he steered elements of the investigation from her couch.

Despite the emotional tension that had characterized their earlier discussion, the mood between them as they passed the hours that afternoon was companionable and easy. They easily fell back into routines and patterns they'd shared when they were dating. Kara cooked and served the soup, and Brady washed their bowls and set them in the drying rack. Kara worked on the crossword puzzle, and Brady stole side glances at her progress and offered answers when he knew them. Kara propped her feet on the coffee table and reclined on the couch to rest her eyes, and Brady pulled her feet into his lap and massaged her arches.

And through the afternoon hours, Brady mulled over what Kara had told him that morning. He hadn't heard her. He'd shut her down, tuned her out when he should have supported her. Would he have taken the interim job as sheriff if he'd really listened to her all those months ago? If he'd made her feel safe enough with him, loved enough to be completely honest about her past and he'd really understood how she felt back then, would he have taken the job? If he'd taken the time to really appreciate what it meant to honor the woman he wanted to spend his life with, if he'd weighed her opinion and preferences when he made his career decision, would he be on the job as sheriff today?

He liked to think he'd have been more understanding, more flexible. But in truth, he'd been so honored to have been asked to fill the position, so eager to use the new post as a stepping stone to boost his career, propel him to better things, he'd all too easily shut her out.

Knowing that truth stung. He'd believed better of himself. He wanted to be more than just a job, a law enforcement star on the rise. He wanted to be a man worthy of a woman like Kara. He wanted to be a good husband, a man of character, someone Kara and his friends could count on and believe in.

He cut a glance to her as she napped in the late afternoon, her tousled blond hair falling in her eyes and her full lips parted slightly as she softly snored. His heart wrenched, knowing he'd hurt her, knowing she'd had reason to believe he didn't respect her feelings. Somehow he had to find a way to make amends. He missed her. He missed…*this*. This rapport and friendship, the quiet evenings and passion-filled nights.

Had he been blinded by ambition? Maybe. Probably.

So…where did that leave him? Did he quit? That didn't seem honorable either. He needed to fulfill his commitment, honor the responsibility he'd been given.

He scoffed and shook his head. Responsibility? For requisitions to buy toilet paper? For parking tickets and bringing Cloyd Werther in *again* on disturbing-the-peace charges so he could dry out in the holding cell? The job hadn't panned out quite the way he'd expected. He missed the puzzle-solving, boots-on-the-ground aspect of working the forensics of a case.

Even now, when he finally had a big case, he was still the one doing paperwork. Wilhite and Anderson had been the ones in the fray. But for all his disillusionment with the job, he couldn't walk away from his post while there was a sniper on the loose.

So where did that leave him with Kara? He rubbed his face, sighing as his thoughts came full circle again.

He heard Kara rouse and met her sleepy gaze as she sat up on the sofa. "You snore."

Her brow crumpled. "Do not."

He grinned and squeezed her foot. "Do, too. But don't worry. It'll be our little secret."

She chuckled and rolled to her feet. "Good." Aiming a thumb toward the kitchen, she asked, "Want one of those pumpkin spice muffins I made?"

"I thought you'd never ask. I've been smelling them all afternoon and drooling."

She lifted one corner of her mouth in a grin. "I know, right? They make the house smell great."

As she approached the kitchen, a loud thump sounded from the laundry room, beyond the kitchen. Jerry came scampering out from the dark back room, and Kara paused, casting a frown toward her cat. "Jer, what's wrong? What happened?"

Brady sat up, pushing his laptop aside as he focused on Kara. "Something wrong? Want me to—"

With a loud crash, the window in the door to her carport shattered. Brady jumped to his feet, drawing his gun, even as Kara screamed and backpedaled.

But not before a large man in dark clothing shouldered through the door, his pistol aimed at Kara. *Dennis Cobb.*

Adrenaline spiked in Brady's blood as he dropped to the floor behind the sofa and leveled his sidearm on the intruder. "Sheriff's department! Drop your weapon!"

Spinning toward Brady, Cobb fired a wild shot. The bullet flew wide and sent a Santa decoration tumbling from the mantel.

Brady returned fire, aiming for Cobb's leg.

In the next second, the sniper had seized a handful of Kara's hair and dragged her up against his chest. While holding his pistol under her chin, he released her hair to snake his other arm around her waist. His grip pinned her arms to her sides, anchoring her in front of him as a shield.

Under his breath, Brady cursed at how quickly the situation had deteriorated. His gut pitched, seeing the muzzle jabbing Kara's throat, angled to put a bullet in her brain before he could blink. "Let her go!"

Cobb barked a humorless laugh. "Why would I do that? I came to kill her."

Kara gasped, her face draining of color. Her body was rigid in deference to the gun pressed to her neck.

"You don't want to do that." Brady kept his tone firm and unyielding, despite the buzzing in his ears, the unsteady beat of his heart. *God, please, not Kara!* "Police around the state are already looking for you."

"Because this bitch fingered me. She earned a bullet for that." He jerked his arm tighter, and Kara winced, wheezed.

Brady drew a slow breath and exhaled evenly. He had to stay in control of the situation. Had to save Kara… "Just put your gun on the floor and step back with your hands up."

Cobb snorted and sneered. "Naw. You first."

"Put. The weapon. Down."

"Go to hell." Cobb poked harder with the pistol and snarled. "She got in my way yesterday, and she put the cops on my scent. She *will* pay."

"You harm one hair on her head, and I swear, it'll be the last mistake you ever make."

A dark, ugly chuckle rumbled from Cobb's chest. "Mighty big talk, lover boy." He walked Kara forward, out of the kitchen and to the end of the hall. He cut a quick look toward the bedrooms, as if checking for someone hiding, ready to ambush him.

Yeah, Brady thought, *backup would be nice about now.* But his phone was lying on the coffee table out of his reach, and he didn't want to make a move that would set Cobb off.

Cobb leaned forward and sniffed Kara's neck. "You know, bitch, you smell nice." He eyed her with a side glance that bought Brady time to shift from behind one end of the sofa to the other. He had a better angle on Cobb now…if only Kara weren't in the line of fire.

Cobb slid his hand from Kara's waist to fondle her breasts. "Maybe before I kill ya, I oughta enjoy the goods."

"You're a pig," she growled.

For her efforts, Cobb knocked her in the temple with the butt of the pistol, then rammed the barrel in her ear.

"Kara!" Brady shouted, his gut churning an icy fear

that jolted his heart. He braced his arms and realigned his shot, waiting for the split second of opportunity he needed.

"What'd you say?" Cobb barked at Kara.

She struggled against her captor's grip, her eyes panicked...until her gaze met Brady's. Even from his position in the living room, he could see the peace and assurance that filled her eyes. She held his stare and gave a tiny nod.

"I trust you," she mouthed, and he knew instantly what she was planning.

Chapter 11

After the shock of having the gunman break into her home and seize her in his vise-like grip, the lightning pain of Cobb's strike to her head shook Kara from her fear-induced paralysis. This was her home, and she would not let this creep manhandle her and terrorize her without fighting back. Cobb might have a gun on her, one she knew all too well he would use, but she had Brady.

She knew the bead Brady had on Cobb with his service weapon was the only reason she was still alive. Cobb was smart enough to know he'd be dead the second he pulled the trigger to kill her. He was repositioning himself, closing in on Brady, checking escape routes, looking for means of distraction, cover…

But Kara was planning, too. Brady gave her a subtle nod, saying he'd read her intentions, was ready for her next move.

Kara wanted to laugh, to cheer. *Hooray for the unspoken connection, the synchronicity they shared!* Brady really was the missing piece of her soul.

Then, without any other warning or provocation, she slammed her head back into Cobb's nose. She followed this instantly by driving her elbow into the startled man's gut. While he sputtered for air, she stomped his instep, kicked back into his kneecap. A bam-bam-bam assault. One move after another, then…she dropped to the floor. Overwhelmed by her surprise attack, Cobb lost his hold on her, and she rolled away from his feet. Covered her head.

As soon as she cleared the shot, a loud blast echoed through the house.

Cobb screamed in pain and answered Brady's fire with rapid shots into the living room.

"Brady!" Kara cried, unable to swallow her dread during the short volley of gunfire.

Then silence fell.

Cobb made a strange gasping sound and staggered back against the hall wall, knocking a picture of her father to the floor where the frame splintered.

Blood streaked the wall as Cobb slid to the floor, his eyes fixed and blank.

Kara struggled to draw air into lungs frozen with horror. Then one thought, one person surged to the fore in her mind. "Brady!"

"Are you okay?"

She scrambled to her hands and knees, rose on trembling legs, desperate to reach him.

Boots thundered across her floor, and he was at her side in a heartbeat. "Kara, babe, are you okay? Your head… how bad did he hurt you? Are you shot?"

His hands were everywhere, gently searching, checking, then pulling her into a tight hug. "I'm okay. My head hurts, but…it's not…" A choking sob cut her off, and her hands groped for him. She curled her fingers into his back, clutching him close. "Oh, God, Brady! I was s-so scared!"

"You're safe now, babe."

"N-no! Scared for you!" She pulled back and searched his face, needing him to understand. "If anything had happened to you... I don't know how...how I'd live without you!"

He was shaking, too, she realized as he rested his forehead against hers. "Ditto, beautiful. When I saw him shove that pistol in your ear, I—" He expelled a harsh breath. "Babe, I think I have a whole new perspective on what you went through with your father's death. Your fears about my job...because when I thought of losing you, of him hurting you—"

She slid her hands to his face and smoothed her fingers over the stubble on his cheeks. "Not something that's easy to forget, huh?"

He shook his head. His eyes were suspiciously moist. "I'm so sorry, Kara. About your dad, what you lived through, and...for not listening earlier. I—"

She pressed her lips to his, holding the back of his head with her fingers splayed in his hair. He reciprocated in kind, his tongue plundering her mouth. Their kiss was deep, desperate. Two souls clinging to each other and savoring the gift of life, the miracle of second chances.

When Kara pulled back, gulping oxygen, she rasped, "I love you, Brady. I never stopped loving you."

His expression melted in relief and joy and affection. "And I love you. So much." He pulled her back into a secure, lingering embrace. Finally he stepped back. With a side glance to Cobb's still form, he sighed. "I need to call this in. I'll drive you to the hospital to get your head checked, then...can you stay with Hannah until the scene here is processed and cleaned up?"

She held his gaze. "I'd...rather stay with you."

The corner of his cheek twitched in a small smile. "Done."

Chapter 12

After the nearest emergency room cleared her as concussion-free and Deputy Wilhite finished taking her statement about Cobb's break-in, assault on her and subsequent death, Kara accompanied Brady to his house on the outskirts of Rusted Spur. Settling on his couch, surrounded by his masculine decor, Kara felt a sense of peace and homecoming. She knew, deep in her heart, her place was with Brady, whatever it cost.

"Brady," she started as he handed her a bottle of water and settled next to her. "I know it won't be easy, watching you head off to work every day, but if you want to be the sheriff or an undercover police detective or an overseas CIA agent, I'll deal with it. Being apart from you is harder by far. I'll manage my worry somehow. But... I need you in my life."

He flashed a lopsided smile and stroked her cheek. "That's good to hear, but...because I shot Cobb, I'm on mandatory leave while the shooting is investigated."

"Oh, right…"

"Just a formality. But until then…" He kissed her nose. "I plan to do lots of making up for lost time…with you." He drew a slow breath. Released it. "And then I plan to throw my support behind Wilhite as the next sheriff of Trencher County."

She jerked back and blinked her surprise. "What? Are you sure?"

"I'm positive. I miss forensics. And I hate paperwork! I was honored to be asked to serve the county in the interim, but forensics, the science, is where my heart lies." He grinned and added, "After you, of course."

She leaned in to brush his lips with hers, whispering, "I like the sound of that."

His phone buzzed, and he glanced at the screen. "I need to take this." His expression serious, he lifted the phone to his ear. "Hi, Nate. Everything okay?" He blew out a breath and nodded to Kara. "That's good."

Another degree of tension inside her released its hold.

"Yeah," Brady said, "He's dead. He came after Kara, and I had to shoot him." His face darkened. "No. He died before we could ask him who hired him." He rubbed the bridge of his nose. "I guess I don't have to tell you that Cobb's death doesn't mean the threat to April is gone. Until we know who hired him, you need to stay vigilant."

Kara shivered. She hadn't considered that aspect of this nightmare. Her friends were still in grave danger. Cobb had just been a pawn in this deadly chess game.

Brady scrunched up his face in frustration. "Right. I'm on leave, but…keep me posted anyway, okay?"

Kara grabbed his arm to get his attention. "Tell him I love them, and I'm praying for their safety, too. That I'll call April later."

He nodded and passed on the message. When he hung up, he pulled Kara closer, and she snuggled against him.

Tipping her head up, she brushed a kiss across his lips. "Now…what were you saying about lost time?" She deepened their kiss and started unbuttoning his shirt.

And they didn't come up for air for a very long time.

Two nights later, Brady escorted Kara back to her house, and she entered the house where she'd grown up with a quiver of reluctance in her gut. Would she ever forget the fact that a man had been killed in her home? Would she ever look at that spot by the bathroom door and not remember how it felt to have a gun pressed to her ear, to know the bone-chilling fear when Cobb had fired at Brady?

Maybe. Maybe not. But this was her home, and she had more good memories than bad here. She wouldn't let the terror Cobb had inflicted on her ruin the warmth and the happiness she'd shared in this house with her parents.

She strolled toward her bedroom to put away the overnight bag she'd taken to Brady's and studied the spot where Cobb had fallen. No visible trace of blood remained. Only the faint lingering scent of the cleaning solution the cleanup crew had used remained.

"Wow." She turned full circle, taking in the rest of the house. The hole in her wall was patched, the broken picture frame replaced. "The crew did a great job."

"Well, not all of it was them. I asked Anderson and Wilhite to patch the hole, and Earlene bought the new frame. She said to tell you it was her Christmas present to you."

Kara smiled. "That's so sweet of her."

After putting her bag in her room, she joined Brady on the couch. He'd turned on her Christmas tree lights, and Kara gave a contented sigh as she snuggled against him and gazed at their soft glow. "I can't believe Christmas is just two days away."

"I know. Right?" He smoothed the hair back from her forehead and dropped a kiss on the bridge of her nose.

As she studied the twinkling lights on her tree, she noticed a small package under the branches that hadn't been there before. "What's that?"

"Hmm?"

She swung her feet to the floor and scurried over to examine the tiny box. "There's no name on it."

"Open it," he suggested, an odd look in his eyes.

"But it's not Christmas yet."

"Close enough. Open it." He patted the sofa cushion next to him, inviting her to return.

A tingle of anticipation and curiosity swept through her as she carried the small box wrapped in red paper and topped with a white ribbon back to the couch. With trembling hands, she untied the ribbon and tore off the thin paper to reveal a jeweler's box. Her breath caught. "Brady?"

He took the box from her shaking hands and cracked open the lid. A sparkling oval solitaire diamond ring winked at her.

"Kara Pearson, I love you with my whole heart. These past months without you have been the longest and loneliest of my life, but they've taught me to value the treasure that you are. I promise to love you, to listen to you and to respect everything about you from this day forward. Will you marry me?"

Tears welled in her eyes, and she threw her arms around Brady's neck. "Yes! Oh, goodness, yes!"

He slipped the ring out of the box, and the diamond caught the colored lights from her tree, sending a rainbow of dazzling shimmers on her walls. She chuckled and whispered, "The rainbow."

He glanced up. "What?"

"A few days ago, we were lost in a terrible thunderstorm. A storm that kinda represented what my life felt like the last few months."

He twisted his mouth in regret. "Mine, too."

"But now the storm has passed, and a rainbow has come out." She wiggled the ring, directing his attention to the spectrum of lights that danced on the walls and ceiling.

He pulled her close, laughing, and kissed her lips. "Yes, it has, babe. Yes, it has."

* * * * *

Dear Readers,

Some of the deepest, longest-lasting relationships I've been fortunate enough to witness didn't begin as romances at all. Instead, they took root in platonic friendships, relationships that grew and flourished over months or even years before one or the other recognized the fragile new buds forming, buds with the potential to blossom into something that cannot be ignored.

In *Rescuing the Bride*, paralegal April Redding is the first to understand that her feelings for Nate Wheeler, the champion bull rider she's known since childhood, have deepened into undeniable attraction. But fear and the geography of their diverging paths keep her from acting on those feelings until one lonely night following her mother's death.

Though Nate is certain he's doing the right thing by proposing to the friend now carrying his child, April balks at settling for a groom who's merely going through the motions out of a sense of obligation. Shaking her head at an altar decorated for the coming holidays, she summons the courage to hold out for the love she's always longed for.

Moments later, the stunned silence erupts with a burst of gunfire from an unknown source. Desperate to save the woman he's taken for granted for so long from a ruthless killer, Nate is forced to come to grips with feelings that run far deeper than he's ever before realized. Feelings that have him putting everything, including his own heart, on the line.

I hope you'll enjoy spending a few hours with April and Nate as they struggle to survive the most dangerous of secrets and fight their way toward a future that will stand the test of time.

Colleen Thompson

RESCUING THE BRIDE

Colleen Thompson

To Michael, who has taught me that
a best friend can be so much more.

Chapter 1

As her uncle walked her down the aisle, the tears in April Redding's vision made the scene a blur of color. Red and green, for all the Christmas poinsettias that festooned the makeshift outdoor altar. Blue and a deepening charcoal gray for the unseasonably warm Texas sky, which was quickly being overtaken by the cold front heading their way, a "blue norther" preceded by a low rumble of thunder.

But why shouldn't the weather open up on them, since everything else had gone wrong? Already a broken pipe had flooded their original venue and left their friends scrambling to set up and decorate an outdoor space at Nate's parents' ranch this morning. Overwhelmed by all the chaos and unfamiliar people, April's intellectually disabled brother Rory had gone into full meltdown mode. As excited as he'd been to be their ring bearer—no matter that he was three years April's senior, heavyset, and six feet tall—she'd been as relieved as he was when her aunt had taken him home before he accidentally hurt himself.

Another sign, she told herself as the friends and family standing at attention and musicians playing barely registered. Instead, her attention zeroed in on Nate himself, so tall and handsome in the black tuxedo he wore with boots, a broad-brimmed Stetson hat and silver-and-turquoise bolo tie. He was smiling at her—the smile that had launched a thousand rodeo fangirls before his accident last December. But there was a tension around his coppery brown eyes, too, along with a subtle shifting of his feet that only a longtime friend would recognize as deep discomfort.

She looked from her maid of honor to her bridesmaids, all in a beautiful deep red to complement the trim on her gown, to the groomsmen and the best man, who were dressed to match Nate. Not one of them showed any sign of noticing the groom's reluctance to be saddled with a woman as far from his taste in females as the Wheeler Ranch's champion cutting horses were from common donkeys.

Or maybe April was just projecting because of what she'd seen from the upstairs room where she was getting ready, when she'd looked out the window. What she couldn't unsee, no matter how hard she tried.

When her long walk finally ended, Nate stepped up beside her, both of them standing before a minister whose words she couldn't hear over the roaring in her ears. As she fought to keep from breaking down, another voice cut through the static, that of the mother whose death had brought her home to tiny Rusted Spur six months earlier.

There's still time to stop this, sweetheart. Still a chance to save this Christmas season and save your heart for love.

It was the shock of hearing her that made April gasp, snapping out of her daze to lay her hand over her middle. Nate turned to look at her, the concern on his face morphing into bewilderment as she blurted loudly, to be heard over an even more ominous growl from the heavens, "I'm so sorry. I can't do this."

A hush followed, the minister gaping, the groom's face draining of all color, and a tall, white-haired man—Nate's father—bearing down on her.

Instinctively, she shied away just as a loud crack split the silence. A thunderbolt, she thought at first. Except the festive floral arrangement behind her exploded, and there was so much blood.

One hour later...

Looking back on his final seconds as a professional bull rider, Nate Wheeler could pinpoint the instant when his life had changed forever, when the whip-crack of a bull's gyration coincided with the massive animal's sudden stumble. Up until that moment, Nate had been a champion with a swagger in his walk and the attention of every buckle bunny on the rodeo tour. Attention he was only too happy to reciprocate—especially when it came to curvy blondes.

It had all changed, that rough-and-tumble, beer-and-brass-balls lifestyle ending in the crunch of bone, the collective gasp of the Saturday-night crowd and a blur of movement as rodeo clown Kara Pearson had appeared from nowhere to save him from being skewered by a pair of wicked horns.

But a goring would be nothing compared to the shock he was feeling now, as he raced to follow the helicopter that had airlifted his injured father from the wedding during a brief break in the stormy weather. A shock that began when Nate's fiancée, April Redding, had blindsided him in front of everyone assembled for their outdoor wedding by saying she wouldn't marry him. Before her rejection could sink in, chaos erupted with the explosion of gunfire—from where, he still had no idea—and people scattering and screaming.

Swallowing hard as the pickup's windshield wipers slapped out a two-step rhythm, he cut his eyes to look at her. The silky auburn hair she'd worn in some kind of fancy updo had fallen down around her shoulders, strands of it clumped with the same blood that had dyed her once-white bridal gown to match its Christmas-crimson trim. Blood that could have just as easily been hers.

"You could've damned well gotten yourself killed," he said, the sharpness of the first words either one had spoken in the past hour making her jump a little.

But he was still pissed, thinking of how she'd left the shelter of the big, bare-limbed pecan where he'd dragged her after the first gunshot. How she'd rejected his instinctive move to keep her and the child she carried safe.

"What were you thinking," he asked, "crawling out from behind that tree after I told you to stay put?"

"Once I saw your father, I didn't stop to think. I acted." She shuddered and wrapped herself more tightly in the blanket Nate had given her. The green wool contrasted garishly with the blood that she was wearing, the clash of colors a lurid mockery of the Christmas season.

He opened his mouth to argue, wanting to lash out, to punish her for her role in what was turning into the worst day of his life. But he couldn't stop seeing her kneeling beside his gasping father, applying direct pressure to the spurting wound in his neck. It came to Nate then that whatever else she'd done today, her quick response had saved George Wheeler—or at least had given him some chance of survival.

Nate clamped his mouth shut, his head pounding as he tried to sort out what he should be feeling and what the hell had happened. When he glanced back at April, he saw she'd returned to staring out the window, mutely watching the rain pound the tough prairie grasses flat.

She looked bedraggled now, so sad and tired that something twisted in his chest to see it. And so pale behind the grime that marred a face that should be smiling, laughing on their wedding day.

"Want to talk about it?" he asked, burning to know why she'd bailed at the last minute. He'd done the right thing by her, hadn't he, proposing once she'd confessed she was expecting?

Expecting his child after one misguided tumble four-and-a-half months ago, both of them half-drunk as they'd lamented the recent changes of fortune that had trapped each of them in tiny Rusted Spur. He still couldn't believe he'd messed up everything, using a platonic friend he'd known since childhood to ease his disappointment.

She looked back at him, her brown eyes damp and worried…and more attractive than he'd ever realized, with contacts replacing the tortoiseshell-rimmed glasses he was used to seeing. Sighing, she moved one hand to the baby bump her A-line gown had concealed so well before she'd gotten soaked.

That simple, protective gesture sent a pang through him, worry for the tiny life they'd both seen on the ultrasound a week ago, the pictures that finally made the abstract child real. A son, according to the sonogram technician, and Nate had instantly pictured himself teaching the boy to ride in such a way it felt as if he and his mount were all one creature, to rope as if the lariat was an extension of his own arm. And to stay the hell off the backs of bucking bulls if he didn't want to ache some days like he was eighty instead of only thirty-two.

April had been smiling that day, too, a smile that lit her whole face as if she'd stepped into a sunbeam. *You're going to be a great mom*, he'd told her, picturing her laughing this time next year, the baby in her arms as Nate wrestled a big tree through the doorway for them to decorate together. *This is going to be all right.*

Damned fool that he was, he'd even made himself believe it. Or maybe he'd just wanted to, which wasn't the same thing.

"You warm enough?" he asked, frowning as he noted how the looming sky had darkened, and the outside temperature on his truck's gauge had dropped yet another ten degrees. "You aren't having any pain or—?"

"I'm sick, Nate, sick to death about this. Wondering how your father's doing, if he'll make it to the hospital."

At the mention of his father, a spiraling sensation hit him. Why would someone do this? And why do it today?

Forcing his attention back to April, he said, "I mean with the baby. Are you all right?" With the trauma center in Lubbock a three-hour drive from Rusted Spur, they'd be lucky to make it there by nightfall, and there were few towns of any size between the two. No medical facilities, either, since he'd opted to take the more direct county road to the old state highway.

"Oh," she said. "I'll be fine."

He glanced toward her to see tears running down her face and reached out to touch her arm. "Then, don't cry. Please, don't, April."

Outside, the rain swelled to a hard, metallic drumming, forcing Nate to slow his speed.

She wiped her eyes, the hand that held the tissues shaking. "I'm crying because—because it's my fault." Her voice cracked as she competed with the sound. "I'm the reason this all happened."

His heart stumbled through an extra beat. "What do you mean, you're the reason? You can't possibly think your getting cold feet had anything to do with some maniac out to kill my father." Though Nate couldn't begin to imagine anyone gunning down a rancher known for charming everyone from his humblest neighbors to the governor in Austin.

She shook her head. "Don't you understand? The shooter wasn't trying to kill your father. He wants me dead, Nate. Only me. Just like Martin Villareal."

April hugged herself and shivered, devastated to think that the same person who had killed her boss might have tracked her to Rusted Spur. Though she was a paralegal rather than an attorney, she could follow the chain of events as well as anybody else.

But Nate was shaking his head, arguing, "His death was ruled an accident. The poor guy was out jogging after sundown on a road without a shoulder."

It had been all over the news two weeks ago, how the hills outside of Austin had been a tragic choice, along with the dark running clothes the well-known attorney-activist had chosen for his usual after-work run. But no matter how often Nate tried to force her to accept it, he didn't have all the facts. No one did but the authorities, even if they'd failed to take her suspicions seriously.

"Listen, April. You've been through a lot," he said. "Losing your mom so suddenly, having to leave a job you loved to come deal with your brother. Then there was the shock of finding out about the baby and—"

Face burning, she straightened her spine. "Don't patronize me, Bull Boy."

As the rain began to slack off, he turned down the windshield wipers. She noticed how he'd clamped his jaw, that telltale twitching of a muscle in it signaling his irritation, the same way it had all the way back when he'd been that rowdy second-grader who'd driven all their teachers crazy.

"Nobody's patronizing you, Geek Girl," he said, reverting to the name he'd called her back then, when she'd worn the world's ugliest glasses, blazed through the contents of their tiny library in no time and always earned gold stars for classroom conduct. "I'm just trying to get you to consider that sometimes, terrible accidents happen—"

"And lots of times, men don't listen," she said, frustration boiling over. "Especially stubborn Neanderthals who've been tossed on their heads once too often by those smelly monsters you couldn't wait to climb back on."

He glared at her, the anger in his handsome face sparking a fear that he might drop her somewhere along the muddy roadside. But Nate could never do that, and besides, there was something more in his eyes. A wound that she'd inflicted, deep and raw and painful.

"I'm really sorry," she said. "Sorry I hurt you when I couldn't go through with that farce of a wedding—"

"Farce?" Nate shot back. "Maybe you should've told my parents that *before* my mom worked herself to exhaustion and my dad insisted he would pay for everything."

But April kept right on talking, desperate to make him understand that things weren't as they seemed. "Out of the corner of my eye, I saw your father coming toward me. Maybe he thought he could smooth things over, get the ceremony back on track. Or maybe he meant to wring my neck. But I ducked away from him just as I heard the gunshots. That should have been my *head* and not his neck."

Nate stared straight ahead, his Adam's apple working, the tension rolling off him like heat waves from a live coal. Watching him struggle to process what she'd told him, she fought to control her body's shaking. She wondered when, if ever, the adrenaline would burn off.

"I don't get why you did it," he murmured, still stuck on her rejection. "I did right by you, April, stood prepared to man up and take my medicine, to give our child my name."

Take my medicine? She made a scoffing sound, tamping down her own pain as he confirmed her suspicions. "I saw how prepared you were when I peeked out the upstairs window before the ceremony started. You were talking to Brady by the barn, fidgeting with that bolo tie like it was strangling you to death."

Nate had lost the tie at some point, and the crisp, white shirt he'd worn with his black tuxedo coat and Stetson was now spattered with blood. There was a smear, too, along his strong jaw, and the wind and rain had tangled his longish sandy brown hair. Still, he somehow managed to look as tempting as a plateful of Christmas cookies—and twice as ill-advised.

A hazy, wine-soaked memory rose to torment her, a memory so achingly sensual, it was enough to make her swear off alcohol, even after she had the baby. And maybe men as well, not that any of Rusted Spur's few candidates were likely to be looking for a woman with the kind of baggage she was toting. Along with someone out to kill her. She couldn't forget that.

"I was only a little nervous, that's all," Nate protested. "My folks invited a ton of their bigwig friends to the wedding."

"Don't give me that, not when you made a career of being the center of attention. It was the idea of settling down with me—settling *for* me—that had you freaked out. Looked to me like Brady was trying to convince you not to jump on one of the horses we had saddled and make a break for it before I could get out there."

"But I *didn't* run. I would've gone through with it."

"What on earth makes you think I want to be anybody's noble sacrifice?" Her vision hazing with tears, she ached for those uncomplicated years of childhood, years when both had been quick to tell anyone who'd listen that they were only friends. At least until she'd first begun to notice the core of decency behind the cocksure attitude and ripped physique that drew all the wrong girls to him. She'd been smart to bury her changing feelings as deeply as she could.

"What about the kid, then?" Nate demanded. "You can't think I'm gonna stand still while you kick him to the curb, too?"

She stared at him, heart thumping. How he could ask a thing like that when she had never for a moment thought of ending the unplanned pregnancy?

Outside, the rain eased, and up ahead, a thin shaft of wintry sunshine punched through the thick cloud layer. But it did nothing to lighten the darkness of her mood.

"Because if you try to adopt him out, I swear to you, I'll fight you in court," Nate vowed. "Our son has a family that wants him."

"A mother, too, I swear it. He'll always have me, Nate. And if you think threatening me is the best way to—" she began before she caught the nauseating scent of the drying blood on her dress. The stark reminder of the horror they had both witnessed had her swallowing hard and struggling to rein in her temper.

"I very much hope," she said, choosing her words as carefully as footsteps through a minefield, "that he'll have you and your family in his life, as well."

Nate turned down the windshield wipers, which had begun to squeak as they passed beyond the heavier shower. "So now I'm supposed to settle for seeing him on weekends and every other holiday? Having to run back and forth to Austin once you get your brother in that group home and move back there for your job?"

"We'll work it out, I promise," she said, her voice shaking. "And as for Rory, I told you before, it could take years, what with the waiting lists for any place I'd let him go."

Though she'd long argued that a group home would help Rory progress socially, she still wasn't certain she could move her brother from the only home he'd ever known. Deeply traumatized after witnessing their seemingly healthy widowed mother clutching at her head and falling dead, he'd regressed to the point where even the slightest change was likely to set him off.

"It's enough I have to deal with it." As much as April loved her brother, giving up the life she'd worked so hard to build to see to his care had been a huge adjustment. She'd managed to do some freelance legal research online, but even that was proving difficult with Rory's interruptions, and the modest inheritance her long-widowed mother had left wouldn't last forever. "You don't need to be saddled with that burden, too."

"I damned well knew what I was getting into. Who better?" he asked, reminding her of how kind he'd always been to Rory, how patient, as Nate had tried to teach him how a real man treats a woman.

No hitting and no screaming at 'em. They're littler than we are, so we have to be strong for them—even when they make you real mad.

As sweet as the memory was, she turned her eyes from Nate, remembering the grim look on his face when he'd suggested they get married. And her worry, even then, that she was only latching on to him to ease the loneliness she felt. Oh, she had friends, good friends who did their best to help out, but her brother's outbursts made her uncomfortable having people over. And she was rarely able to get out on her own, with her aunt and uncle, the only other caretakers Rory was used to, living too far from town to come by more than once or twice a month so she could stock up on groceries and run a few essential errands.

Nate cleared his throat before admitting, "I know it wasn't all flowers and romance, the kind of proposal that a woman dreams of. And I know it was a little late in coming, too."

"It's all right," she lied. "I understand. The whole thing was so—so unexpected." She flushed, remembering that mortifying moment when she'd woken up, limbs tangled with his, and realized that both of them were naked. Rory had been pounding at her bedroom door, pleading for her to come out and make him his favorite French toast.

"No, it isn't all right," Nate told her, "just like it wasn't all right that as soon as they got wind that I'd proposed, my mom and—and dad took over."

The conversation stopped, derailed by the mention of his father.

But as April mulled what Nate had just said, something else sprang to the forefront of her mind. "Wait," she said. "You mean they didn't *make* you propose?"

Nate snorted. "I might be living on the property while I run the ranch now, but make no mistake about it. Nobody tells me how to run my life. This seemed like the right thing, and we've always gotten on all right. Well, mostly, anyway."

She rolled her eyes at that, reminded of how he'd reacted when she'd first told him she was pregnant and planning to have and raise the child. *Oh, that's great*, he'd said, as if it had nothing in the world to do with him. *Then you're back with, what's his name again? That computer guy you used to see in Austin?*

Considering the trouble she'd gone to to rid herself of the lovelorn Kevin Wyatt—a nightmare that had ended up involving two changes of phone numbers, one move and a sternly worded letter from one of the attorneys in her office—April could have strangled Nate for bringing him up like that, even though he knew none of the details. Instead, she'd calmly wiped the dumb grin off his face, broadsiding him with the fact that there had been no one else for more than a year. No one except him.

"Besides, my folks have always liked you," Nate said with a shrug of a powerful shoulder. "Pretty sure they were relieved I at least picked a nice girl from a family they knew instead of one of those—they were none too fond of the kind of girls I used to run around with."

"In all fairness, Nate," she said, remembering one of the few she'd met, "I'm pretty sure nobody from your parents' generation wants a daughter-in-law named Bambi."

He chuckled at a memory, adding, "Or Chardonnay. Or Honey."

April bit back the reply that came to mind, the ragged scraps of her good humor evaporating at the thought of Nate with any of those bimbos.

The wheel appeared to jerk in his hands, and Nate's smile turned to a scowl. "What now?"

His question was quickly answered by a rhythmic thumping, a thumping that could only be a—

"Flat tire," they both said at once.

Nate groaned as he pulled to the shoulder. "I damned well knew I should've stayed in bed this morning."

But what abruptly came to April was how isolated they were out here, with nothing on the horizon but a sea of gold-brown grasses, the herd of cattle grazing in the distance…

And a prickling instinct warning her that just maybe, coming up behind them, was the anonymous emailer who'd claimed to want her dead.

Chapter 2

"Don't worry. I'll take care of it," Nate said, taking some comfort in the fact the rain had dwindled to a drizzle. But icy crystals had formed in it, and according to the dashboard gauge, the temperature had dropped below freezing—a forty-degree plunge in less than three hours with the front.

If April heard him, she gave no sign as she darted nervous glances at the road behind them. "Sitting ducks," she murmured. "We're sitting ducks here."

He shot her a glance. *What the hell?* "What is it?"

She unlatched the seat belt and reached back to where the luggage had been stashed in preparation for the short honeymoon he'd planned. Coming up with the big leather tote she used as a handbag, she started digging through it. "We have to call Brady. Tell him that we're stuck out here, so he can send help."

One of his groomsmen and a friend for years, Brady McCall had recently been named Trencher County's new interim sheriff. But they'd left him back in Rusted Spur on the shooter's trail. "You're not making any sense. You want to call the sheriff of a county more than a hundred miles behind us to deal with a flat tire?"

She dumped the tote's contents in her bloodstained lap, her frantic movements setting off alarm bells in his head. In all the years he'd known her, he'd never seen her like this. Even after today's shooting, she'd been quick, decisive, keeping her head while others shrieked or sobbed or stampeded to safety.

"Calm down and talk to me a minute," he said, worried that this might be some form of delayed shock.

"My phone's not in here." Her voice shook. "I must have left it at your parents'. Or maybe he took it out, so we couldn't call for help."

He grasped her arm until she looked at him, her eyes wide. "Or maybe *who* took it?" he demanded. "You mean the shooter, April?"

At her nod, he pulled his smartphone from the inner pocket of the black jacket he was wearing. "I've got mine right here. Brady's in my contacts. See?"

She jabbed a finger at an icon showing zero bars. "There's no signal. What if—what if this was all planned?"

Nate cursed himself for taking them through an area so remote, cell towers were a rarity. His gut clenched as it hit him that his father could be dead already. Or his mother, who'd been so hysterical she'd had to be sedated, might have gotten worse, and he would never know it. And from the look of April's pale face, there was more bad news to come.

"What's this really all about?" he asked, all too conscious of the blood soaked into her dress. There was so damned much of it. But he saw something else in her lap, too, that alarmed even more. "Wait a minute—is that a can of Mace? Why would you have that?" As far off the beaten path as Rusted Spur was, it struck him as odd that she would feel a need for personal protection.

"Pepper spray, from Austin," she corrected, quickly tucking it back into her bag.

"Tell me everything," he ordered.

"I tried before. But all we ended up doing is arguing about the wedding."

"You've got my full attention now. I swear it."

She shook her head. "We should change that flat first. Get out of here in case he's coming. I can help you—"

"I've got it," he assured her.

"But your back, Nate."

"I'm no cripple." After all the sweat and pain he'd put into fighting his way out of that wheelchair and building himself back up, he'd be damned if he'd allow a pregnant woman in her wedding dress to change a tire for him. "But I'm not loosening one lug nut until you slow down and explain this. How could the shooter possibly predict we'd have a flat, much less know where we'd—?"

She was out of her seat belt and out of the truck, leaving him no choice except to follow and start to work on the tire as she'd demanded.

"Come on, April. It's freezing out here," he said, taking the blanket she had left behind and tucking it carefully around her bare arms and shoulders. "Get back inside where it's warm."

"What if he followed us from the ranch, hoping to catch us alone?" She shivered, ignoring his suggestion and pulling the blanket even tighter. "Waiting for his chance, just like he did with Martin."

"Villareal again," Nate said, opening the truck's hood to grab the tool he'd need to remove the under-bed-mounted spare tire. "Why would you think a flat has anything to do with your boss?"

"After all the publicity last summer, we got threats at the office. Dozens of them."

"The Chambers case?" he guessed, remembering how quickly public opinion had turned against the Texas Justice Project when a man they'd helped to free from prison had gone after the eyewitness who'd put him on death row and beaten the thirty-six-year-old woman within an inch of her life.

"Right," April said, a world of regret crammed into a single syllable.

"Sure, I remember that. Who doesn't?" Nate headed for the rear of the truck. Even in the rehab center where he'd been at the time, the sad spectacle of the victim's family's distress had played out on every TV, from the husband's anguished fury to their cute blond kids' tearful pleas for their mama to wake up from her coma.

"The police were no help at all. They were still mad that we publicized how those two cops fouled up everything from the DNA collection to the—" Cutting herself off, she shook her head. "A person might think they'd want to fix it when they ruin someone's life by sending the wrong man to prison. Instead, they decided *we're* the enemy, trying to destroy careers and embarrass the department."

As he squatted down behind the truck to lower the spare, he asked her, "So when Villareal was run down, you're saying they didn't do anything about it?"

"I do think they made a good-faith effort then," she allowed, "but with no witnesses or cameras out there, they didn't have a lot to go on. And they saw no connection to some threatening emails we'd gotten months before."

Their conclusion made sense to Nate, who'd long since learned that the universe could at times be cruel and random. Seventeen-hundred-pound bulls flattened champion riders a few days before Christmas. Seemingly healthy fifty-eight-year-olds like April's mother died of undetected aneurysms, witnessed only by the disabled son she had spent decades insulating from the harshness of the world.

But a few hours earlier, those poinsettias behind April *had* exploded, an instant after his father had stepped into what Nate realized could have been a line of sight from the barn. In his mind's eye, he pictured the landmark, famous around the county for the Texas flag painted on the roof and twinkling lights hung every Christmas season. Had the hayloft door been open, the killer waiting inside?

Distracted by the thought, he pulled himself underneath the truck bed and retrieved the spare, in spite of his back's jabbing protest. "You said 'threatening emails *we'd* gotten,' right?" He came to his feet with a grunt. "Were you talking about the office as a whole, or just Villareal, or—"

"I received my share, too," she admitted, following as he rolled the tire and leaned it against the driver's side front fender, "addressed specifically to me."

Alarm jolted through him. So that was why she carried a canister of personal protection. "But why you? As the public face of the organization, Villareal would naturally draw fire. But why would anyone single out one of several paralegals working in the office?"

April's sigh made a hazy plume in the frigid air. "Ordinarily, you'd be right, but there was that horrible Trial TV special that aired back in July."

"I didn't catch that one." At the time, Nate's full attention had been focused on the grueling work of relearning to walk. April had visited him in rehab, offering smiles and hugs, even lame jokes like a six-pack tied carrot-fashion to a stick to encourage his progress. But she'd never said a word about what was going on with her. "Why didn't you tell me?"

"Because it was embarrassing, that's why. I was interviewed about nailing down Chambers's alibi and proving he couldn't have possibly been anywhere within a hundred miles of the original crime scene. That was just one piece of the puzzle, along with the new DNA testing and the witness's admission that her ID might've been influenced by those two cops breathing down her neck. Only the way the show was edited, they made it sound like I practically broke open the whole case by myself."

Nate retrieved his toolbox, unsurprised by her discomfort. Even back in school, April had always preferred to work behind the scenes, letting others hog the glory. It didn't surprise him either that the TV people would keep their story—and their cameras—focused on a pretty young face like hers as much as possible.

"The trouble was," April continued, "by the time he was finally released, twelve years of prison had twisted Ross Allen Chambers in ways I can't even comprehend. I mean, we knew he'd been repeatedly attacked there, but we had no idea he would—"

"If prison was so rough on him, why would he risk going after the eyewitness in broad daylight the way he did?"

April blew out a breath. "Who knows what set him off? Alcohol. Frustration. PTSD from the assaults. Whatever it was, he'll never breathe free air again. And that poor woman's life will never be the same."

Nate squatted down to start work on the lug nuts. And finally saw what he should have noticed earlier. What he *would* have, if he hadn't been so damned distracted by the conversation.

But when he looked up to tell her, he saw her horrified

face staring down the roadway as an older pickup slowed and glided toward them, its window rolling down.

"Back in the truck, April," Nate warned, his instinct to protect her bringing him to his feet, the steel wrench clutched like a weapon in his hand.

It can't be the shooter, not coming from that direction. Though she moved around to the passenger-side door, April was worried enough about Nate that she couldn't force herself to climb back inside, not until she was certain that everything would be all right.

The old brown pickup's brakes squealed as the driver's side window rolled down. His attention focused on Nate, an older man with a feed store cap called, "Need a hand there with that tire? Don't look like you're quite dressed the part, son."

When April stepped back into view, his gaze snapped to her gown, his amiable expression freezing.

Nate lowered the wrench and said, "No, thanks. I've got it covered."

The man's wide-eyed gaze latched on to the blood-spattered tuxedo shirt, the color draining from his face. An instant later, tires spun, and the old brown pickup roared off, belching a puff of smoke.

Nate gave April a once-over, his gaze moving from her wrecked hairdo to the ruined gown. "Can't imagine what could've got into that guy. Hasn't he ever seen a zombie wedding before?"

Despite the horror of their situation, April broke out laughing. But then, Nate's droll delivery had always gotten to her, all the way back to those days when he'd lean forward to whisper something awful in her ear to crack her up in math class.

Above them, the clouds parted, a patch of cold blue

overhead. Sunlight illuminated the rolling prairie, its grass sparkling with the ice coating golden-brown stalks. For a fleeting moment, the beauty of it sliced through winter's bleakness, touching off a fresh ache in her heart.

Before she could read too much into it, Nate abruptly sobered. "And the next time I tell you to get back in the truck, you do it. No arguments, no stalling."

Annoyed, she made a scoffing sound.

"I'm serious," he said. "Come over here and see why."

She cautiously approached, her heartbeat picking up speed as Nate pointed out the tire he had just pulled off the truck. "See this. That's a sliced-through sidewall."

"So I was right, then. Someone did intentionally cut it."

"Nicked it, maybe, for it to leak so slowly. But it's also possible that something from the road flew up and hit the tire just right."

"Sure," she said, not buying the coincidence for a moment. "Just like that broken pipe this morning—on a night well above freezing—*could've* been an accident."

Nate tightened a lug nut on the spare tire and quickly started on another. "I've thought about sabotage at the church, too. Remind me to ask Brady about that when we reach him."

Frowning, April bit her lip. "If the tire was cut at the ranch, though, why wouldn't it have gone flat right away?"

"If the shooter was in a rush, worried he might be seen, his cut might've come in at too shallow of an angle."

She nodded. "I can see that."

"And the dropping temperatures would've slowed the leak down even more. But that would mean he'd have no way of guessing where we'd end up stopping. Besides, my bet's that Brady's got this guy on the run—or better yet, in custody by now."

Despite the queasy feeling in her stomach, April nodded, admitting to herself that Nate was likely right.

Grimacing, he rubbed his lower back, turning his head in an attempt to hide his expression. Remembering how no one had been sure he would even make it last December, with two vertebrae, his right hip and a femur broken, April knew he had to be in agony, squatting and lifting as he had been. But she fought back her impulse to offer help again, not wanting to add insult to injury by hurting his stubborn cowboy pride.

Still, she couldn't stop herself from laying one hand on his shoulder and giving it a squeeze. Instead of shrugging off her touch as she more than half expected, he gave an exhalation that fogged the frigid air. A moment later, he returned to the task before him, the way he had so many times before.

Standing beside him to keep watch over the road, April wondered if he would ever get past the pain she had inflicted on him today. And if his father didn't make it, what then would become of this fragile, temporary truce between them? Would Nate's sense of obligation toward her give way to resentment that the sniper's bullet hadn't struck her down instead?

Chapter 3

Once they were under way again, April felt the tension in her shoulders ease when they finally turned onto the more heavily traveled road that would take them into Lubbock.

Ten minutes later, Nate pointed out a tall steel frame in the distance. "Cell tower, dead ahead."

"Got it." She snatched up his phone and called Brady's personal cell number, then groaned in frustration. "It's going straight to voice mail."

As Nate muttered a curse, she left a brief message asking Brady to get in touch as soon as possible.

"Try the main sheriff's department number," Nate suggested. "We've got to let him know what's really going on."

Once she reached one of Brady's deputies, she hurried to fill him in about her belief that the shooter had been aiming for her. When she brought up the flat, Deputy Anderson sounded skeptical about the theory that it could be part of the shooter's scheme to catch them on the road.

"That part sounds a little far-fetched," he said, "especially since you haven't run into any other trouble yet. Or maybe the shooter got caught behind our roadblocks."

"So he's still not in custody?"

"Not unless Sheriff McCall's caught up with him. What with the bad weather fouling up communications, we're having a little trouble locating him."

"You can't reach him, either?" Fear prickled along the back of her neck. A shooter brazen enough to open fire during a well-attended wedding wouldn't hesitate to kill a lawman.

"We think we've got at least one guest missing, too."

"Who is it?" she asked, trying to recall who she'd seen after the shooting stopped. The trouble was, she'd been so hyper-focused on Nate's father at the time, she'd tuned out everything else until the moment she'd impulsively jumped into Nate's truck to follow the helicopter.

"We're still confirming, checking names off from the guest list, trying to account for everyone," Anderson said.

"But who do you *think* it is?"

Before she could get an answer, Nate reached for the phone. "Let me have that."

Hearing the urgency in his voice, she relinquished his cell.

"What do you hear about my father?" he asked the deputy. "Did he make it to the hospital alive?"

April froze, heart thumping wildly. Why hadn't she thought to ask about Nate's father first?

At Nate's indecipherable grunts, the knot inside her stomach tightened.

"My mother, then?" he asked. "Can you at least tell me how she's doing? Her blood pressure's been an issue even before all this—hello?"

Nate glanced down at the screen. "Of all the—the

damned battery's gone dead now." As they approached a sign reading Lubbock City Limits, he added, "I guess we'll know soon enough."

Hearing the dread in his voice, April said, "He'll make it. He's a strong man—and so kind, no matter what anybody says about his—"

"His what? You mean his business?" Nate asked, instantly defensive. "Why the hell would you bring that up? You, of all people, should know he's been out of the private prison industry for two years."

April cringed, angry with herself for mentioning the touchy subject of Correctional Solutions, the source of much of George Wheeler's wealth. "You're absolutely right," she told Nate. "Forget I said anything about it."

"I'd like to forget everything about today. But somehow, I don't figure there's a chance in hell that's happening. Do you?"

She blew out a sigh, wishing she could purge much of the past year from her brain. Yet she wouldn't take back everything…like the unborn child she'd already come to love so deeply that just the thought of holding him took her breath away.

After parking outside the hospital about twenty minutes later, they hurried into an expansive lobby, with April using the blanket to hide as much of her bloody dress as possible. Hampered by all the material, she scrambled to keep pace with Nate's long-legged strides…

Until he stopped in his tracks so abruptly that she nearly bumped him from behind.

"What's wrong?" she asked, only to see him staring at the children's choir that stood in front of a beautifully lit Christmas tree. In the cavernous space, the boys' and girls' sweet, clear voices echoed off the glass and marble, the strains of "Joy to the World."

When he didn't answer, a chill rippled through her as she remembered how Nate's mother had brought a little stereo to his bedside last year, insisting that a nonstop barrage of holiday music would cheer him and speed his recovery. But April couldn't help but wonder, did he think back to the death of the career that had so long defined him every time he heard a carol?

He glanced over at her. "Sorry," he explained. "Just looking for a sign for the emergency department."

She didn't buy it any more than she'd believed his weak reasons for not wanting the musicians to play any Christmas music at their wedding. But he was looking around now, his gaze zeroing in on a desk marked Information.

Before he could start toward it, April caught his arm. "You go on ahead," she said. "I'll catch up after I find a place to get out of these sticky clothes."

"Maybe you should get the doctors to check you out first, as is. Just to be sure everything's okay with the baby and—"

"I wasn't the one hurt, Nate, but I really need to change."

Deciding to back off for now, he noticed she hadn't brought her suitcase. "Into what?"

"Into something that won't get me detained and hauled off to the psych ward," she said, half expecting the children's choir to break out screaming over the bloody gown at any moment. "I stuffed an outfit into my bag while you were working on the tire."

"Go ahead," he told her, his voice hoarse and his coppery eyes glazed with what she recognized as fear—this from the same man who had faced down the meanest bucking bulls the rodeo circuit had to offer. Who had faced down potential death and the chance of permanent paralysis without betraying much more than the sometimes-annoying cockiness that was his response to every challenge.

She ached to reassure him it would be all right, that he'd learn the father who had so patiently taught him everything he knew of horses, who had steadfastly supported Nate through so many ups and downs, would make a full recovery. But she didn't know that and couldn't say it, not when both of them had seen the entrance and the exit wound in George Wheeler's neck. Not when they had heard the rasping and the rattling of a man struggling not to choke on his own blood.

With no words to offer, she acted on impulse, hugging Nate instead. To her surprise, his arms wrapped around her and instead of one of the polite, all-for-show embraces they had shared during their brief, so-called engagement, they squeezed each other, drawing comfort from the years of friendship they had shared.

In the low swell of her belly, April felt a flutter, a stirring that made her gasp.

"Didn't mean to squash you. Sorry," Nate said as he let go.

"It wasn't that. I just—" *I just felt our baby, for the first time, moving. I'm sure that had to be it.*

Excitement rippled through her, and she badly wanted to tell him all about it, to be like any other first-time expectant mother gushing to the father of her child. But they would never be that couple, and even if they had been, this wasn't the right time. "See you in a few," she said, standing on her toes to place a kiss on his jaw.

He hesitated for a moment, studying her face before turning away. She stood, watching him for a few heartbeats until he broke into a jog and disappeared.

After washing up as best she could and changing into the casual green sweater and jeans she'd packed, April found Nate in a small waiting area where she had been directed. Alone in the room, he was rubbing his back, his expression so grim it hurt to meet his gaze.

"Any news?" she asked.

He nodded. "He was breathing when they took him into surgery. That's something, right?"

"It's everything," she said before asking if she could borrow his phone again to give her aunt and uncle her contact information. A few minutes after she'd finished texting them, an angular, dark-haired woman in blue scrubs came out and introduced herself as Dr. Han, the surgeon who had worked on George Wheeler.

Ignoring her suggestion that they sit, Nate said, "Just cut to the chase and tell us. Did my father make it?"

"Please," April added, uncertain whether she was being polite or begging for the answer they'd both prayed for.

The surgeon nodded, her expression somber. "Your father's survived the surgery to repair the compromised blood vessels and damage to his trachea."

"The trachea?" asked April.

"The windpipe, but for now he's breathing through an opening created in an emergency tracheotomy."

Nate's face drained of all color. "Then he wasn't breathing. Is he—is his brain still…?"

"Before we can do any neurological assessment, we need to worry about stabilizing his vital signs. For now, he's under sedation, and a ventilator's assisting him with respiration."

Nate stiffened. "You mean a machine's doing his breathing for him?"

"It's assisting his own efforts," she explained patiently, "to give him time to heal. He's also had a blood transfusion—"

"I can give blood," Nate blurted, "all the blood he needs."

"Not single-handedly, I'm afraid, but any donations to our blood bank are certainly welcome."

Fearing Nate's emotions were getting him off track, April asked, "Was that the only damage, to the blood vessels and the trachea?"

"That's the most critical at this point. The rest we can worry about once we've gotten him through this period."

"And what would you say his chances are?" Nate asked.

"It's very early to predict."

Frowning, he shook his head. "Just spit it out, doc. Please. Should I be offering my mother hope? Or preparing her for the worst?"

Dr. Han nodded, her large, dark eyes locking with his equally intense gaze. "It's a very serious injury, Mr. Wheeler, and with the added question of how long he may have been deprived of oxygen, there's no way to be certain. But I will tell you I've seen patients survive traumatic injuries that on presentation looked worse."

"Survive them with a decent quality of life?" Nate asked. "Because I can tell you one thing. My father's always said he'd never live hooked up to machines and wires. He's—he's said he'd rather... He had some papers drawn up."

"Don't get too far ahead of yourself," Dr. Han advised him. "And don't ever lose hope, Mr. Wheeler. At times, I've seen it take my patients further than any medical intervention we've come up with."

In a quiet alcove outside the Trauma ICU, Nate found a spot to plug in his phone and made several calls. By the time he'd finished, he had convinced himself that the best thing for everybody would be to send April home before his mother arrived the next morning, thanks to a sympathetic friend of his father's who'd offered to fly her in his private plane.

But as he returned to his father's bedside and watched

the rise and fall of his chest—the whoosh and odd pauses of that damned ventilator and the beeping of his monitors at odds with everything he would have wanted—Nate's resolve gave way to an even greater sadness, a sickness of his soul almost impossible to bear.

He couldn't deny that over the course of the afternoon and evening, April's presence had been a comfort. Sticking close, she said little, but when she laid a hand on his back, somehow sensing those moments when doubt and grief threatened to consume him, or when she bathed his father's pale face and combed back his thick, white hair, Nate felt the warmth of her sincerity…and felt grateful, too, to have someone by his side who wouldn't try to fill the space with words.

Yet for all of that, the anger came over him in waves, and he found himself replaying that awful moment she'd told everyone, *I'm sorry. I can't do this.* As if he were the worst damned thing that could ever happen to a woman.

Just as Nate convinced himself that he was letting his wounded pride blind him, he would think about how April had endangered all of them by not mentioning something as important as the threats to her own life. Was she even fit to be a mother, putting their child at such a risk?

But he wouldn't leave her vulnerable by forcing her to drive home alone. And with his best man, Zach Rayford, tied up with a wife in labor and Brady heaven only knew where, there was no one available that he trusted to come pick up April. No one capable and competent to defend her with a gun, if it came down to an ambush.

Nate looked down toward where she sat, only to see her staring through him, her eyes glazed over as if she were deep in thought or utterly exhausted.

"You haven't touched the dinner I brought you," he said,

keeping his voice low so the charge nurse would continue to tolerate their after-hours presence.

She eyed the tray, its grilled chicken salad still locked in a plastic clamshell, a look of revulsion twisting her mouth. "I can't."

"You need to try. I know you haven't had a thing since breakfast, if you even ate this morning."

"There's no way I could keep it down," she said, though as far as Nate had heard, what little morning sickness she had suffered had passed weeks before. "My stomach's upset as it is from the milk I drank."

"Later, then," he suggested. "That chair reclines, I think. Why not lean back and try to rest a while?"

April straightened as she rubbed her arms. "I tried while you were on the phone, but every time I close my eyes, I hear the shots and the screams. I see all that blood." Her gaze slid to his father, with the thick, white bandages encircling his neck.

"You have to take care of yourself, for the baby's sake, if not yours—"

"Don't act like you own my body," she said, her brown eyes fierce.

"There's no need to get upset. I never said I owned it."

Coming to her feet, she placed her hand over her small bump and glared at him. "Never even wanted it, once you sobered up."

He took a step toward her.

She lifted her chin, defiance crackling in her expression. But when he moved in closer, he saw something rawer shimmering behind it. A brand of pain that had a knot forming low in his gut.

Raising a hand to brush a stray auburn strand from her face, he asked, "You think I've never wanted you? That's what this is all about?"

The hurt that bloomed in her eyes told him he'd scored a direct hit. "Why would you possibly want me," she asked, "when you had all the groupies you could handle?"

He snorted and gestured around the room. "You see any of those gals here with me now, standing by me through this? You run into any at the hospital or the rehab center when you drove for hours to visit?"

She turned and walked over toward the dark window, putting her back toward him. But hiding her face did nothing to disguise the drooping of her shoulders or the slight trembling that led him to believe she might be weeping.

The knot in his gut tightened, and he came up behind her. Telling himself that, between the hormones and the situation, she was as likely to go off on him as the average hand grenade, he hesitated for a moment, then surrendered to the impulse to put his arms around her and place a kiss atop her crown.

She tensed at first while the whoosh and hiss of the ventilator remained as steady as the thumping in Nate's chest was erratic. After a few moments, he felt her relax, her breathing slowing until it found a natural rhythm. Until it matched his own.

With the scent of her shampoo in his nostrils—a lemony-clean smell that reminded him of summer—and her soft heat pressed against him, Nate felt desire stirring, his body remembering what his mind barely did.

Closing his eyes, he whispered into her ear, "I do love you. You know that, don't you, April?"

She jerked away from him and spun around, as if he'd gone and pulled the pin. "Love me like a sister, right? Or the way you would an old friend you never meant to sleep with?"

Up until a few months ago, he couldn't have denied it. But now, with his libido assuring him that things had changed, Nate wasn't certain how to answer. Because he shouldn't want this woman, the woman who had spurned him in a way half of Texas must be buzzing about by now. The woman whose secret had left his father fighting for his life.

But from the hurt look in April's eyes, his hesitation was all the answer that she needed. "I'm heading home tomorrow," she said. "I don't belong here with your family. Not after what I've done. Please, tell your mom how very sorry I am for everything."

"Stay," he told her, wanting to add the words *I need you.* But with so much bitterness between them, what came out instead was, "At least until I can see to it that you make it back home safely."

"I'm perfectly capable," she told him, "of making my own arrangements."

"I know you are, but that doesn't mean—" he started before the now-recharged phone in his pocket began to vibrate.

"Don't go anywhere," he said as he pulled out the cell to check it. Seeing the words *Trencher Co. Sheriff Dept.* on the screen, he added, "This could be the news we've been waiting for on Brady."

As he stepped out to take the phone call, she waited inside the room. Praying, he supposed, as he was, that their friend hadn't been another casualty of a wedding that never should have been.

April's heart leaped to her throat, her anxiety building for what seemed like an eternity before Nate returned.

"First, of all," he said before she could ask, "they're safe, Brady and Kara both."

"You mean *Kara* was out there with him?" April could scarcely believe that her friend had been the missing guest.

Considering how Kara had begged off an invitation to be a bridesmaid because she couldn't deal with being around Brady after their recent breakup, it was tough to imagine that anything short of life and death circumstances could have driven the two of them together.

"They're okay," Nate assured her, "and you're not going anywhere, especially not back to Rusted Spur on your own."

"What?" she asked, in the hush between his father's machine-assisted breaths.

"Brady says Kara saw the shooter—and she recognized the guy from your boss's funeral."

April blinked hard, the nausea she'd felt earlier threatening to overwhelm her. "Who was it?" she asked, wondering if it could have been someone she knew. Someone who'd pretended to be there grieving Martin Villareal's death?

"Brady doesn't have a name yet, but they're working hard to figure this out and find the man before he gets the chance to finish what he started."

"What about Kara?" April thought of the danger to her friend, who'd accompanied her to the funeral when Nate had a ranch emergency involving an injured colt. If the shooter had seen her, too, she could easily be a target. "Will she be safe?"

"As safe as anyone can be with Brady looking after her. Just the way I'll be looking after you until this guy's behind bars. He was aiming at you, April. Brady says the shot's trajectory had the shooter lining up with your head just the way we suspected."

But April's thoughts had already flown to Rory and her aunt and uncle, who were staying with him at her home. "What if this person goes to my house looking for me and finds my family there?"

Nate put his hand on her shoulder. "I forgot to tell you

earlier. When I called the house to check on my mom, the friend staying with her said that your aunt and uncle were taking Rory out of town to their place. He'll be safe there, April, even if he does freak out a little about having to sleep in a strange bed."

She hugged herself. "I have to go and help them. Uncle Jimmy and Aunt Sylvia aren't young anymore, and Rory's—"

"Their kids will pitch in, right?"

"Maybe. If it's convenient," she said, thinking of the many times her cousins had bailed out when anyone made the mistake of taking them up on their halfhearted offers of help. How could April trust them now, with Rory still so emotionally scarred by their mother's death? "At least until I can get there."

"You're going to have to let them rise to the occasion," Nate said, giving her a look that brooked no argument. "Because I've already told you, you're not leaving my sight for one minute. Not until the man who wants you dead is behind bars."

Chapter 4

The sun had barely risen the next morning when Dr. Han came in to check on Nate's father's condition.

"Glad to see he's held his own through the night," she reported, keeping her voice low so as not to disturb April, who had finally nodded off a couple of hours earlier. "Vitals are improving."

"That means he's getting better?" Nate asked, coming to his feet so he could watch the doctor's eyes as she answered.

"It's certainly an encouraging sign," Dr. Han said, choosing her words carefully, "as long as the trend continues."

"How soon before you can take him off that ventilator?" The wires and monitors were bad enough, but Nate didn't want his mother hearing the machine's troubling artificial pauses and disturbing whooshing sound. Didn't want her to face the guilt Nate himself was grappling with for listening to the surgeon rather than his father's stated wishes.

"You need to understand, Mr. Wheeler, your father's body is still recovering from a critical injury, shock from blood loss and the surgery to repair the wounds. Infection is a risk as well, and we don't yet know about what damage lack of oxygen might have caused—"

"In other words, you don't know whether the man that wakes up—*if* he wakes up—will still be the same person who—the same guy who—" Embarrassed by his burning eyes, Nate turned his head away, remembering how his dad had been there every minute through those dark days last December, how he'd been the one to make Nate believe that no wheelchair would ever hold him.

To Nate's surprise, April was right there beside him, slipping an arm around his waist. And it felt so right, that she should be here, standing by his side, even though he knew it couldn't last.

"I think you'll find that none of you will be the same person," Dr. Han said, her dark eyes thoughtful as she looked at the two of them. "Crisis changes people, but that doesn't mean your family has to fall apart."

Attempting a smile, he told the surgeon, "I think you might've missed your calling. Or did you minor in counseling?"

She smiled back at them and nodded, then excused herself to finish her rounds.

By the time Nate updated his mother, who'd recovered from the sedative she'd been given and would be leaving with his father's longtime friend, Joe Mueller, in a few hours, a new nurse arrived with the shift change. After giving Nate and April a once-over, she wasted no time issuing marching orders.

"Cafeteria first," she said, her steel-gray bob of a helmet and no-nonsense manner hinting that she'd been at this for decades. "Then try the Restway Hotel. It's clean and new and nice as any. And I'm not having any arguments. You won't be of use to anyone if you crash and burn the first day."

"You're making it sound like you think this could go on a while," Nate said.

"Better a long recovery than a swift conclusion. That's what we tell everyone in the trauma ICU."

Nate glanced down at April, noticing the smudges of exhaustion beneath her brown eyes. And he could use a few hours' sleep himself, if he was going to be in any shape to support his mother later.

"I think we'll do that," he told the nurse before securing a promise that she would call his cell phone if there was any change in his father's condition.

After a quick breakfast downstairs, he and April headed for the address the nurse had given them for the hotel. While they waited for the man behind the desk to finish with another customer, April surprised Nate by pulling out a credit card.

"I should at least pay for my own room," she said, eyes shining with the reflection of the white Christmas lights hung around the lobby. "I've already cost your family so much, with the wedding, and—"

"Put that away. For one thing, I was serious when I said I'd be sticking close." For another, there was no way he was letting a woman he knew was staring down the barrel of money issues pay when he had plenty.

She gestured toward the lobby. "Really? Do you honestly think this assassin is lurking behind the greenery, waiting to hop into the elevator and follow us upstairs? It's bad enough to have you hovering outside when I'm in the restroom."

Nate checked out a new arrival, a paunchy business type who'd just exited the elevator.

"I'm not taking chances with my son's life," Nate said, but it was the thought of April, of someone cruel enough to leave her like his dad or worse, that put him more on edge than ever.

"With your son's life…well, that's just *fine*," she said, the color staining her cheeks telling him he'd once more managed to say the wrong thing. "But make sure to get us a room with two double beds."

"Come on, April. We're both totally exhausted, so what do you have against a king?" he asked.

She treated him to a withering look before saying, "Nothing in particular. I just don't want *my son's father* hurting his back sleeping on the floor."

Up in their room, April used the shower first before coming out wearing a silky-looking red nightgown that clung to her new contours. Curves that had Nate's full attention, though he'd been half asleep.

When she caught him looking, she blushed. "It's what I had packed for, you know, the *honeymoon*." She used her fingers to sketch out the final word, as if she'd expected that their three days at the lakeside spa would be an even bigger sham than their engagement.

"It's—it's nice," he said. Too nice. He would've had her out of it in no time. "You look amazing in it. Gorgeous. And yesterday…that dress you wore was…"

Noticing her stricken expression, he remembered how the bridal gown had been her mother's, though April had had the new trim added when she'd had it altered. "Did you save it?" he asked. "Maybe we could find a cleaner who could get out all the—"

"I threw it away. I had to. A nurse caught me outside the restroom and explained it was a—a biohazard, with all that blood. Besides," April added, shaking her head as she crossed her arms, "you can't think that I could ever wear it again. Or even stand to look at it after…"

As she wound down, he said nothing. Had nothing to offer. Nothing that she wanted, anyway.

By the time Nate shaved and showered, April had shut off the lights and closed the curtains. She lay huddled on the bed nearest the window, the covers drawn so high, he could only see the top of her head. She looked so forlorn there, so isolated in her misery, that he was tempted to crawl in beside her and pull her into his arms. To tell her he was sorry.

But the temptation of the curves beneath that silky red gown had him rethinking the idea. Instead, he claimed the other bed and tried in vain to relax. With the shooter still on the loose, every odd noise snapped Nate into full alert mode, from what proved to be a maid pushing a squeaky-wheeled cleaning cart to a door closing down the hall, the room's occupant yakking on her cell phone as she headed for the elevator.

When he did finally drop off, disjointed images spun through his dreams, each one more disturbing than the last. At one point, Nate jerked awake, his body shaking as he snatched up the silent phone beside him, panicking to imagine he had missed a call from the nurse.

Finally, he sat up in bed, raking his fingers through his sweat-damp hair, torn between the desire to rush back to the hospital to stand vigil and his inability to leave April here to rest alone. And he couldn't bring himself to wake her when she so clearly needed her sleep—not yet.

But when he glanced over toward her bed, he saw that she'd rolled to face him.

"Can't wind down?" The voice floating through the darkness was barely louder than the low hum of a vacuum cleaner from somewhere down the hall.

"Sorry if I'm bugging you." Frustration ground his words down into harshness. "Every car door slamming outside takes me right back to the gunshot. Every time the heat kicks on, I hear my father's ventilator. I think about my mother on her way here and the guy out there, staring down a barrel and taking aim at you. Part of me hopes Brady won't catch him, so I can kill the bastard with my own two hands."

The heat chose that moment to come back on, its quiet drone going on so long that Nate began to suspect she had fallen back to sleep.

At last, she whispered, "Close your eyes, Nate. Let it go now. Let it go so you'll be able to help your mother when she comes."

He sighed, wishing it were that easy, but he humored April and lay down again. A moment later, he heard the squeak of her bed and the pad of bare feet on the carpet.

When his mattress dipped, he held his breath until she had slipped beneath the covers beside him. When she lifted his arm and snuggled to let him spoon her, he moved to pull her back against his chest. It wasn't her back, though, that fired his imagination but the urge to explore the changing landscape of her pregnant body. To taste the sweet new fullness of her breasts—would they be more sensitive to his touch?—and stroke the growing swell of the new life forming, to marvel at a miracle two parts bourbon and three bitter disappointment.

But it wasn't disappointment he felt as his fingertips glided over the surprising firmness of her belly. Wasn't disappointment that had him pressing his mouth against her neck, his teeth lightly pinching the flesh until she gasped.

In the small sound, he heard surprise, and maybe the same desire he was feeling. The need to obliterate the memories, if only for a while.

When she turned her head toward him, he captured her mouth with his. The contact was explosive, the heat and pleasure of it burning off every other thought. Everything except his need to have this woman, body, heart and soul.

She moaned and wriggled against him, the sounds of her excitement only serving to inflame him. His fingers, kneading her breasts, found the tight bud of a nipple. Kissing his way down her neck and chest, he drew the hard tip into his mouth.

But she was pushing at him, pushing him back and saying, "No, please, no, I never meant for—"

Confused, he pulled back. "But I thought—"

"You're way too sober for this, aren't you?" she asked, a cynical edge to the words.

He noticed she was breathing hard, too, and that kiss— he could have sworn she'd been responding, feeling the same rush of raw attraction he had. "Then why did you come over?" he asked. "You're the one who insisted on the separate beds."

"I just wanted you to be still," she said, turning away from him. "You were bothering me with all the tossing and the turning."

He scoffed at her words, knowing a bald lie when he heard one. "What is it you're so afraid of? It's not like you can get *more* pregnant."

"I wanted to help you sleep. That's all."

"Are you sure about that, April?" He nipped the lobe of her ear gently, shifting enough to let her feel what she was doing to his body.

She rolled away and sat up on the bed's edge, and even in the dim light, he saw her shaking her head. "I'm not going to do this. I won't be the woman that you go to when you're trying to forget things. The old friend who's only good enough when no one better is around."

"Is that who you think I am?" Nate asked, not realizing until the words were out that maybe he had been that guy for a good chunk of his thirty-two years. But even if he could reclaim the life his final ride had stolen, he could no longer quite remember why it had seemed so important. "And who says any of those girls I dated were half the woman you are?"

"Too little, too late, Bull Boy," April said, padding back to the bed where she'd been sleeping. "So go to sleep. On your own side of the room."

"I will, then," he said, trying to hide how much it bugged him that she wouldn't believe what he had told her, "but I promise you, you don't know what you're missing."

"If it was so darned fabulous the first time, don't you think I'd probably remember?"

Nate winced, reminded of why he'd so abruptly sworn off drinking, then rolled over in his own bed. "Guess it's a good thing, then, I left you with a little souvenir."

He lay there, sleepless, for a long time, the pleasure of getting the last word in turning to ashes in his mouth. Because for all he'd told himself these past few weeks that he had manned up and done the right thing by April, he saw now it hadn't been enough. Not nearly.

It hadn't been a tenth of what a heart like hers deserved.

It needed to be wrapped up, the man behind the desk knew as he rose to grab his jacket. The target had to die. No more screwups like the wedding. No more trying to make a statement by having it done where cameras would be rolling and witnesses on scene to talk to the reporters. Where the bereaved groom would be so stoic, breaking hearts as he spoke with the press. His handsome face and ill-fated final pro ride were already famous among fans of rodeo, and the media would be sure to pick up on his grief, splashing visuals from his days on the circuit across their blood-soaked newscasts.

And the perfect statement to get across to anyone who guessed that he was coming for them, too, if they didn't back off. Or sending someone, anyway, someone he could trust to get things done and get away without leaving a trace.

With the shooter he'd sent missing in action—either scrambling to save his own neck or out to salvage what he could—the man locked up his office and headed for his sleek Mercedes, taking comfort in the fact that he'd used an intermediary. But then again, he was no amateur, to leave a trail for the authorities to follow.

He opened a brand-new burner phone, also purchased via a third party, to call his contact once more and make a backup plan. This time, however, he specified that it must be done as expediently as possible, with no fuss and no fanfare. Just as long as the target was eliminated...with the biggest bonus he could manage, if it was finished before Christmas Day.

By the time the two of them returned to the hospital a few hours later, April was still fuming. Nate, too, seemed in a bad mood, though not for the reason she expected.

"I was in the wrong," he said as they approached the building's lobby doors, both of them wearing the jeans and warm jackets they'd had packed away, "poking at you like that earlier. We've got problems, grown-up troubles that it's time for us to deal with, so no more arguing like a couple of schoolkids. There's way too much at stake to mess this up."

Cold as it was, April's face burned. Who would have ever guessed that Nate would be the one pointing out the high road? The one who was proving he had changed more than she'd thought possible.

"It wasn't just you," she admitted, reminding herself that she'd already inherited the responsibility for Rory, and in a few short months, she'd be a mother, too.

On some level, though, she understood her and Nate's squabbling was a form of self-defense. A way to keep the real issues at bay as long as they could. But as badly as she'd wanted to bury the feelings he had stirred with his touch, sniping at him hadn't helped her. Nor had it erased her gnawing doubts about the way she'd backed out on their nuptials.

If you hadn't, you'd be dead now, and my first grandchild with you. It was her mother's voice again, sending chills skating along April's backbone. A ripple of nausea had her placing her hand on her stomach.

When she stumbled, Nate took her arm. "You okay?"

"Just a little clumsy, that's all, tripping on my own feet."

He studied her a moment, his sharp, brown eyes assessing, and it struck her again how mouthwatering he was, whether in the black tux he'd had on yesterday or the jeans and button-front red shirt he wore with a distressed leather jacket. Between his handsome face and the muscular, trim body, she half expected to be set upon by a pack of the man's former groupies any minute.

"There's no need to worry," he said, ignoring the canned strains of "Have Yourself a Merry Little Christmas" floating through the lobby. "I've got your back now, April."

As they walked, she noticed, too, the way his gaze touched on every person they passed, and she, too, kept her eyes peeled, her body tensing when she spotted a man she thought resembled the photograph Brady had sent via text while the two of them were sleeping. A deputy had called last night with a name, too: Dennis Cobb, a man with a long criminal history in Austin. But April, who'd been so emotional about her boss's death that her memories of the funeral were a jumble, had never seen or heard of him in her life. Or had she?

"It's not our guy," Nate assured her, sounding more confident than she felt. But April trusted him, just as she trusted what Kara had said about spotting Cobb at her boss's funeral.

Had Cobb been there gloating over his kill—or hoping for a chance to take another of the Texas Justice Project team out? April wondered, could she have died that day, if he'd only caught her alone?

Some forgotten detail buzzed in the back of her brain like a rattler in the tall grass, a detail that slithered away when the elevator doors hissed closed behind them.

"Hope we beat my mom here," Nate said. "Joe promised he'd take her to get something to eat before he had to head home, but you could sooner shoehorn a mule inside a minicar than get my mother to do anything she doesn't want to."

"I'm sure she's anxious to see your father," April said, remembering how only days ago, the kindhearted Ella Wheeler—a woman famous around Rusted Spur for delivering a homemade apple-pecan cake and King Ranch casserole after every blessed event or family loss—had taken April aside and told her how proud she was to welcome her into the family. *I can never replace your own mother. I know that, but I hope in time you'll come to think of me—that you'll allow me to claim you as the daughter I never had.*

April's eyes slid closed, her heart twisting at the thought of another victim of her own wretched timing. If she'd mustered her courage and called things off last week, or even an hour before the ceremony, none of this would have ever happened. "I only hope she can forgive me."

"There's nothing to forgive," Nate said, as gallant now as he'd been exasperating earlier.

April only wished that that were true.

When they reached the room, they found his mother standing with her back to them, holding her husband's hand. With a fresh blond hairdo she'd gotten especially for the wedding, she wore one of her usual Western-styled blouses and a calf-skimming skirt with hand-tooled boots. But there was nothing usual about the quaver in her voice as she murmured what April recognized as a prayer. Here and there she caught a few words in the spaces between the ventilator's breaths.

Her heart twisted as she saw that Nate's father looked the same as when she and Nate had left him, the chalky pallor of his face so different from the vibrant, robust rancher she'd known for so many years.

Nate went to his mother and wrapped his arms around her shoulders. A tall woman of generous proportions, she had never looked so small. "I'm sorry, Mom, so sorry. But the doctors say there's still hope."

The moment was so raw, so laden with emotion, that April wished she could back out of the room and give the family privacy.

But Ella Wheeler put her grieving aside the moment she spotted April just inside the door. Pushing herself away from her son, she straightened her spine to glare down with her blazing blue eyes.

"What on earth would make you think you're welcome within a mile of my family?" The anguish in Mrs. Wheeler's voice brought tears to April's eyes. "After what you did, I couldn't believe it when I heard you had the nerve to climb into the truck with my son, but this—you in the same room with us. I can't—"

"Please, Mom," Nate started. "Not now. They'll make us leave, and Dad needs us."

"I can't have this. I won't have her here. Not after she destroyed what should have been the happiest day of all our lives."

April started to speak, to apologize for the unforgivable, but Mrs. Wheeler was having none of it.

"You humiliated my Nathaniel, made a mockery of us in front of all our friends." Trembling with anger, she moved to wag a finger in April's face. "This, after you went and got yourself pregnant out of wedlock."

Heart pounding, April shrank back, speechless in the face of the wrath of a woman who had never before spoken a harsh word to her.

But Nate was quick to step in. "Now, come on, Mom. April *did* have a little help in that department," he said with one of his most charming smiles. "Let's not do this. Dad would want all of us to pull together—"

Tears flowing, Mrs. Wheeler turned on her son. "Don't you stand there grinning like a fool, like your behavior is something to be proud of. And don't you dare try to tell me what your f-father needs. It was supposed to be *his* day, too, George's day to—to share with everyone that he…"

"To share what?" Nate asked her, passing her a clean bandanna from his pocket.

She looked back toward her husband before blotting the fresh tears in her blue eyes. "Your father was—he was going to—the governor's called on him to…"

After many false starts, many more tears, and much more prompting from Nate, she finally got across that Nate's father had been asked to fill the remaining term of a US Senator from Texas who'd resigned in disgrace after an embarrassing sex scandal.

"He—we've thought about it for weeks," Mrs. Wheeler said. "About moving to Washington, giving up our retirement to embark in politics, a world neither of us knows a thing about."

"I'm not so sure about that part," Nate said. "You know how Dad loves running down to Austin for all those party fund-raisers, how he comes alive whenever he's helping the bigwigs plan strategy. And heaven only knows how much money he's donated to political campaigns over the years. Everyone there loves him."

April shook her head, her thoughts skipping like stones across the crests of troubled waters. What if—was it possible that things weren't as they assumed?

"Not quite everyone," she put in, thinking back to her own years in Austin. "There are people who won't be so pleased. People who might question Mr. Wheeler's connection to the private prison industry, especially with the proposed federal legislation on the minors crossing the—"

Two steps and Mrs. Wheeler was on her, the loud crack of her slap registering before the sting. April cried out, backpedaling as Nate yelled, "No, Mom, please, don't do this."

He grabbed his mother, physically restraining her as the hair-helmeted nurse ordered all three of them out.

"You ruin everything, and now you blame him?" Nate's mother kept screaming at April as Nate did everything he could to protect her.

While the nurse rushed away, shouting that she was calling security, Mrs. Wheeler sobbed. "He could die now, *die*, and you still won't be satisfied. George told me about that—those people you worked with, how they thought he was some monster, responsible for those poor men cooking in their cells."

"Not Mr. Wheeler, no." Tears running down her face, April shook her head empathically, not believing for a moment that the man she'd known all her life had been the person responsible for the cost-cutting efforts that had led to last summer's deaths of four prisoners in a metal building where temperatures had been measured at more than one hundred thirty degrees. Not that law-abiding taxpayers had been inclined to care much about the fate of the convicted, no matter how much noise advocates like Martin Villareal made about the conditions within for-profit prisons, but there had been lawsuits filed and could be more to come. "I defended him, even when my boss said he should've been one of the players named in—"

"Enough," Nate said, hauling his mother toward the exit when she struggled to break free.

"George had his misgivings about your—your priorities," she said, "but I told him you've always been a good girl, the kind of girl we'd want for the mother of our grandchild. But how do we really even know that baby's my son's? How can we— Stop pulling on me, Nathaniel!"

Mrs. Wheeler jerked her arm free, making a break for the restroom a few steps down the hallway. Hearing her echoing sobs, April started after him, but Nate put out an arm to block her way.

"Let's give her a little time to calm herself down," he suggested.

Adrenaline coursing through her body, April couldn't control her shaking. "But I have to explain to her—I have to make her understand—"

"No, April. You've done enough."

"I have?" His tone had her shaking her head in bewilderment. "You didn't see her hit me?"

Nate nodded, the muscle in his jaw twitching as the sobs of weeping echoed from the restroom. "I'm sorry, April. So damned sorry, and I hope she didn't hurt you."

"She *hates* me, Nate."

"She's—she's not herself right now. I've never in my life seen her like this."

"I understand she's upset. But she can't—the things she said to me."

He shook his head. "Yeah, but did you really have to mention those idiots who blame my father for things he never did? Did you have to mention it while he's lying in there, fighting for his life?"

April knew that her timing had been horrendous, but Nate was missing the entire point. "Don't you understand? This political appointment could mean it wasn't me the shooter was really gunning for."

"I know you're feeling guilty, but don't try to shift the blame from yourself, April. Not when my mother's facing—when for all we know, she'll be widowed before the day is over."

Her jaw dropping, April jerked back as if she'd been struck again. How could he think for a moment that she'd only been trying to make herself feel better? How could he pretend that he knew her at all? "I thought you were my friend, Nate. Or at least that you could be again, for our child's sake. Or do you need a DNA test now, too, to prove I didn't lie to—"

She jerked her head to the left, catching sight of a pair of uniformed guards hurrying their way. But Nate's eyes were boring into her. Wounding her with the anger burning in them.

"This whole damned thing's nothing but a train wreck," he said, with the sobbing from the restroom louder than ever. "I wish to hell I'd never touched you in the first place."

She stiffened. "And you wonder why I backed out? Why I never trusted for a minute that you could ever love me?"

Turning away, she ran toward the elevator, thinking of nothing but escaping the unbearable pain.

Chapter 5

The words were scarcely out of Nate's mouth before the wrongness of them sank in. But like bullets that had already left the chamber, there was no calling them back.

I wish to hell I'd never touched you...shouted at the mother of his child.

Other than that first stunned moment, when he'd babbled some pig-stupid comment regarding a boyfriend he'd known full well had been history for the past year, he'd accepted that April wasn't lying. That the life she carried—*his* kid—belonged to no one else.

So when she turned and ran from him, he tried to follow her, to tell her. To beg her to forgive the emotional insanity he'd been caught up in in that moment.

"Freeze!" a deep voice shouted. "One step, and I swear I'm gonna Tase you, Cowboy!"

Looking from April's retreating form to a pair of uniformed security guys who both looked more than ready to make good on their corn-fed blond leader's threat, he tried to explain, "I have to stop her. She's in danger."

"What'd you do? You hit that woman?" His spotty, toad-faced partner nodded toward the ladies' room door, his lip curling back into an ugly sneer and what looked like some sort of tactical flashlight pointed Nate's way. "'Cause if there's any danger, bro, I'm guessing it was you."

"No!" Nate argued, realizing they'd misread the entire situation. Pointing in the direction April had taken, he said, "My fiancée? Didn't you see her? Only yesterday, someone tried to kill her. I have to—"

"I said *freeze*," roared Corn-fed, his voice closer than Nate would have imagined possible.

Desperate not to lose track of April, Nate tried to make a break for it. But pain shot through his damaged back, telling him he'd moved wrong. And slowing him enough that what he'd taken for a flashlight sent enough amperage coursing through his body to drop him to the floor.

By the time she took a cab back to the hotel, April was still shaking, so upset over the confrontation that she'd walked straight past two different people who'd stopped to ask her if she needed help.

She didn't want anybody's help. She needed to escape this. To jump into her car and drive a thousand miles from the mess she'd made of her life. Except her car was hours away, parked back at the house where she had left it. The house that—because of the trusting, vulnerable brother who came with it—anchored her to a community where everyone would blame her for the hell she'd put the well-liked Wheelers through. Especially once word got out that the bullet that had struck Nate's father had been meant for her.

In a town the size of Rusted Spur, it was likely that such talk had spread far and wide already. Even if April was no longer completely certain that it was really true. But she couldn't think about that now, not with her head pounding and her cheek still stinging. Checking the mirror in the bathroom, she was surprised to see no trace of what she'd half expected would prove to be a glowing handprint.

Still, it hurt, that shocking blow, the crack of it echoing in her ears as loudly as the sniper's gunshots. Yet, upsetting as the slap was, it was Nate's anger that had drawn blood.

I wish to hell I'd never touched you... Gritting her teeth, she found a phone book and called a rental car company to arrange a ride. It would take an hour, the agent told her, long enough for her to try to pull herself together.

She was nearly finished tossing assorted clothes and toiletries back into her suitcase when she felt the fluttering again, a flurry of what she felt more certain than ever was the movement of her son. Distracted, she went still, a hand over her middle. As the wonder of it blossomed, she thought of Nate's words from the lobby as the cheery Christmas music struggled to convince them they were happy. *There's way too much at stake to mess this up.*

Was she acting like a child now, running from her troubles? Or did she owe it not only to herself but to the tiny life in her womb to try to fight her way through the storm of emotion to some semblance of sanity?

Sitting on the bed's edge, she took a shaky breath and glanced toward the room's door. After settling his mother, would he come after her to talk or at least call the room's telephone to try to reach her? To beg her to forgive him for lashing out as he had? She should apologize as well, she thought, realizing that she could have at least given his mother time to adjust to the distressing sight of her poor husband, lying there with all those tubes and bandages and wires, before blurting something that seemed to denigrate the man.

Awful as April's timing had been, she couldn't yet stop thinking that her idea had had merit. She kept up with her former coworkers well enough to know how troubled many were about a movement for the government to privatize the care of unaccompanied minors who'd crossed the country's southern border. They'd be horrified to learn that someone with George Wheeler's prison industry connections could be put into the position to funnel the warehousing of children to his former cronies.

Horrified enough for one of them to end Wheeler's future in politics with a well-timed bullet? Though April couldn't imagine anyone she knew resorting to murder, every movement had its extremists, and extremism attracted crazies. Could Dennis Cobb have been sent by one such unbalanced individual?

She kept running it through her mind, but it was almost impossible to focus with the telephone sitting there, so stubbornly silent that her nerves frayed. Should she try calling Nate instead to extend an olive branch by checking on his mother? Or would doing so only throw more fuel on the flames?

When she heard a rattle from the room's door, April was so relieved she leaped to her feet as it began to open. "I'm so sorry, Nate. I'm sorry," she cried.

But her apology turned into a panicked scream, for the tall man bearing down on her wasn't Nate at all.

In a tiny room attached to the office of hospital security, Nate sat rubbing at his bruised elbow, frowning at the police officer who'd just come back in. "Are we done here? I need to head upstairs and check on my mother." But Nate's real concern was April. Was she safe back in their hotel room, or off somewhere where Dennis Cobb might find her? Or maybe it wouldn't be Cobb at all but a different paid assassin sent by whatever head case was behind this. Nate would never be able to live with himself if his cruel words got her hurt—or worse.

An older cop who smelled of cigarettes and the minty gum that he was chewing in an effort to disguise it pushed a sheet of paper toward him. "Here's what we worked out. In light of this being an emotional time for your family, the hospital brass wants you to sign this, saying you won't sue their pants off for their security guys getting a 'little overzealous'—that was the administrator's spin on it, not mine. Then, they'll let you back in with your father, as long as there are no more disturbances upstairs."

"So, no charges, then?" Nate asked, uncapping the pen left on the small table.

"No charges," the cop told him, "even if I think you ought to get a free chance at leaving those two knuckleheads twitching on the floor."

Pleasant as the thought was, Nate signed off on the agreement without bothering to read it. For a moment, he considered asking the officer to help him with the search for April but quickly discarded the idea, figuring it would take far too long to explain. He had wasted too much time already, trapped in this airless room.

"I've got something for you here, too," the officer remembered, pulling out a phone Nate recognized as his and handing it over. "One of the guards picked this up for you. You're lucky the shock didn't fry it, or it didn't break when you hit the floor."

"Funny," Nate said as he took it, "I'm not feeling all that lucky today."

Once he was free to go, Nate hurried out, not even taking the time to glare at the guard with the itchy stun gun finger. He had to head next door fast, to bring April back where she belonged. His mother, who'd been mortified by her own behavior, had tearfully sworn she would beg April's forgiveness the moment he brought her back. He told himself they'd sort it all out, as soon as he could find her.

He hurried through the lobby, his throat tightening as he caught the sound of a female singer belting out "All I Want for Christmas Is You" over the speakers. The moment he reached the exit, he ran for his truck, ignoring the pain of every old injury reawakened by the jolting his body had taken. As if to compound his discomfort, snow flurries were coming down, too, falling from low, gray clouds.

Falling as he breathed a prayer that he would find his bride in time.

It was Kevin Wyatt, here in April's hotel room, the stalker she'd been certain she'd put behind her more than a year before. The same guy who'd driven her half-crazy with his drunken, weepy 4:00 a.m. phone calls, hundreds of lovesick texts, and the flowers he'd piled in front of her apartment door until it looked as if someone had died there.

But never before today had she had any inkling the man she'd only dated a few times might turn out to be violent. Both a vegan and a pacifist, he'd left her more exasperated with his continuing attentions than afraid.

"Get out, get out, get out of here!" she cried, shaking uncontrollably as she fought to shove her unwelcome visitor back out the door. Though he had a working key card— she could only imagine that he'd found a way to hack into the hotel's system using his computer skills—she hoped the chain lock could keep him long enough for her to call for help.

But in spite of his thin build, her former boyfriend had a wiry strength she couldn't hope to match. And something in his gray eyes—open far too wide and glazed as if he'd taken something—sent raw terror cascading through her system.

"Stop fighting me, damn it!" he ordered, his jaws clenched as he made a grab for her wrists. Clamping down on one, he added, "And don't be scared. Please, don't be. I'm only here to save you from whoever's—"

Her free left arm rising, she struck his jaw with the heel of her hand, then pulled away as his head snapped to one side. By the time he recovered to come after her, she'd run to the bed where she had left her purse. She fumbled for her pepper spray, but he was on her before she found it. Grabbing both her arms, he shook her, his shaggy, jet-black hair flopping as he shouted, "Why'd you do that, April? I want to help you. That's all."

"I'll press charges. I swear I will. You'll go to jail this time!" she warned as the purse spilled near her feet.

He kicked it out of the way and pressed her up against the wall, the anger in his eyes making her wonder how she could have been so completely wrong about Kevin's commitment to nonviolence.

"You—you did it, didn't you?" she asked him. "Tried to shoot me at my wedding."

"I didn't shoot at anybody. You know how I feel about guns," he said, a face she'd once found handsome twisted in disgust. "When I heard about it on the news, though, I knew. Knew it was a sign we were meant to be together."

"You mean, *you* were meant to be committed," she said. "Because you're crazy if you think I'd ever for one second—"

"They're saying that you jilted him. That you couldn't go through with it."

Though her heart was pounding like a snared rabbit's, she felt regret wash over her. And anger that the media would pick up on such a humiliating detail. *Forgive me, Nate. Forgive me.*

"Because you weren't over me," he said, his eyes swimming in deluded hope.

"That had nothing to do with you," she told Kevin, wishing desperately that she hadn't been so embarrassed, so inclined to blame herself for somehow encouraging his attentions that she'd never mentioned him to her friends. "Nothing at all, so get out of here. Go now, and I promise you, I won't call the police."

It was a lie, of course, but with terror pounding through her, she'd say anything to make him leave.

"But you need my protection. With someone out to hurt you—"

"How did you find me here?" she demanded.

"That was easy," he said. "It was on TV that that Wheeler guy was flown to the nearest Level I trauma center, and when I called your aunt, she said you'd gone there."

"How did you get my aunt's number, much less convince her to tell you—oh, never mind." April knew that Kevin had a knack for what he called *social engineering.* He'd bragged about his "mad skills" on their last date, until she'd informed him that she saw nothing admirable about conning people out of passwords and private information. And nothing to be gained by continuing to see him.

She thanked her lucky stars that he'd revealed himself for who he was before they'd slept together. As it was, her skin was crawling as he studied her like a butterfly trapped beneath a bell jar.

"I'm here to save you," he repeated. "I drove through the night from Austin, staked out the hospital lot for hours—"

"If you want to help me, please, let go. You're hurting my arms."

He leaned in even closer. "But—but I've waited all this time to hold you."

The unsettling gray eyes seemed to darken as his gaze

traveled down her body. "You don't know the things that I've imagined…how many times I've dreamed of us together. Me and you—it'll be so perfect. You'll see."

Alarm rocketed through her, adrenaline sending her pulse soaring. She felt as if she would be sick, but she couldn't afford to let her panic get the better of her.

"I'm pregnant," she said, desperate to dissuade him.

He jerked back, letting go of her to look hard at her belly. "You're—you're *pregnant*? But we never—"

"Pregnant by another man," she clarified, wondering again what on earth this guy was on. Or maybe he was off whatever medications allowed him to mostly pass for normal. "A man I—I care for deeply."

It was true, she realized, in spite of the horrible scene she'd fled at the hospital and everything that had happened at the wedding. A part of her would forever be bound to Nate, no matter how big of a mistake he thought their child.

But Kevin Wyatt's face told her she'd made a far bigger mistake just now. A mistake that left her terrified she was about to learn how very violent this so-called pacifist could be.

Chapter 6

Nate knocked lightly at the door first, figuring that after everything that had happened, he at least owed April the courtesy of a little warning.

"You in there, April? It's me," he said quietly. "I just want to—I'm so sorry. Let's sit down and talk this through."

From inside the hotel room, neither voice nor the sound of a movement hinted at her presence. Drawing a deep breath, he used his key card to let himself in.

Seeing no one, he felt a stab of disappointment. After checking the closet and the bathroom and finding all her things gone, he cursed, the slim hope that she might have only stepped out for a moment burned off in a puff of gritty ash. But was there still time to catch her if he hurried?

Racing for the elevator, he headed back down to the lobby, where he was relieved to see the same slightly built, meticulously groomed balding man behind the desk who'd checked them in yesterday.

"Do you remember me—Nate Wheeler? And the woman

I came here with—about five-five and pretty, auburn hair and—"

"How may I help you, Mr. Wheeler?" asked the man, whose dark suit bore a brass tag naming him a Guest Relations Manager. The creases around his eyes and those that lined his forehead gave him a concerned expression.

"You can tell me where April's gone," Nate said. "It's important that I find her before...before someone else does."

Mr. Guest Relations pursed his lips, air hissing out his nostrils.

"What is it?" Nate demanded, his heart pounding. "Please. Someone tried to murder my fiancée only yesterday, and I—if something's happened to April..."

Eyes flaring slightly, the balding man looked around the lobby, as if making certain no one was around to hear. "You should have said something when you checked in. That way, we might've taken additional precautions—or recommended a more secure hotel."

"What's happened to her, damn you? Don't sit there and lecture me when I don't even know whether she's—"

"She seemed fine when she left here. And she certainly didn't complain about the accommodations."

"Left here how?"

"A woman from the rental car agency came to pick her up. I called the room myself to let her know."

A rental car. Nate's hopes crashed. Had April already left town? "When?"

"The police were still here then, so that would have made it around one."

"The police?" Nate burst out, leaning over the countertop, his fists clenched to keep him from grabbing the man behind it. "Why the hell—? What happened?"

Mr. Guest Relations frowned. "A man came down the

elevator to the lobby. He was muttering and pacing. I didn't recognize him as a guest, so I asked him if I could help him. He became belligerent, weeping and shouting all sorts of abusive language. Two of our employees were able to detain him until the police arrived and found…"

"Found what? Tell me all of it."

"Let me just say that as far as I'm aware, this has never before happened at one of our hotels, and the matter will be investigated thoroughly—"

"*What's* never happened?" Nate felt his face grow hot, and his hands itched to shake free the whole story.

"This intruder had a blank key card, no logo, but somehow, it opened—this person had a master, and he wouldn't tell us where he'd gotten it. So naturally, we had him arrested for criminal trespass and whatever else the officers come up with."

Fear slammed Nate like a freight train. Fishing out his phone with shaking hands, he showed the manager Dennis Cobb's mug shot. "Was it this guy? Look carefully."

The bald man stared for a few seconds before shaking his head. "Definitely not him. The man today had black hair, and he was thinner, like a distance runner. Kind of twitchy, too."

Nate tried to take comfort in the fact it hadn't been Cobb. "What about April? Did she report anything unusual? Anything that might have led you to believe she knew anything about this stranger?"

"She didn't, but—" Once more, the manager looked around before lowering his voice. "She stood staring for a long time when they took this man to the police car, and she was rubbing her wrist. I would have gone to question her, but I had other guests to deal with who'd been frightened by the intruder's ranting. By the time I had them settled down, your fiancée was gone."

"You said before, a rental car agent had come for her. Which company?"

Mouth tightening, the manager said, "I'm afraid I've said too much already. We value guest privacy, and this is beginning to sound more like a police matter. Could I get you the address to the station, or would you care to call from—"

His patience at an end, Nate reached over and grabbed the man by his lapels, jerking him close enough to get in his face. "That man you let waltz right by you, the one with a skeleton key to all your rooms. That sounds to me like a lawsuit waiting to happen—or a reason to plant my size-thirteen boot up your—"

The name of the rental car company squeaked out in record time, along with the address of the office.

Thanking him, Nate sprinted for the door. As he headed outdoors, his thoughts swirled like the snowfall beginning to dust the vehicles. Once he climbed inside his truck, his phone started ringing. After checking the caller ID, he was quick to answer.

"Brady. Everything okay with you and Kara?" April had borrowed his phone last night to check in with Kara, but Nate needed to hear it directly from his friend.

"We're fine, but my cell didn't fare as well, so you might want to make a note of this new number."

"Will do." Nate started the engine. "And I'm glad you made it back in one piece."

"Your father—how's he doing?"

"Still critical but hanging in there. I need to tell you, though, April took off—it's too complicated to explain why. I think she's rented a car to head home or to her aunt and uncle's."

"What the hell?" asked Brady. "You swore to me you weren't going to let her out of your sight."

"Hard to manage when you're doin' the electric two-step on the floor." After clicking to put the call on speaker, Nate gave him the short version of the security guards and the stun gun incident.

Under other circumstances, the two of them might have laughed about it over a beer. But the Trencher County interim sheriff's reaction was deadly serious. "Get me the name of the rental car company she used, and I'll start working on a court order to have them check the GPS location of the vehicle."

"The company can do that?" Nate asked, checking for traffic before he pulled onto the street.

"Most of 'em do," said Brady, "in case the car is lost or stolen, but in cases like this, where law enforcement believes an individual's in imminent danger, they'll cooperate— at least, if the right judge signs off on the paperwork."

As Nate drove, he gave Brady the name and added, "I'm afraid I have some more news for you." He gave a brief rundown on the intruder at the hotel and then added, "I don't know that this guy had anything to do with her, but I don't know for sure he didn't, either."

"Hotels get hit a lot with addicts looking to score an easy wallet or something they can pawn, but I don't like the coincidence," Brady said. "Let me put in a call to Lubbock PD and see what they've got. And change hotels, too, both of you, as soon as you find April."

"Thanks," Nate said, hoping it would prove unrelated. "One more thing. Before April left, she brought up something else here about my dad. She's got it in her head that he might've been the target."

"I'm more convinced than ever she was the one that Dennis Cobb was gunning for. That's what I called to tell you. Austin PD's telling me there's an internal affairs investigation into one of their detectives, a Frank Vaughn, who made some threatening statements. Turns out he was the brother of the witness who was beaten half to death after the Chambers exoneration."

"Are you thinking this detective might've had some connection to Dennis Cobb?"

"A serial thug like him would've crossed a lot of cops' paths. And a cop like Vaughn would likely know just who to turn to if he wanted people taken out. And let's not forget that Kara spotted Cobb at Martin Villareal's funeral."

Nate's gut churned to think of it. "Any sign of Cobb around there?"

"Not yet, but we're looking hard. And I'm keeping close tabs on our witness, too, just in case he makes a run at getting her out of the way."

Something in Brady's voice convinced him that his old friend had more than a professional interest in keeping Kara Pearson safe, but Nate had way too much on his own plate to say anything about it. After promising to keep each other posted, the two of them ended the call.

Before he reached the rental car agency, another call had him pulling out his cell again.

This time it was his mother, sounding terrified. "It's your father, Nate. I need you to come back here. I need you to come now."

Once April had the rental car squared away, she circled the lot to reassure herself that Kevin Wyatt hadn't somehow talked the police into letting him go and returned to harass her. She was still shaking from their confrontation, worried out of her mind that at any moment she would look up to see him in her mirror.

"Please, let him be gone for good," she prayed aloud, thankful that he'd been so disgusted to learn she'd allowed another man to touch her, he'd turned and stalked out the door after swearing he was done with her forever.

She should have reported the attack, but the idea of explaining the whole convoluted mess unnerved her. And as creepy as Kevin could be, she couldn't imagine for the life of her that he had anything to do with Dennis Cobb.

After signing the paperwork at the rental car office, she'd gone to claim her car—her freedom—wanting only to put distance between herself and Lubbock. But on the way out, she hesitated, then asked for directions to a discount store. Having a phone on the long trip would be far safer, and she should at least let Nate know she was all right in case he was worried.

If he was so worried, he would have come after you. Or at least called the room to check on you. Pinching her lip between her teeth, she blinked back the threat of tears.

As a few flurries spiraled downward, she parked the car and told herself not to be such a girl about Nate. If he didn't want her—and *had he ever*?—she would find a way to live with it, solving her problems on her own. Still, she couldn't help but wonder if it was possible that he could cut her off, cold turkey, without even caring about what happened to their child.

That part didn't sound like him at all, not after he'd threatened legal action if she tried to give up the baby for adoption. He'd said he loved her, hadn't he? Even after her rejection.

After passing a bell-ringer in a Santa suit on her way into the store, April stopped and went back to him, then stuffed a few bucks in his red kettle. Perhaps it was too late to hope for instant karma, but April figured that it wouldn't hurt to cover all her bases.

Inside, she picked up a cheap, no-contract phone before hurrying back to the small silver sedan. With the defroster melting the snowflakes that landed on her windshield, she activated her new purchase. But instead of calling Nate first, she tried her aunt and uncle's house. When Aunt Sylvia answered, the sound of her voice—so similar to April's mother's—had her dissolving into tears.

"What is it?" her aunt asked. "Has poor Mr. Wheeler passed away?"

"No," April said. "I mean, I don't know. Everything else has gone so wrong."

They spent the next few minutes talking, with April's aunt doing everything she could to reassure her. Hearing that Rory was adjusting and her aunt and uncle were safe, April felt at least one weight lifted from her shoulders.

But when it came to her fallout with Nate, April's aunt minced few words. "If you're not sure, you shouldn't marry him," she said, "but you're a fool if you don't go back and try to work things out with that family. He'll always be your baby's father. You can't cut him from your life."

Before April could formulate an answer, her aunt went on to say, "And you can't afford to risk it, either, running off on your own with that shooter still on the loose. If you can't care for your own sake, think about your child, Rory, *all* of us."

After promising she would be careful, April ended the call, thinking about her aunt's clear belief that she herself had been the shooter's target. Most likely based on something she'd heard from the sheriff's office.

It made April wonder, was Brady pursuing any other theories? Had Mrs. Wheeler even told him about the political future that her husband had been planning, or had she been too distraught or drugged—April vaguely remembered someone calling for a doctor to administer a sedative during the chaos following the shooting—to pass on that information?

April picked up the cell again, thinking she should

call the sheriff's office. But after her aunt's scolding, she couldn't face the idea of Brady lecturing her, too.

Not until she had more evidence, if there was more evidence to be found. She wasn't certain where to find it… but she knew just who to call.

He spotted her in the parking lot, not paying the least bit of attention. Anyone could walk up, finish her and drive off, leaving the settling snowflakes to cover up his tracks.

Nate's stomach flipped as he imagined some security guard coming across her slumped over the wheel, her body cooling as blood droplets dripped down the—

He cursed under his breath, angry with himself for letting his imagination run wild. And even angrier with April for putting herself in this position. He was half-tempted to pop her bumper with the front grill of his pickup just to wake her up.

But he came to his senses, remembering his promise to the young guy he'd found moving returned rental cars, that there would be no trouble, before convincing him with a couple of twenties to describe the last vehicle they'd sent out and the woman driving it. Sympathetic to Nate's story about wanting to make things up to her after he'd done something stupid, the clerk had mentioned her confirming directions to a nearby megastore.

Then he'd wished Nate luck—and for once it had been with him. He'd found her within ten minutes, despite the crowded lot filled with those taking advantage of the final weekend shopping day before Christmas.

Walking up behind her, he rapped sharply on the driver's-side window. He should have been gratified when she jumped and dropped the phone in her lap. But when she turned to look at him, her eyes wide, all he really wanted was to pull her into his arms and hug her tight against his chest.

He reminded himself she wouldn't welcome it, not after the way they'd parted. The wary look she gave him confirmed the suspicion.

When he motioned for her to roll down the window, she hesitated before unlocking the doors and nodding toward the passenger side instead. By the time he climbed into the small car, she was wrapping up her conversation.

"If you find anything, you call me. Day or night, Max. Please."

Nate felt his temper rising, hearing that she'd called another man for help while he'd been worried sick about her. It hit him hard, mixed with a flare of fear. The realization that he might not be her only option.

"Do you have any idea how much you—" He shook his head, too upset to admit to the panic crowding into his chest. "While you were chatting away, *anybody* could've walked up. Anyone at all."

"No need to yell at me. I'm fine. Or as fine as I can be, after you frightened me to death."

"Turnabout's fair play after the scare you gave me, disappearing the way you did. I've got Brady working on a court order to make the rental people give up your GPS location. He's worried, too," he told her.

She winced and shook her head. "I'm sorry. I didn't think—not about Brady, anyway."

"So you did think about me? Or were you too busy reaching out to your ex-boyfriend?"

She flinched, a tide of redness rising until it covered her face. "For your information, Max Hager's a colleague, a private investigator I used to work with when I was—"

"Why so flustered, then? I haven't seen you flush like

this since—" He stopped short, seeing her eyes danger-ously close to overflowing.

"He saw it on the news, Nate, what happened at the wedding."

"Who did? This Max Hager?"

She shook her head and wiped at her eyes. "Not him, no. My—my ex-boyfriend, if you can call him that. Somehow he tracked me down at the hotel and came to *save* me, if you can believe that."

"Wait a minute. You mean that guy the cops arrested at the hotel? Did he hurt you?" When she didn't answer, he felt his own face heat up. "Did he touch you, April?"

"He frightened me, that's all. He's always been…not violent, but a little off. It's why I dumped him after only three dates."

"He sounds more than a little off." Remembering some-thing the hotel manager had said, he added, "Let me see your wrist."

Her hand pulled back inside the sleeve of her blue jacket like a turtle withdrawing to its shell. "It's fine—I'm fine. I swear it."

Letting the issue drop for the moment, he asked, "Why didn't you talk to the police?"

"I—I was still so upset about the hospital, and then— I just wanted to get away from all this. I wanted home. I wanted—"

Unable to stop himself, he reached out and pulled her into his arms. "You should've called me, April. Should've let me know."

"But you said—you told me you wished you'd never touched—"

"I know what I said." He'd thought of little else since he'd gone looking for her. "And I swear to you I didn't mean it. People say things in the heat of anger."

She pulled away to look him in the eye. "They say things they really mean, too. Things they're normally too polite to let out into the light of day."

"Well, that could be the first time any woman's accused me of being too polite," he scoffed before his voice softened. "And if I'd really meant it, would I have come for you? With my father heading into surgery?"

"Oh, no, Nate. What's gone wrong?"

"His blood pressure's started dropping. What with the transfusion he had, they're thinking that the pressure from the stronger flow broke loose the vessel they stitched. If the surgeon can't control the bleeding…"

"I'm so sorry, Nate. You shouldn't be here. You should have stayed. Your mother needs you."

"She begged me to come find you, to tell you how horrified she is about what happened in my dad's room," he said, focusing on his mother rather than his own desperation. "She's scarcely stopped crying since it happened. What she really needs is for you to forgive her. And so do I. I'm sorry."

On the side windows, snowflakes linked into a frozen lace, and their combined breath fogged the inner surface. The tip of her nose reddened, but it was the shimmering in her eyes that commanded his attention.

"Of course I forgive your mother. I understand, and what I said about your father—I never meant for a moment to run him down. I was only thinking of other possibilities."

"Like this ex-boyfriend of yours?"

"Kevin Wyatt might not have an off switch, but he's no shooter, I'm sure of it. I was referring to your dad. That's why I called Max."

Bothered as he was that she hadn't said that she forgave him, Nate forced himself to hear her out and to really listen this time.

"He's a great PI," she said, "discreet and thorough, and he didn't think my idea about someone wanting to keep your dad from taking office was such a crazy one. But then, Max's seen the ugly postings related to the latest scheme to use private prisons to warehouse unaccompanied minors crossing the border like adults, even kids as young as eight and ten."

Nate had heard about the plan, which supporters claimed would save a lot of money and would discourage the influx of illegals from making the dangerous border crossing. "But what would that have to do with my dad?"

"I know he's out of the industry, but think of his connections. It's not a stretch to imagine he'd be sympathetic to the idea of the same private companies with experience housing adult prisoners taking charge of juveniles."

"Why would anyone imagine that my father's got that kind of influence?"

"If the vote comes down to party lines—and that's what everyone is thinking—your father's could be pivotal. And other senators might be influenced by his experience in the industry."

"And these people you're talking about, you think they're nuts enough to shoot somebody?"

"That's the million-dollar question," she said. "I'll admit, it seems a little far-fetched, but the debate's gotten pretty heated, and all it takes is one crazy willing to settle an argument with violence."

Nate thought about it before nodding. "I see where you're coming from, and it's not such a bad theory. Except that Brady's found out something I think might change your mind."

"Brady's found out what?" she asked, her hands tightening on the wheel.

"I'll tell you about it on the way to the hospital. Let me take you in my truck, though, with this weather. We can pick up your rental later. Or better yet, return it."

She hesitated for a moment, then hit the wipers to clear the windshield of the slushy mess before saying, "I don't know about that, Nate. I wanted my own wheels for a reason—"

"Come on, April. This little clown car'll be skating around on the ice like it's trying out for the Olympics, and my truck has four-wheel drive."

She frowned at him but acquiesced, even allowing him to put her suitcase in the back seat of the pickup.

As more snowflakes tumbled down around them, Nate headed for the exit and explained what Brady had told him about the Austin police detective currently under investigation, along with the officer's possible connection to the suspected shooter.

"So Brady thinks this man—this angry cop—is trying to avenge his sister?"

"Right. Between that and the fact that Cobb was at your boss's funeral, Brady's surer than ever you're the target after all."

"The funeral..." she said.

"What about it?" Nate asked as he pulled onto the freeway feeder road.

"I can't help thinking there's something huge that I'm forgetting. Something I was too overwhelmed that day to really register. I've tried my best to think back, to remember who was there and what was said, but...it's so frustrating."

"Maybe if you quit trying so hard, it'll pop back into your head," Nate suggested. "But based on what we know,

I think the pros have this right, April. Brady and the Austin PD's theory makes a lot of sense."

She let out a sigh that sounded utterly exhausted. "So while I've been off chasing mirages, someone could still be trying to—to—"

"To kill you, yes." Nate took a chance and reached out to touch her arm. "I'm sorry, April. I am. But this isn't about fault. It never has been. It's about some cop lashing out in his pain because he can't get to the guy who really hurt his sister."

She wiped at her eyes. "And on and on the damage goes, one injustice piling on so many others. And now your father, too."

"You need to know," he said, "I'll never blame you, even if he doesn't—if he—"

"You say that now," she said, her voice shaking with emotion, "but if he doesn't make it, every time you look at me, all you'll think about is how, if he hadn't stepped in front of—"

"Don't talk like that. Please, don't. I would never, ever wish that you'd been hurt instead."

They rolled along in silence, slowing as Nate passed a car that had slid sideways on the icy roadway.

"Soon as we get to the hospital," he warned her, "I'm going to get in touch with Brady. Tell him I have you with me, safe and sound."

"Tell him that I'm sorry, too, for worrying you both."

Once they arrived, she fiddled with her new phone while Nate made the call. When the phone went to voice mail, he instead reached out to Deputy Wilhite at the sheriff's department. After relaying the message that April was safe with him, Nate asked if he had any further updates.

"Cobb's fingerprints were on a car we found abandoned

about a half mile from your family's ranch. We're taking that as confirmation of the witness ID."

Nate wrapped up the call and related what he'd heard to April.

"I hope Brady's looking out for her," she said. "You know, the two of them were…"

"I know." Nate remembered how happy his friend had been when the two of them had been together. And how miserable since then, though he did his best to hide it. "But Brady's a professional. He'll take care of Kara. Just like I plan to take care of you. Whether you like it or not."

Chapter 7

As they hurried into the hospital, April's stomach was in knots. No matter how Nate tried to reassure her, she knew their relationship would never heal if something had happened to his father while he was off chasing her down.

They were soon directed to a private waiting area set aside for families of the most critically ill patients. Inside, she spotted Nate's mother leaning forward in a padded chair, her hands covering her face.

"Mom," Nate said, crossing the room to sit on his boot heels and take her hands. "I'm here. We're both here. Have you—have you heard anything at all yet?"

Ella Wheeler looked up, her wrecked mascara ringing both eyes. Her blond hair, normally sprayed within an inch of its life, was sadly mussed, too, and part of her blouse had come untucked. But when her blue eyes found April's, Nate's mother swiftly came to her feet.

"I'm so sorry," April told her, "about everything. Please believe me."

Uncertain whether she would be hugged or slapped again, she sighed when Ella Wheeler's strong arms squeezed her.

"Thank God," Nate's mother said, stroking her back as if she were a small child. "Thank God that horrible man didn't find you before Nate did. I was so worried about you."

April leaned her head against the taller woman's shoulder. "So you knew the shooter was aiming for me?"

"Of course. I heard this morning."

"So you know it was my fault."

Nate's mother pulled away to look at her, shaking her head emphatically. "No, you don't. I won't have you blaming yourself. You weren't the one who pulled that trigger."

April swallowed hard, knowing that she wasn't blameless. She'd had her share of doubts about her boss's death, so why had it never occurred to her that she might be in danger, too, even though she'd moved back home?

But it was Mrs. Wheeler who was begging her forgiveness. "I'm sorrier than you can ever imagine about what I said and did earlier. And I swear to you, if I'd known for a single moment that there was a bullet flying toward you, I would have knocked my George out of the way. Would have laid down my life gladly to save you and our grandchild myself."

Touched by her outpouring, April sniffled until Nate passed them both a box of tissues.

"About time, you two," Nate grumbled, with a gruff look April suspected was meant to hide the emotion she spotted gleaming in his eyes. "Now, about Dad's surgery. Do you know if he—"

"We're about to find out, I think." Mrs. Wheeler grasped their hands, one in each of hers as she stared toward a translucent window, where an approaching figure loomed large before the door swung open.

But the expression on the man's face told them all they needed to know.

* * *

By the time the surgeon finished explaining that the procedure had been successful, Nate was breathing again. Not only had April and his mother found a way past their earlier blowup, but it also sounded as if his father had a good chance of surviving.

"His heart is strong, and his vitals are steadily improving, now that he's not leaking blood," the doctor told them, sounding more upbeat than Dr. Han had. "If he continues improving, we could be weaning him off the ventilator by this time tomorrow."

"He'll wake up then?" Nate's mother asked.

"I can't make any guarantees, of course, but I'm guardedly optimistic."

Nate wanted to ask the question weighing on him about the condition of his father's brain, but Nate couldn't bring himself to plant this fear in his mother's mind. Better she should hold on to the hope that they'd been given than worry all night over other possibilities.

After thanking the doctor, the three of them returned to the ICU area. Only this time, the charge nurse—the same man who'd been on the unit last night—informed them that Nate's father could have no more than two visitors at a time.

"If this is because of what happened earlier," Nate said, "we've got it all ironed out."

"I'm sorry," the nurse told them as he looked up from his computer after Nate's mother and April both vowed that there would be no more arguments. "I have it right here from hospital admin. They said absolutely no exceptions, no matter what the situation."

"It's all right," said April, as the nurse went to check a patient. "Why don't you both go in, and I'll stay in the waiting area—"

"Are you out of your mind?" Nate asked her. "I'd rather get Tased again than have to worry about—"

"Wait a minute." Her eyes went wide, her face flushing. "Someone shocked you? Right here at the hospital?"

"It's a long story," Nate told her, his face burning with the memory.

"One you'll have all evening to tell her," his mother said, sounding stronger and more confident than the basket case she'd earlier resembled, "because I don't want you leaving her alone a single minute. Go get some dinner and some sleep. I'll be just fine with your father on my own."

"Don't be ridiculous. I'm not leaving you here alone."

"I don't see why on earth not. I'll sleep next to him in one of the chairs. I'm sure I can get a blanket and a pillow from one of the aides." Frowning at Nate, she added, "I've had a lot of practice at waiting around in hospitals, mostly thanks to you."

He winced at the reminder. "I'm sorry, Mom, but I can't remember a time I've seen you as upset as you've been."

"Of course I've been upset. My husband—he's lying in there right now, *alone*, while we stand here and argue. And I'm telling you, if only one of us can go in, it's absolutely going to be me."

"The nurse did say two," April corrected, "so I could sit with you if—"

"Not a chance you're leaving my sight," Nate said.

"He's right," his mother affirmed. "Now, you two go get some rest. Spend some time together, and relieve me in the morning."

Nate snorted, amused by his mother's pointed look as her gaze slid from him to April. Clearly, his mom was feeling better, if she was trying to push them back together. Or more likely, trying to push herself back into a starring role as doting grandma.

But was it even possible, after everything they'd gone through? Judging by the uncomfortable look on April's face, Nate wouldn't lay money on their odds. What surprised him a lot more was how hard her reluctance hit him. And how his heart leaped at the thought of really wooing her for the first time.

Was he a glutton for punishment or insanely stubborn? It reminded him of all the times he'd stubbornly climbed back on board an angry bull after recovering from a broken wrist or ruptured spleen—until the last outing had nearly killed him.

But Nate remembered, too, the rush it had given him, the electrifying thrill of the risk, the ride, the glory. And what higher stakes could he be playing for than his own role in his son's life? *You're not thinking straight*, something in the back of his brain told him. It wasn't his son that was the key here, but the girl he'd never really looked at beyond taking her friendship for granted. He needed to convince April that he wanted her, that he could love her in the way she needed and deserved. Even if a part of him wasn't sure if he could take being tossed off this ride again.

"I guess we'll go, then," he told his mother, "but we're bringing you back dinner, and I don't want any arguments about that."

She put a hand on one generous hip. "You ever hear me arguing with food, kiddo, you'd better have somebody check my pulse. But don't go to any trouble. A sandwich would be just fine if the cafeteria's still open."

Smiling, April promised, "We'll find something better than the cafeteria. How 'bout barbecue or Mexican?"

"Guess you know me better than I thought," his mother agreed before saying that either one would be great, whenever they were finished eating.

By the time they headed back down to the lobby, the sky

outside was dark. But nightfall did nothing to diminish the irritating strains of "Rockin' Around the Christmas Tree." Nate could scarcely wait to get the holidays behind them.

There were a number of older people coming in from outdoors, their heads covered in Santa caps and their arms full of boxes containing little gift bags.

"Let me get that door for you," Nate said, holding it as the seniors kept coming.

"What is all this?" April asked a woman with shining eyes and short gray hair, whose red-and-white hat rested at a jaunty angle.

"Best part of a volunteer's year," she said, "is handing out homemade treats to the patients. Want to come along and help?"

"Thanks. I wish we could." April's smile said she meant it. "But you and your friends have fun."

A sassy smile lit the woman's wrinkled face. "You can bet that good-lookin' cowboy on your arm we will." Dropping her voice to a whisper, she confided, "For one thing, I can tell you not all of the rum in my kitchen ended up in this year's rum ball cookies."

As they started toward the car, April laughed, sounding delighted. "I want to be just like her when I get old."

Nate smiled back at her, but it was the darkest shadows that drew his eye. The shadows where a killer could lie in wait, looking to make certain that she didn't live to see her senior years...or even Christmas morning, only five short days away.

As they drove around looking for a place to eat, April cringed at Nate's story about the security guard shocking him right outside the ICU. With his typical self-deprecating humor, Nate tried to minimize what had happened, but all

she could think about was how he could have been hurt—
or even shot, if things had gone any further.

Furious on his behalf, she said, "Those people should
be fired. Or sued. What if you'd reinjured your spine, or
hit your head in the fall? What if you—"

"Darlin'," Nate said, "how 'bout we stay away from
what ifs? Because it seems like we've got plenty on our
plates to worry about as it is. Now, what about this place
for dinner? From the looks of that crowded parking lot,
I'd be willing to bet the food's good."

She grimaced at the change of subject, the justice
worker in her fighting his desire to drop the subject of the
stun gun incident. But he had a point, she realized. They
couldn't afford to get distracted over injuries that hadn't
happened. Not while the man who'd shot Nate's father was
still on the loose.

Another point she agreed on was that any restaurant
as busy as this one on a Sunday evening was bound to
be a winner.

Once they were seated, April ordered the chicken-
tortilla soup she'd been craving. But Nate insisted on getting enough tamales to share, saying it wouldn't feel like
the holidays without them.

"Oh, definitely, tamales," she said, reminded of Carlos,
who'd worked for the Wheeler Ranch for as long as she
remembered. Every year, the old *vaquero*—the Spanish
word for cowboy—would deliver foil-wrapped packages
of the spicy meat-pie-like favorite, each one swaddled in
a dried, golden corn husk. His wife and daughters made
them by the score each season, and invariably a package
was shared with April's family, as well.

"Rory's going to miss his this year," she said, saddened
to imagine her brother spending Christmastime away from
home for the first time ever.

Nate dipped a chip into some melted *queso*. "I'm sure I can talk Carlos into making a special out-of-town delivery, just this once, for him."

"Thank goodness for Carlos, then, and you, too, Nate. You've always been so great with Rory."

"Why wouldn't I be?" Nate asked. "He's not only my good buddy, he's my number one fan."

It was true, April knew, thinking of Rory's huge collection of pro rodeo tour memorabilia, almost all of which Nate had given to him over the years. He'd invited her brother to rodeos, too, making sure that Rory and April's mother both got complimentary tickets and their transportation was taken care of. Though travel with her brother could be challenging, the trips he'd made to what he called "the big show" were some of Rory's most cherished memories.

"You were nice to him before, too," she said, "even back when too many other people weren't. I still remember that fight on the bus, what you did to those three guys who were calling him such horrible names."

Nate shrugged at her. "You know I only did it to get out of school—three days' suspension."

There was something about his wink that got her heart racing...even though the thought of him using it on untold legions of buckle bunnies got under her skin. "I'm calling BS on that, Bull Boy. Why can't you just let me compliment you on being a good guy back then? And now, too, come to think of it."

"Messes with my roguish reputation."

"There you go again," she said, more irritated than she should be. Because that day back on the bus when they both were only thirteen, she'd lost a piece of her heart to Nate. A piece he'd never seen fit to notice. "Can't you ever be serious with me? Be serious *about* me?"

He pushed the basket of chips aside to frown at her, the muscle twitching at the corner of his jaw. "How can you possibly think I'm not serious about you when I've been right by your side when we got to hear our baby's heartbeat and had our first glimpse of his sonogram? How can you imagine I didn't mean it when I stood there at the altar, watching the most beautiful woman I've ever seen coming down the aisle toward me—"

"Come on, Nate." Her face heated at his over-the-top praise. "I'm not beautiful, not like those other girls you—"

"Not like them, no, because you're *real*. You're genuine and generous, not a flash of fool's gold, and everything that's beautiful about you shines through from the inside."

April's knee-jerk reaction was to tell him that was a very kind way of telling her the outside wasn't especially appealing. Not to him at any rate. But the waiter arrived then with their entrées, forcing her to bite her tongue. And to think about the advice Kara had once given her. *You need to learn to take a compliment. To just say thank you and be quiet instead of coming up with ten different ways to minimize what's been said.*

The waiter placed a steaming bowl of soup before her, along with a plate of diced avocado and shredded cheese to spoon on top. The fragrant warmth had her empty stomach rumbling, but she made no move to lift the spoon. "Thank you," she told Nate awkwardly, but she couldn't make herself leave well enough alone. "That's very kind of you."

"It's not just *kindness*, April," Nate said, his face reddening with what looked for all the world like temper. "What do I have to do to get it through your head that I'm finished chasing heartbreakers and hangovers? Even if I weren't some washed-up cowboy, I'd still—"

"You're a first-rate rancher, breeder and trainer of some

of the finest quarter horses in the country. So, what are you talking about, *washed up*?"

He winced. "Poor choice of words, maybe."

April crossed her arms, skeptical. *Or maybe you're not as finished grieving for your lost dream as you think.*

"What I was getting at," Nate told her, "is that all I'm chasing now is a chance to be as good a person, as good a father as the man who raised me. And a chance at the kind of happiness that lasts…with you."

Seeing the earnest look in his eyes, she reached across the table and brushed her fingertips across his knuckles, wanting to tell him he *would* be a good father, whether or not his own father lived to see it. And whether or not they ever found a way to move past the wounds they had inflicted on each other.

"You're already a good man," she assured him, wanting to believe that he really had changed—or was changing, right before her eyes. Living up to the potential she'd first glimpsed on that bus ride, the potential she had feared he never would grow into if shackled to a woman he didn't really want.

They ate in silence, with April finishing her soup and two tamales, surprised to realize how hungry she had been. Nate polished off his meal, too, before ordering an enchilada plate to take back to his poor mother, who waited by her husband's side alone.

At the thought, April felt anger building at the idea of what the shooter—and especially the coward who had sent him—was putting her and Nate and all their loved ones through. *All of us…* Her heart fell. How could she have been so wrapped up in her own drama that she hadn't given a thought to her coworkers?

Digging in her purse for the new cell phone, she said, "I need to contact everyone I worked with on the Chambers exoneration about what's happening. Because who's to say that I'm the only target Cobb was stalking at Villareal's funeral or that he won't go after one of them now, while I'm out of his reach?"

"Since Brady's been in touch with the Austin PD, I'm sure they've notified anyone from the Texas Justice Project they think might be in danger."

"I wouldn't bet on that," April said, shaking with the panic ripping through her. "Remember what I said about the police not liking that we showed them up? And surely there are those who sympathize with the cop whose sister's in a coma."

"I see your point, but calm down. Let's think this through a minute." Nate scowled at a trio of mariachi musicians, who were heading their way singing "Feliz Navidad." Stopping short when he shook his head, they took their guitars, accordion and cheerful Christmas music in the opposite direction.

"So who was at the funeral?" he asked April. "We'll make a list of who to contact."

"At the funeral? There were hundreds paying their respects to Martin—family friends and colleagues from the legal community, volunteers, even professional rivals, from criminal prosecutors whose convictions we've worked to overturn to…" She stared straight ahead, her mind miles away as she thought back to that day, to how touched she had been to see old enemies acknowledge her mentor's humanity and talent. Old enemies like… She frowned, her mind snagging the dim memory of a flash of light. And a familiar face.

"Your father was there, too," she told him, a shiver rippling across the surface of her skin.

"He was?" Nate asked, lines furrowing his brow. "I knew he was in Austin all that week, but I thought it was for one of his political powwows."

"He *was* there. I'm sure of it now." It came back to her now how he had hugged her, squeezed her shoulder and whispered his advice to be good to herself and his grandbaby, before moving on to pay his respects to Martin's family.

Still, something else nagged at her, a buried memory or her stubborn mind's attempts to deny the fact that she was in danger?

The waiter returned with the boxed meal and bill and thanked them both for coming before hurrying off to deal with another table.

"I'm not surprised," Nate said. "He's always been a class act that way, and it would be just like him to acknowledge a man he thought of as a worthy adversary. But let's get back to your colleagues. Who was there that had worked on the exoneration with your team?"

"I'll try Sienna. She'll know." While Nate tucked some bills inside the bill folder, April tried the number of her fellow paralegal for the Texas Justice Project, who had also been her maid of honor at the wedding.

Though Sienna was bursting with questions and worried out of her mind about her, April did her best to keep their conversation as brief as possible.

Before she could hang up, Sienna said, "I know it's hardly the time to ask, but have you given any thought to the latest offer we sent you?"

"What?" April asked. "What offer? I haven't checked my email in a week, what with the wedding and everything."

"I wondered why you never brought it up. But since you, um, seem to have changed your mind about this marriage business, maybe you should take a look. We could really use your help here, and I know the extra money would really come in handy."

April frowned, wondering how many times she would have to refuse her former employer before the new director would get it through his head that she wasn't abandoning her brother to move back to Austin.

After promising she'd call again as soon as possible, April hung up and told Nate, "Thank goodness Brady's so on top of things. One of his deputies spoke to Sienna, and she's contacted all the others. They're all safe, but everyone's on guard, especially those of us who appeared in that Trial TV show."

"That's good news," Nate said as they headed for the exit and the dark parking lot beyond.

"Hold on just a minute," he said, snagging her arm before she reached the door. "Why don't you wait here and let me have a look out there first? Or better yet, I'll pick you up. It's seriously cold out there, and there's no need to risk you slipping on the ice."

She nearly argued that she was pregnant and not ninety, but she was stopped by his serious expression, along with a memory of how far from the door they'd been forced to park and how dark the corner of the lot was.

"You be careful, too," she said, reluctantly agreeing. Before he left, their gazes caught, an unspoken mutual reminder of the dangers that still lurked.

Chapter 8

While April waited for Nate inside the restaurant's door, the new phone buzzed in her pocket, and her thoughts flew to her brother. Instead, Max Hager's name and number flashed up on the screen, leaving her to wonder what the private investigator could've learned so quickly.

"I've been working the phones since you called," he said without preamble, "and I've got a couple of pieces of news you're gonna want to hear."

"About George Wheeler? Because it turns out there's an Austin cop under investigation connected to Villareal's death."

"I've got a contact in the PD who told me the same thing," Max said. "I don't have any details, but I'm hearing they're about to make an arrest on the Villareal hit-and-run—"

"Then they're finally willing to admit it was a deliberate killing?"

"It's always been a serious crime—failure to stop and render aid's a felony when someone's killed."

"It was a murder, pure and simple," she said. "The attempt on my life proves it."

"That was my first thought, too. At least until I got a tip about George Wheeler's recent trip to Austin."

"He was at the funeral that day," she told Max. The flash of light, a reflection off metal, glinted in her memory, but once more, the specifics refused to come into focus.

"That's not the only thing he was up to that week. Seems there were a number of bigwigs connected to the private prison industry all in town at the same time. And all staying at the same hotel." Max named an expensive downtown property known to cater to the many lobbyists who routinely descended upon the state capital.

As Nate pulled up in the truck, she headed out and climbed in, the phone still pressed to her ear. Though he looked curious, he didn't interrupt when she gestured for him to go ahead and drive.

"So they were meeting there," she said to Max, her heart sinking at the thought of George Wheeler involved in some scheme to carry their agenda from the state capital to DC.

"Appears so. But I can tell you, it wasn't all hearts and flowers. There was an altercation."

"About what?" she asked as she pulled the lap-and-shoulder belt across her body.

Seeing her distraction, Nate took the latch from her hand and clicked it into place for her before heading in the direction of the hospital, where they would deliver his mother's dinner and check on his father's condition one last time that night.

"No idea," Max said. "But it got heated enough that the cops were called about a disturbance in a meeting room there—yelling and what could've been a fistfight. My cop pal didn't know for sure because by the time officers arrived, everybody'd gotten their stories straight and couldn't imagine how hotel security could've *possibly* mistaken their audiovisual presentation for a real live dustup." Max snorted in what sounded like amusement.

April might have laughed, too, at the thought of a bunch of rich old white guys—as they almost assuredly would all be—whaling away at each other over who would get the fattest slice of government pie. But there was nothing remotely funny about Nate's father's current condition, or the possibility, however slim, that someone from the group might have decided that Wheeler's rise to the US Senate might give Correctional Solutions an unfair competitive advantage.

Once she thanked Max and ended the call, Nate was quick to ask, "Bad news?"

"More like confusing news," she said. "That was my PI friend again. He's told me the Austin police are close to an arrest in the Villareal case."

"That cop—the beating victim's brother?"

She shook her head, though she could tell Nate was too intent on the icy road to see. "I guess so, but I'm not sure."

"But if the officer's really the person who sent Cobb to our wedding, this could be an end to it, right?" Nate said. "At least, if Cobb's caught—and he's not the only thug this guy sent."

"That's still a lot of *if*s, Nate," she said, "but it's definitely a step in the right direction."

"I'll rest better when those bastards are all behind bars. And you and I are safe to figure out a future."

He glanced her way as he said it, the Christmas lights from a shopping center they were passing reflected in his eyes. But she saw hope there, too, as well as a bone-deep need to put the nightmare events of the past two days behind him. It was enough to convince her not to mention what Max had said about Nate's father's recent activities in Austin. Enough to want to spare him the worry that the man he most loved and respected had been brought down by corruption.

Or was she instead afraid that Nate would push her away forever if she said one more word that questioned his father's integrity?

After stopping by the hospital, Nate suggested that April might want to change hotels after her earlier experience. "Not that I think you'll have any more issues with this Kevin Wyatt, but you'll probably sleep better."

As the pulled into the Restway's parking lot, April groaned aloud. "To tell you the truth, I'm so darned tired, I don't even care. He's cooling his heels in jail, isn't he?"

"We don't know for certain how long they're going to hold him unless you go in to press charges," Nate said, wishing he'd gotten the chance to ask Brady what he'd found out about the arrest.

"I'll call tomorrow," she promised. "Maybe that will finally convince him to get the help he needs. But you're right. We should move tonight. I've had enough nasty surprises to last me for a good, long time."

Knowing how exhausted she was, he said, "Don't worry. I'll take care of everything."

In less than an hour, they had moved into a hotel a few miles away. When the only available room proved to be a top-floor suite, Nate didn't quibble about the price, telling himself that after all they'd been through, they deserved a little extra comfort. Besides, after seeing how much better his father's color had looked, Nate felt optimism surging through him—the hope that all of them would live to put this nightmare behind them.

Nate locked the door behind them and set down each of their bags.

"This is nice, Nate, really," April said, her gaze drifting around the generously sized room, with its sitting area and marble-topped bar, before coming to rest on the king-sized bed. "But I'm a little… Maybe they'd bring up a roll-away if we called to ask."

Seeing the worry in her eyes, he said, "I can sleep on the couch, April. There's plenty of room there, if that's what you want."

"Or I can sleep there. After all, I'm shorter. And you've been paying for—"

"Take the bed," he told her. "I'm not arguing about this."

April smiled, then shook her head and muttered something about "stubborn cowboy chivalry." But after kicking off her shoes and settling on the bed, she sighed, her eyes sliding closed and her head nodding as he unpacked a few items from his suitcase.

Judging her to be asleep, he headed for the bathroom to brush his teeth. When he came back out, he spotted April still lying in the same position.

Still sleeping, he supposed, until she suddenly sat up with a gasp, her hand darting toward her belly.

"You okay?" he asked, going to the bedside. "You aren't— aren't having any pains, are you?" Between the stress and her exhaustion, could she be having issues with the pregnancy?

The thought struck him like a kick to the ribs, the possibility that she might lose the child he'd never known how much he'd wanted. That he could lose his only claim to a woman he'd taken for granted for far too long.

"No, not that." She looked up at him, a look of wonder lighting her face. Making her absolutely gorgeous, whether or not she would believe it. "It's the baby, Nate. I feel him. Just a flutter now and then, but I'd swear it's getting stronger each time."

"Can I—do you think I could feel it?" he asked, sinking

down to sit beside her. He raised his hand, but she shook her head before he dared to touch her.

"Not yet," she said. "He's still too tiny. Maybe in a month or two—I don't know. I've never done any of this before."

He smiled. "Well, don't look at me to be the voice of experience. The only little ones I know about tend to bark or whinny."

When she laughed, he put an arm around her shoulder, the enormity of his relief making him careless as he squeezed her in what could have been a friendly hug.

Could have been but wasn't, as she looked up at him with worried eyes. Beautiful, brown eyes, with their long, dark lashes. Desire stirred as he wondered how those lashes would feel as they brushed against his heated skin.

"I really want you, April," he admitted, the words out before he could think them through, shaken loose by the pounding of his heart. "Want you, want this—want my best friend for my lover." *For now and forever...*

He felt her body tense, felt her gaze searching him for any sign that he was lying. And knew to his core that of all the seductions he'd embarked on, this was the only one that mattered. As well as the first aimed at a woman's heart, not just her body.

Reaching up, he smoothed a lock of sleek, auburn hair behind her ear, leaning close to whisper, "Only this time, I mean to be stone-cold sober, so I can remember every second of it...and every gorgeous inch of you."

She shivered at his words, whether in horror or desire, he had no idea.

"Nate, your father..." she began. "He might've—"

"You heard the surgeon. He'll be breathing on his own tomorrow. He'll be our family's second Christmas miracle." He remembered how badly he'd frightened his friends and parents last December—how scared he himself had been, not of dying so much as the possibility that he would spend his life dependent on others, a burden to his parents rather than a help as they aged.

He pulled her close enough that he could feel her heart pounding against his chest. Close enough that all he would have to do was tip his head an inch or two to claim the kiss he ached for.

She opened her mouth to say something, but Nate beat her to it. "Or maybe it'll be the third," he said, his voice barely above a whisper, "that is, if I get to count you, too."

She sighed and said, "I want this, Nate. I want to believe you."

"Then you'll have to take a chance, too, or you'll never know for sure."

Their gazes met, so close now, so intense, that he felt the desire arc between them. Or maybe he was crazy, imagining she would ever dare to trust him. Imagining he hadn't just set himself up for more rejection.

Imagining until she pushed forward just enough to bridge the gap between them.

She should have told him, April knew. Should have shared what she had learned about his father before she got in any deeper.

But seeing the vulnerability in Nate's eyes, hearing him put his pride on the line, stopped her. Or maybe it was the dim memory of the way he'd used that taut, hard body that made her need to find out if they'd really been as good together as she suspected.

As their kiss caught fire, she realized she'd been off—way off—in her expectations. Because the word *good* didn't begin to encompass the desire blazing through her for his hands, his mouth, his body to move with her, over her…inside her.

She had a moment's misgiving, worry that her changing shape might be a turnoff to a man more used to a flat stomach and perfect, plasticized breasts. But the speed with which he had her top and bra off, the hunger as he cupped and suckled, had every last doubt burning off in the white heat of their frenzy.

Her hands curled into fists full of his shirt, which she tugged until he paused to strip it to reveal a lightly haired chest so chiseled, a six-pack so well defined, she could scarcely believe it existed outside of fantasies.

But it was the smoldering heat in Nate's eyes, a heat that lasered straight through every last layer of her self-doubt, that assured her that this time, there would be no stopping what was happening between them. No stopping the inevitable, no matter how much either one of them might regret it later.

She reached down to grasp the silver buckle of his belt and said, "The rest, Nate. Please, now."

"Yes, ma'am. If that's what you want." A wicked grin split his face as he undid the keeper and pulled the leather strap free. "Every inch and every atom are now at your disposal."

Pulling the belt from his hand, she tossed it onto the floor. The rest of their clothes followed suit as every other worry faded to the background...

Including the one that should have concerned both of them most.

Chapter 9

His mistake had been in trusting others, the man behind the desk realized. Trusting led to failures like the last
attempt. Or excuses, such as those made by his contact
when he'd insisted the target die before the coming holiday.
The harder he had pushed, the more money this so-called
professional had attempted to extort from him.

But regardless of how much he'd thrown at the problem, no one could be found to get the job done in a timely
manner. "It's the Christmas season," the man had whined.
"People have families, shopping, too. Can't your problem
keep until after the new year?"

Ridiculous, the sniveling over sentiment. Or maybe it
hadn't been that, but instead a test to see how desperate he
was to get this unpleasantness dealt with before someone
put it all together. And before the first of the year, when
the trial would begin.

Where he would be the scapegoat, while his betrayer
would be rewarded...

A betrayer who wouldn't live to revel in his destruction, to dance away, into the spotlight...

Even if the man behind the desk had to see to it himself.

Nate was in the chute, climbing aboard a writhing, snorting mass of muscle that wanted nothing in this world except to cast him from its back and stomp him into the dust of the arena. The roar of the crowd captured his attention, the people screaming for him, three women in the front row blowing kisses his way.

A few voices distinguished themselves: his father pleading that he needed him to run the ranch, his mother crying that he'd break himself in two. April was sitting a few rows back, her sad brown eyes doing the talking for her as she clutched a bundle close to her chest. A child Nate wanted desperately to see. A child he started to climb off the bull to get to.

But it was too late. The chute opened, the beast charging out and leaping, plunging, kicking. Caught off guard and off balance, Nate knew he had to hang on—or at the very least not let himself land badly.

Just one more second. Now another. Hold and—

He was spinning through the air, arms flailing, forgetting everything he'd ever known about how to fall. But instead of the train wreck he expected, he wafted gently down to earth, relief flooding through him...

Until he looked up to see the bull barreling toward him—a bull bearing a stranger's face. A stranger now distracted by April jumping into the ring, dressed in Kara Pearson's rodeo clown clothes.

Except that April, unlike Kara, had no idea what she was doing as the beast turned toward her. And Nate lay paralyzed and helpless as he watched the monster charge and realized that April still held their child in her arms.

* * *

Startled awake by Nate shouting, "No. *No!*" in his sleep, April struggled to extricate herself from his arms. But Nate's hold only tightened, his arms binding her like the strongest lariat. Instead of a rope, though, it felt as if he was using a boa constrictor to squeeze the breath from her.

"Nate," she cried out, her voice slicing through the darkness. "You're hurting me. You're—"

He jerked and moved his arm, relieving the pressure on her rib cage. "What? What's going on?"

"Nightmare, from the sound of it." She could still hear him breathing hard, could still feel his heated body, damp with perspiration.

"Nightmare. Yeah. You were—you had the baby with you, and this bull, the one with the man's face—it was... never mind. You're here. You're okay now."

"Now that I can breathe, especially," she said, touched by the pure relief in his voice. And a little concerned to think he was still dreaming of the bull riding that had nearly cost him his life. But even if the idea of being with her, building a family together still scared him, he was here with her this moment. With her after they'd made love with a fevered intensity that make her dizzy to remember.

The question was, had it only been a release, an outlet from the enormous stress that both of them were under? Or was it possible their mutual desire—and she had no doubt at all that he had wanted her, at least in the moment—might form the foundation of everything she hoped for?

As Nate sat up against the headboard, she glanced at the clock and saw that it was only four-fifteen. Too early to get up, yet her brain was buzzing, the worries over Nate's parents, Brady's investigation and Kara's situation pushing her further and further from the dark borders of sleep.

"Are you okay?" she asked, doubt creeping into her

voice. Because she wasn't just asking about the nightmare. Propping herself up on her elbows, she added, "Are *we*?"

He pulled her into his arms and kissed her temple. "I want us to be, April. I want that as badly as I've ever wanted anything."

"But?" she added, giving voice to the word she felt crouching in the darkness, waiting to spring at any second.

"But nothing, April. I love you, and I want you in my life. Not just as a friend, either. Those days are behind us."

She laid her head against his chest, then lifted it to ask him, "Then why is your heart still pounding?" *And why can't I let myself take your words at face value?*

"Because I'm worried as hell. And furious to think there's somebody out there besides Dennis Cobb—some faceless stranger I can't get my hands on—who wants to take everything away. To take *you* away, you and the baby both."

"Brady's on this, Nate. And you heard what Max said about the Austin PD being close to arresting that cop who—"

"Did your PI friend really say that? Because before, you told me an arrest was imminent in the hit-and-run. For all we know, the driver was just another thug sent by this bad cop. Which means there could be more."

She blinked hard, jolted into awareness that she'd been making a dangerous assumption in thinking this was almost over. "Thanks a lot," she told him. "I was just beginning to think we might get back to sleep tonight."

"I didn't bring it up to scare you. But you need to understand, we can't afford to sit back and assume that law enforcement's going to keep you safe."

"I know you're right." Her own pulse ratcheted higher, but she told herself that forging a real relationship with Nate, the kind of relationship she wanted, required her to trust him fully. Even with those truths she knew he'd find hard to swallow.

Still, she hesitated, the memory of his reaction to the sore subject of his father's business dealings too raw. All she really wanted was to be with him, in this moment, without starting up another argument. Without giving him another reason to doubt they had a chance.

But April had worked in the service of truth for too many years to allow her fears to put a muzzle on her. So, girding her strength, she told him, "There's something else Max told me. Something it's only fair to let you know."

She felt Nate's muscles tensing.

"Watch your eyes," he said before letting go of her and reaching over to switch on the bedside lamp. "Go on."

She blinked until her vision cleared, only to see him staring at her so hard it had her skin pebbling with goose bumps. She took in a deep breath and started, telling him about his father's presence at a meeting of those involved in the private prison industry. And about the alleged fight that had resulted in hotel security calling the Austin police.

"So you kept this from me, why?" he asked. "Because you think it's some kind of proof my dad's corrupt?"

"It's not proof of anything," she admitted, though surely, Nate must realize how this revelation might be perceived if the media found out his father had been hanging around with his old cronies while he was presumably in talks with the governor about his appointment to the US Senate.

"Of course, my father still has friends, people he worked with for years inside the industry. Why, Joe Mueller, the man who flew my mother here from Rusted Spur, worked with Dad for years on—"

"I don't doubt it for a minute. And we have no way of knowing what this supposed altercation could've been about or if your dad was even around for it, much less somehow involved—or if any of it has something to do with your father's future in politics."

"We don't even know my father has *any* kind of future."

"Maybe the wrong people were worried they'd be cut out of a deal. Because that blowup at the hotel—it could've been about—"

"You're grasping at straws again," Nate said, "but I do have a good idea of a guy who might be able to shine some light on this, at least if I can twist his arm enough to tell me the whole story."

He reached for his phone, which he'd left charging beside the lamp.

"Nate, it's not even five o'clock yet," she reminded him, thinking that people awakened from a sound sleep might not be inclined to be helpful.

"The truth's way too important to worry over interrupting Joe's sleep."

They both jumped as Nate's phone rang, their muscles tensing with the expectation of bad news.

Chapter 10

As the cell continued ringing, more adrenaline shot through Nate's bloodstream. But it was nothing compared to the guilt he felt for even considering the possibility that the father he knew and loved could be nothing but another schemer out to claw his way to power.

"Answer, Nate," urged April. "It could be Brady."

She was right, he realized. Seeing that the caller ID read Trencher Co. Sheriff Dept., he picked up.

"What's up, Brady?" Nate said, knowing that his friend would never have called at this hour unless the matter was urgent.

"This is Deputy Wilhite. Sheriff asked me to call and fill you in."

"What's happened? Is everyone all right?" Remembering Brady's worry about protecting the woman he'd once—and still might—love, Nate asked, "Is Kara safe?"

"They're both going to be fine," Wilhite said, "but I can't say the same for Dennis Cobb."

"You caught Cobb?"

At Nate's mention of the shooter's name, he felt April's nails dig into his arm. She was sitting close beside him, her nude body stiff and chilly, judging from her goose bumps.

As Deputy Wilhite explained the situation, he tugged the bedcovers higher to wrap them around her.

"Well, that part's bad news," Nate said, "but at least we don't have to worry about him hurting anyone else."

He thanked Wilhite and accepted the deputy's wishes for his father's recovery.

The moment he ended the call, April asked, "What's happened?"

"Dennis Cobb is dead," Nate said. "Wilhite couldn't give me many details, but apparently, Brady was forced to shoot the man to save Kara's life."

"Kara must be terrified." April's eyes gleamed with tears. "Is she all right? She wasn't hurt, was she?"

"She has Brady to look after her. They'll both be fine." *Eventually*, Nate thought, understanding that the use of lethal force was something his friend would take very seriously. Especially since, with Cobb gone, there were still unanswered questions about who had really sent him and what his reason was for wanting April dead.

If Brady was right and April had been the target from the start.

April rubbed at her arms, worries clogging her throat. But knowing that Dennis Cobb had never left the Rusted Spur area had her dialing back a little on her paranoia.

Still, she wasn't about to rush over and open the drapes to greet the new day. Even if she were dressed for it, she'd be a fool to take such a chance before Austin PD had Police Detective Frank Vaughn, or whoever was behind the shooting, safely in custody.

Nate looked down at his phone. "I've got a text here from my mother. Dad's out of the ICU and in a private room on the third floor."

"That's good news, right?"

"Sure is. She says he woke up briefly, squeezed her hand in answer to her questions. And he's able to move his legs and feet, too, which tells them the spinal cord was spared."

"Thank goodness." April knew Nate's father wouldn't be able to speak until the ventilator was removed, but she prayed he would soon be out of danger.

"I don't know about you, but I'm way too wired for sleep now," Nate said.

"Me, too."

"What do you say we get ready and go grab an early breakfast? Then we can relieve Mom and lend her the truck to head back here."

"Here?" she asked.

"I'll get her her own room, of course," Nate said. "She probably won't come until after the doctors make their morning rounds, though."

"So there's time for a shower first?" April asked. Running her gaze over his bare chest, she was tempted to invite him to join her. To make another memory that wouldn't dissolve with sobriety. But the news about her friends' ordeal had left her rattled, and the thought of Nate's mother, alone with his father all night, had her anxious to check on the couple.

Nate stepped into yesterday's jeans. "You go ahead. I want to make a call, and then I'll shower and shave, too."

She looked at him uncertainly, wondering if he still intended to call his father's friend to question him about the Austin trip. Wondering if he'd be better off with her by his side when facing the possibility that his dad had been in on some shady dealing.

"Go on, April. I can handle this," he assured her.

Deciding to take him at his word, she gathered clothing for the day and headed for the bathroom to pull herself together. A half hour later, she was dressed in dark jeans and a red sweater. She had taken time to do her hair and makeup, too, leaving her auburn hair shiny and smooth over her shoulders.

"Did you reach your dad's friend?" she asked.

"Yeah," Nate said, "for all the good it did me. I've known Joe Mueller for a lot of years. Can't tell you how many times he brought his wife and kids to backyard barbecues at the ranch. But I have no idea whether he was telling me the truth about my dad this morning."

"So, what did he say?"

"That it was news to him Dad's been asked to accept the governor's appointment to the Senate. Said he was blown away to think my old man could've kept it from him, of all people. I told him I'd had no idea, either. Probably the governor insisted Dad keep it under his hat, so it didn't end up getting leaked to the media too early."

"Did Joe admit your father had met with him and the other private prison executives in Austin?" April asked.

"He claimed they had a few drinks together one night, but it was purely social. Dad's never tried to second-guess Joe since he bought him out to take over Correctional Solutions."

April tapped a nail against the dresser top as she thought about it. "What about the fight at the hotel?"

"I asked him about that, if my father was there when it took place. He immediately popped off, 'When what took place?' Acting like this was the first time he'd heard of any altercation."

"You don't buy it, do you?" she asked.

Nate's mouth twisted as he pondered. "He really did

sound surprised, but then, maybe Joe wasn't in the room when this thing happened. Or maybe your PI's source was wrong—they did deny it."

"Or it could have been no big deal, just a couple of competitors who'd had too much to drink or something," she admitted.

"We'll ask my dad ourselves," Nate said, "as soon as he can talk."

Though April had her doubts about his father's ability, much less his willingness, to answer questions on the topic, she said, "That sounds like a good idea," which seemed to satisfy Nate for the moment.

While he headed off to clean up, she decided to test her new phone's internet capabilities by logging in to her email account. Sighing at the glut of unread messages, she scanned the list, looking for any that seemed important. With so much junk to wade through, however, she ended up deleting message after message.

She clicked on a message from Helping Friends Community, not with any real hope of getting Rory into one of the best group home programs in the state, but because she figured she could quickly dispose of yet another reminder of how rarely openings became available. Instead, she blinked in surprise at what turned out to be a very different sort of message.

Dear Ms. Redding,

In memory of the long board service and fundraising efforts of Martin Villareal, we would like to offer residency to your brother, Rory Redding, at Helping Friends, beginning February 1st.

April raised a hand to cover her mouth, then went on to read that the director felt it was a fitting tribute to Martin's work to offer a scholarship in his name. Because of the facility's long waiting list, however, they were going to need an answer by January fifteenth—after a visit from Rory, who would have the final say.

January fifteenth? Her heart beat out a rapid tattoo. That wasn't nearly enough time to get her brother used to the idea of a trip there, much less to push him toward a decision that would impact the remainder of his life.

And mine, she realized, feeling panic spinning through her. But why was she so afraid when this was what she'd hoped and prayed for: a chance to reclaim the life and work that had once given her so much satisfaction?

A chance to raise the baby on her own in Austin, away from the mess she'd made of her life in Rusted Spur...

Away from Nate and all the Wheelers, if that was still what she wanted.

On their way to pick up April's car after breakfast, Nate glanced over to see her staring out the window. "You've been awfully quiet. Is anything the matter?"

"Just a little sleepy. I really miss my coffee."

He slowed his speed, eyes peeled for black ice, though the streets were mostly clear this morning. "I thought the obstetrician said you could have a cup in the morning if you wanted."

She shook her head and wrinkled her nose. "Maybe I could, but I can't stand the smell just lately. Must be some weird pregnancy thing."

He snorted. "Good thing I can't get pregnant, then. I'd probably go into withdrawal and die."

She barely smiled, her gaze miles away. Probably still worried over Kara, he thought, or wondering whether Dennis Cobb's death would put an end to this nightmare. Or if he'd really meant the things he'd told her, or it had only been this crisis pushing them together.

Nate refrained from bringing up the subject again, telling himself that it hadn't been words that had earlier convinced April of his reluctance to jump into marriage, and it wouldn't be words that would convince her that he was all-in now. She would have to decide whether or not to take a chance that he was a changed man, a man who wanted her and their son more than he'd ever wanted any championship buckle.

But was his sudden interest in her sparked by the challenge of her unattainability? Hell, no, he told himself. The ground had shifted beneath his feet, with his father's injury just the latest event that had driven home the things that really mattered in his life.

"I got an email earlier," she said as the light changed and Nate turned onto the freeway feeder, "concerning Rory's placement."

She explained about the Helping Friends Community, telling him about the wonderful family atmosphere, the residents' chance to work with animals and raise and sell fresh produce at farmers' markets outside of Austin while working to improve social and life skills. It sounded like a perfect place, tailor-made for Rory...

Yet the more she talked about it, the more the bacon and eggs he had just eaten congealed into an indigestible lump. Because he knew what this might mean for him, knew that if this worked out, April had another viable option. A choice that wouldn't include him, except in the marginal role of part-time father. The thought of losing her—the woman he had only reluctantly proposed to—made his blood run cold.

"And I'd be able to help with his transition," April continued, "if I returned to work at the Texas Justice Project—"

"At the same place that almost got your head blown off? There's no way I'm going to let you—"

"*Let* me?" she demanded, the look in her eyes a warning.

"I don't mean—or damn it, maybe I do. Because if anything happened to you, April, to you and the baby—"

"I can't let one man's misguided vendetta, or one exonerated man's crime, cancel out all the good the Texas Justice Project's done. That's like saying Martin Villareal's life's work meant nothing, like saying all those men and the one woman we proved were wrongly convicted didn't matter."

"Of course they matter. All of them, but that doesn't mean *you* have to risk your life after everything we've been through."

"So I'm supposed to, what? Hide out forever in Nowhere, Texas, while other people take their chances?"

"But what about your brother? What about staying home and helping him move past his grief at his own pace the way you said you would? Isn't that important work, too? And what about our—"

"Maybe being stuck in that same house where he watched her die is what's holding Rory back. Did you ever think of that, Nate? Isn't the chance at making new friends and having a real sense of purpose, a reason to get up and get moving every morning, better in the long run?"

"Are you talking about Rory or yourself here?" he asked, remembering what she'd said about missing the job she'd called her passion that night they'd sat drinking together. The night he'd acted on an instinct buried so deep beneath the surface that he was only now just beginning to understand that what he'd done—what they'd created—had been no accident. "Because the way I see it, being a good mother to our child and a good sister ought to be enough for any—"

"Are you kidding me?" she blasted back. "What do you know about being a good mother or a good sister? Enough to say there's one right way for every woman? One way that makes me dependent on your deciding to 'man up and take your medicine,' or however it was you put it."

Nate knew he had said the wrong thing on more than one occasion and was bound to do it again. But when the two of them had made love, he'd been so damned certain he'd forged a connection, a bridge between his thoughtless words and what was in his heart.

"I've told you that I loved you," he said. "Told you in no uncertain terms that I want you and our son both, want us to be a family. But that's not really the issue here, or the reason you turned tail at the altar, is it? The truth is, you haven't yet decided whether *you* think of me as anything more than just a friend. Or whether you just agreed to our marriage in the first place because it was the only real choice that you had."

"So you're telling me that if your doctor suddenly called you out of the blue and told you there's a new procedure that would guarantee you wouldn't end up a paraplegic, you wouldn't risk your life—" She made a face that let him know how much she hated the idea. "—going for another shot at the brass ring?"

He flicked on a turn signal to head into the shopping center parking lot and thought it through for a moment, expecting to feel the familiar pull of the bright lights and the big crowds, the adrenaline coursing through his system and the drinking and carousing he'd used to bring himself down from that high.

He thought, too, of holidays far from friends and family, of makeshift celebrations that somehow left him feeling hollow, no matter how loud and boisterous they got.

"No, I wouldn't," he said, surprised that the idea didn't even tempt him. "For one thing, I've already caught the brass ring. Now I'm going for a gold band." Using his thumb, he touched the ring finger of his left hand. "Besides, my parents were there for me through my recovery, and I mean to be there for my father's, no matter how long it takes. Just like I mean to be there for my son and you—in Rusted Spur, with all of us together. The real question is, what do *you* want, April, if you had the choice between returning to the life you had as a single mother and moving forward with me?"

He pulled up beside her rental car, one of only a dozen or so vehicles in the parking lot at this time of the morning. Putting the pickup into park, he studied April intently, wanted to grab her hand in his, to shake the doubts out of her. To force her to admit that she loved him as much as he'd come to understand that he loved and needed her.

As the engine idled, she stared up into his face, and then reached up to run a hand along his freshly shaven cheek. "I just want time to think about this, Nate. Time to make sure we're getting this thing right."

His memory arced back to the altar, to that moment when she'd turned from him. To the pain of a rejection that had seemed to send his whole life into free fall.

He jerked his head away from her hand, frustration mushrooming into anger.

"Just remember," he said. "Time's a finite resource. And so's my patience, April. You either marry me by Christmas—in front of the hospital chaplain, the justice of the peace, or whoever we can round up—or forget I ever asked."

She speared him with a look that was every bit as angry. "And here I'd thought your last proposal could not get any worse."

Chapter 11

By the time she stalked into the hospital lobby, April was still too irritated about Nate's ultimatum to wait for him to catch up to her. This morning, a group of teenagers stood before the giant tree with their bright eyes and guitar accompanist, their song taunting her with the promise of a holiday filled with peace on earth and good will to men.

For the first time, Nate's dislike of holiday music made sense to her. She felt it, too, a smoldering resentment for the artificial cheer, the twinkling lights and festive decorations only serving as a terrible reminder that four days from now, when Christmas dawned, her mother wouldn't be here. Though Nate's father might well survive his injury, neither he nor his family would ever be the same after the violence visited upon him.

Neither will I, April realized, no matter how she tried to roll back the months to a time she had been happy. Because there was no going back to that life, no pretending that recent events had not forever changed things. Forever changed *her*, whether or not she could let herself admit the way she felt every time Nate touched her or spoke to her—at least when he wasn't letting pride and frustration turn him into an insufferable jack—

Feeling the flutter once more in her belly, she turned around to see him striding toward her, a pained expression on his handsome face. Or was that aggravation? Either way, she was sure to get a lecture for daring to come inside on her own, as if an assassin or even the relentless Kevin Wyatt was going to jump out from behind the *Peace on Earth, Good Will to Men* choir and attack her in broad daylight.

Dreading the thought of a public scene, she reluctantly headed his way. But Nate abruptly stopped, then said, "Just a second. Don't move," before turning to his left and trotting after a man who had been walking past him.

She wrinkled her nose in confusion—and not a little annoyance that he imagined she was taking his orders. April stood watching Nate call out to a man who looked for all the world like an older cowboy, with his chocolate-brown felt hat, a thick silver mustache that drooped down well beyond the corners of his mouth, and a pair of dark-wash jeans ironed with a crease. A second look, however, assured her this was no common cowhand, not with those boots, which looked to be made of something exotic and possibly endangered, the leather jacket and an expensive-looking silver buckle with a lone star worked in gold at its center. Whoever this guy was, he had money, the kind of serious but understated wealth she'd come to recognize from all the Texas Justice Project fund-raising galas she'd attended.

As he shook Nate's hand, she took a closer look, wondering if that was where she knew the man from. But he was already turning and striding toward the elevators by the time Nate had veered in her direction.

"About what I said, April," he started. "I shouldn't have—"

"Who was that?" she interrupted, a glint of metal—gold on silver—flashing through her memory. *That belt buckle*, she realized. She'd seen it before, along with the man who wore it. With the thought, her stomach pitched like a life raft on a storm-tossed sea, and a sick chill rippled along her nerve endings.

"Joe, you mean?"

Ignoring the vibration of her phone in her back pocket, she asked, "Was he there, at the wedding?" Maybe she'd met him that morning when they'd been frantically working to set up the outdoor ceremony after the church flooded or spotted him afterward, in the mayhem that followed the shooting.

"I don't remember seeing him there, but I must be wrong. That's Joe Mueller, my dad's old business partner, the one who—"

"The one who flew your mom out in his private plane, right? I thought you said he'd left Lubbock after flying her here," April said, uneasiness crawling around the bottom of her stomach. Because it hadn't been the wedding where she'd seen him. She was certain of it.

The sick chill returned, bringing with it nausea.

"I thought so, too," Nate said. "That's why I stopped him. He said he'd cleared his calendar to be here for my family. Funny, though, he didn't mention he was on his way when I talked to him earlier."

"I've seen him somewhere else. Recently," she murmured as she fought to place the memory.

"Could have been at my folks' place for a barbecue or even at the hospital last year after I got busted up. He and my dad go way back, from long before he bought Correctional Solutions."

"Correctional Solutions—*he's* the current owner?" she asked, while in her back pocket, her cell phone's vibration ramped up to a loud tone, until she pulled it out to mute it.

She recognized the number. "It's Max again. Could be important," she said and walked farther from the still-singing choir to answer before the PI disconnected.

"Did they make an arrest yet?" she asked him, praying that the Austin PD had locked up the officer who'd surely sent Dennis Cobb to kill her. That the threat to her had already been contained, leaving her free to figure out what she would do next—and free to walk away from Rusted Spur and its painful memories rather than give in to Nate's demand.

At the thought, her mouth filled with the bitter taste of loss. For along with grief and violence, friendship had taken root in her hometown, too, including a relationship that had grown to bear such achingly sweet fruit that her vision shimmered.

"Good morning to you, too," Max said. "But, yeah, that's why I called you. It's all over the news here this morning, and you'll never believe who—"

"Officer Vaughn?" she asked, her heart racing with the fear that maybe she'd been right before about the police covering for their brother of the badge, giving him free rein to exact vengeance on the people he blamed for Ross Allen Chambers' exoneration.

"No, not him. You won't believe this. An eighty-six-year-old man's daughter brought her father to police headquarters. Old guy was a total basket case, crying his eyes out when he confessed he didn't see Villareal running on that dark road until he heard the thud and felt the tires bump over his—"

"Max, please," she said, sickened by the detail. "It can't be. Why wouldn't he have just called 911 then?"

"I'm afraid it's true, April. The old man claims he panicked. He thought his daughters would use the accident as the excuse they'd been looking for to take away his driver's license."

"His *license*?" she cried, her voice slicing through a choral rendition of yet another carol. Those listeners nearest the singers turned disapproving looks her way.

Nate put his arm around her and walked her farther away until they were mostly hidden by the lobby's Christmas tree.

But April shrugged off his touch, too upset to be pacified. "That—that old man could've saved Martin's life, or at least saved him from dying alone. How could anyone with a heart possibly—are the police sure? False confessions happen, especially considering all the news coverage and the public pleas for any witnesses to come forward."

"My source tells me they went to the old man's house, where he still had the car parked inside his garage. He said he hadn't been able to bring himself to drive since, could barely eat or sleep or anything. And the car had—there was body damage. Blood and hair, too, and when they tested it, the detectives knew he was telling the truth."

She closed her eyes, the mention of blood and hair making her feel sicker than ever. "So, for all his spouting off threats, it wasn't Officer Vaughn?"

"He's still on leave over his comments, but Internal Affairs has cleared him of any involvement in Villareal's death."

"Then that means," she said, a prickling awareness shimmering in the air around her, "that could mean that Dennis Cobb really wasn't aiming at—I was never the intended target."

"We don't know that for certain," Max warned. "We have no idea who sent Cobb up there to Rusted Spur."

But April did have an idea, blazing through her brain in a fiery crescendo. Because she remembered now, where she had previously seen Joe Mueller.

Not only where, but with whom, on the day of Martin's funeral.

The stricken look on April's face changed to one of horror before she ended the call. "We—we need to—" she started, her trembling hand cradling her belly as she struggled to catch her breath.

"Slow down, April. I've got you." Nate placed a hand at the small of her back. He'd gleaned enough from her phone call to understand that Martin Villareal's death hadn't been a premeditated murder but a tragic accident instead. "Just take your time and tell me."

"I—I saw him—at the funeral."

"You saw who? The car's driver?"

"Not the old man from Austin. The guy who was just here. Joe Mueller."

"That would make sense, though, wouldn't it? If he was at the conference with the other private prison execs, he might've gone to pay his respects with my father."

April shook her head emphatically, her brown eyes wide. "That's just it, though. He *wasn't* with your father. He was talking to another man. And now that I think about it, it was Dennis Cobb."

"The shooter?" Nate asked. "But I thought you never saw Cobb."

"I *did* see him. I'd just forgotten. But Mueller, I remember, and seeing him again now brings it all back. I remember looking up just as he pointed out someone to Cobb."

Confusion spun through Nate's brain as he tried to make

sense of what April was saying. "*Who* did he point out? You?"

But what sense did it make that Joe Mueller would want April dead? Surely, he couldn't blame her in particular for her boss's criticism of Correctional Solutions' treatment of prisoners. And even if he did, to have their wedding shot up—a wedding hosted by his longtime friend—

"He was pointing toward your father, Nate," April explained, "and the look on Mueller's face—it was pure contempt, not friendship."

"He pointed out my father? To Dennis Cobb?" Nate's heart drummed a counter rhythm to the eerily soft strains of "Silent Night." Because what April was saying made no sense at all to Nate when Joe and his father were the best of friends. Surely, his father's rise to the senate would only serve to bolster Mueller's own business opportunities.

Or would it? Nate thought about something his father had said recently, something about having sold out of the business just in time. At the time, Nate had thought his dad was enjoying his retirement; he now wondered, *Just in time for what*? What was coming down on Correctional Solutions—and the old friend who might have felt he'd been left holding the bag?

April made a visible effort to pull herself together, straightening her spine to tell him, "We have to get upstairs. We have to catch him before he—he could be here to finish what Cobb started."

A surge of pure adrenaline shot up the column of Nate's spine, along with a bone-deep instinct telling him that if he didn't act—and quickly—he'd regret it for the rest of his life. But before he did, he grabbed April's arm and said, "I want you to go to the security office. It's down a few doors in that direction." He pointed out a hallway across the lobby from them. "Get them to send a couple of guys up to room 309 right away."

April opened her mouth, looking as if she might argue, before nodding. "You're going up, then?"

"I am, but don't you dare. Not until I give you the all-clear. You get that?"

She shook her head. "But, Nate—"

"But nothing, April. If we're wrong about this, you can go ahead and call me an overcautious idiot. But Joe Mueller's an avid gun collector—so the chances are he hasn't come unarmed."

She gaped, her face paling, and he ducked to plant a kiss on her forehead. Then he ran toward the elevator, praying he would be in time.

Pounding heart in her throat, April hurried in the direction Nate had pointed out. But what if she was wrong, if her mind had manufactured one of the false memories eyewitnesses were infamous for coming up with?

She thought of the young woman who'd been so convinced she'd seen Ross Allen Chambers leaving the house where a couple had been murdered, an eyewitness whose mistake had cost Chambers his freedom and herself a violent assault. Like her, April could have just set into motion a confrontation that would erupt into heaven only knew what violence.

But the more she thought about that glint of sunlight off Joe Mueller's belt buckle, that hateful look on his face as he pointed out his supposed friend George Wheeler, the more the memory solidified into something terrifyingly real. Mueller *had* been there, at the graveside service, where she'd spotted him using the occasion to point out the man he'd wanted dead to a man willing to do anything—even shoot up a wedding—if the price was right.

Thrusting aside her doubts, she pulled on the door of the office marked Security, only to find it locked. Frustrated, she smacked and pounded at it, shouting, "Open up! Please!" But no one came to answer.

Panic ripping through her, she glanced up and down the hallway. A door swung open, and a slim, fortyish woman in a dark, skirted suit and hip-looking glasses stepped out. "What's all this noise about? Is there some sort of problem I can help you wi—"

"I need security right away, upstairs in Room 309. A man went up to see George Wheeler, a shooting victim, and we think he's—he could be the person responsible." Tears burned in April's eyes, but with Nate and his entire family counting on her, she didn't dare to break down.

The woman stared, jaw dropping, before shaking off her shock. "I understand. I have the number. Let me call and see where our security team is right now and how fast they can get up there. Meanwhile, why don't you dial 911 and have them send a unit to assist?"

April wanted to argue that they needed someone upstairs *now*, not in the twenty minutes it might take police to arrive. But with no better option, she made the call as asked before following the woman into what appeared to be a small administrative office.

Putting down her phone, she looked at April, all seriousness behind the trendy glasses. "Security's dealing with a fender bender in the parking lot, but I told them to head straight up."

A fender bender? April's stomach dropped as she thought about how large the hospital lot was and how long it might take for them to get there.

"Police are on their way, too," April said, hoping she'd done the right thing by saying that Joe Mueller was armed. She thought of how, only yesterday, hospital security had misinterpreted the situation and ended up shocking Nate with a stun gun...

Would police be just as apt to consider a tall, athletic-looking younger man more of a threat than the smaller, older Mueller? What if another mistake was made, this one involving bullets?

"Here, why don't you have a seat?" the woman invited, concern in her brown eyes. "Can I get you some water while you're waiting? You're very pale—"

But April was already backing toward the door again, head shaking. "No. I can't afford to wait—there's too much—he's the father of my baby, and I never even told him that I love him."

"Stop," the woman said, coming out from behind her desk.

Out of the corner of her eye, April saw a well-manicured hand reaching for her, but she moved more quickly, hitting the hall at a dead run.

Chapter 12

Too impatient to wait out a slow elevator, Nate went for the staircase, taking the steps three at a time. Heart slamming against his ribs, he burst out onto the third floor, then dodged a man in green scrubs, only to bump the edge of a wheelchair the orderly had been pushing and send it spinning down the corridor.

"Hey, watch it!" the guy in green yelled. "What's wrong with you, dude?"

"Sorry, ma'am. You okay?" When the chair's passenger nodded, Nate took off again, relieved he hadn't jostled the frail-looking, white-haired woman too badly.

As he rounded a corner, he saw there was no one at the nurses' station, but he did spot his mother pressing the call button for the elevator.

"Where's Joe, Mom?" Nate asked as he hurried toward her, sweating with exertion. "Have you seen him?"

"Oh, morning, Nate. Of course I have," she said, looking a bit rumpled after her night at his dad's bedside but not at all alarmed. "Joe's in with your father. I needed to stretch my legs, so I'm heading downstairs to get some coffee for both of us."

"That's good. You go on," he told her, wanting her as far from harm's way as possible while he confronted the man he believed responsible for his father's condition.

But her eyes narrowed suspiciously, as if somewhere in her head, an internal mother's alarm was bleating out a warning. "What's wrong, Nate? You look—is everything all right with April? You didn't muck things up again, now did you?"

More than likely, he thought, but with no time to get into it, he said, "If you run into her downstairs, she'll explain things."

Seeing the skepticism in his mother's blue eyes, he sweetened the deal, adding, "I think she needs help with baby names. She wants to call him Humphrey, after her late grandpa."

"*Humphrey*? For a baby? My grandchild can't be saddled with a name like that." The moment the elevator dinged and opened, she charged onboard, a woman on a mission.

Nate waited for the doors to close and then raced toward his father's room.

At the threshold, he stopped short, his heart pounding at the sight of Joe Mueller, his back to the door as he leaned over his old friend's bedside, speaking quietly to the sleeping man. The scene looked so calm, so ordinary, that Nate stood staring for a moment, certain that April had been wrong about what she'd seen.

Except the few words that drifted his way made a mockery of Mueller's soothing tone. Angry as they were profane, they lured Nate slowly closer, his movement careful so he wouldn't be heard. And with the prayer that he'd be able to grab Joe's right arm, which appeared to be holding something on a level with his father's chest, before he opened fire.

"Thought you'd sell me out to buy yourself a seat in congress, didn't you, you bastard? Well, I'm here to tell you, I know all about your deal with your buddy-boy, the governor—and everything about your so-called *secret* deposition to those sons of bitches out to ruin me, you backstabbing piece of—"

Behind Nate, footsteps approached, causing Mueller to turn and peer over one shoulder. But it was the sight of Nate, now rushing toward him, that had Mueller's hidden right hand rising.

Teeth gritted, Nate grabbed for his wrist as a woman screamed behind them.

"No!" she cried as Mueller ducked beneath Nate's arm. Speaking to someone outside the room, she shouted, "Call security!"

Nate felt a stinging bite in his thigh, but there was no gunshot, no gun at all in Mueller's hand, only a syringe, its needle gleaming like a fang, a drop of venom at its tip.

"What the hell did you just stick me with?" he demanded, grabbing Mueller by the collar and shaking him until the syringe clattered to the floor. "Tell me now, or I swear, those nice, capped teeth of yours are goin' down— down your throat."

Already, he was breaking out in a cold sweat and feeling dizzy, but Nate told himself it was only the backwash of adrenaline. Surely, whatever this SOB had meant to shoot into his father's IV couldn't work so quickly when injected into muscle.

Kicking the syringe beneath the bed, Mueller fought to free himself from Nate's grip. "Let go, you son of a bitch," he yelled, tearing loose just as Nate sent a haymaker flying toward the man's face. But the punch missed, leaving him so off balance that when the desperate man launched himself at him, Nate fell sideways across a chair, splintering something inside it and sending it—and him—crashing to the floor.

Nate struggled to his feet—fighting weakness that made his body feel weighted down with a lead suit—his vision blurring as Mueller grabbed the tubes connecting his father to the ventilator.

"No, don't! What are you *doing*?" shrieked a voice he recognized as April's.

Get out! Nate tried to shout at her, but he couldn't find the energy to make a sound. Crumpling to his knees, he saw Mueller turn away from his father. Instead of another hypodermic needle, Mueller pulled a pistol from his jacket and took aim at April's chest.

Nate struggled to move, focusing every atom of concentration on the effort to take Mueller down while he was distracted. Instead, Nate's vision began to gray out, the lead suit dragging him down, down, toward the blackness faster than he could break his fall.

The gun in Mueller's hand, the wild look in his eyes, should have been enough to make April run screaming from the room. But the sight of Nate on the floor struggling to rise slipped an icy blade of fear between her ribs, and she couldn't turn away from him. Couldn't budge for fear that he'd been shot just like his father, and this man, this *animal* would finish both the Wheeler men the moment she turned her back.

"Out of the damned way," Mueller said, lowering the gun slightly. "Don't think I won't take out all three generations here and now."

He means to kill my baby, too. With the shock of his

words detonating inside her, in the place of her cold terror, a fiery rage exploded. A rage that had her pulling out the hand she'd slipped inside her bag and raising the pepper spray to shoot it at his face.

He fired at the same time, but Nate had rallied enough to slam himself into Mueller's ankles, knocking him off balance and sending the shot wide. And the room filled with screaming, both hers and Joe Mueller's as he clawed helplessly at his eyes and struggled to kick free from Nate.

An instant later, someone grabbed April from behind, yanking her several steps back.

"Over there, miss. Now," one of the two uniformed security officers ordered, pointed out the nurses' station.

Too stunned to obey, April froze in place as the men raced into the room and disarmed and cuffed the shouting, cursing Mueller. When she saw he couldn't inflict more damage, she raced back inside, kneeling beside Nate and shaking him.

"Wake up!" she cried. "What's wrong with you?"

But his flesh was cool and clammy, and his eyelids barely twitched.

"He needs help," she shouted. "Help! We need a doctor!"

One of the security officers looked over. "Has he been shot?"

"I—I don't know." She scanned him, her heart pounding so hard, she thought it might burst in her chest. She couldn't lose Nate now. "I don't see any blood, but something's very wrong." Glaring at Mueller, she shouted, "What did you do to him?"

But Mueller was rubbing at his red face and running eyes and ranting about George Wheeler destroying his life. Within seconds of the security officers hauling him from the room, a woman and two men in scrubs rushed in, one checking on the still-unconscious George Wheeler while the other two turned their attention to Nate.

As a thin man pulled out a stethoscope, the woman said, "Please, miss, give us room to work."

"But he doesn't know I love him," April protested, still holding Nate's cold hand. "He doesn't know I want to be with him forever."

Say the words, then. Chills blasted through April's body at the sound of her mother's voice in her ear. *Trust your heart, not your fears, and tell him before it's too late.*

With the strength of certainty flowing through her, she clutched Nate's hand for dear life and did exactly as her mother—or maybe her own subconscious—told her.

Though Nate's eyes remained closed, she felt him squeeze her fingers…barely. But it was enough to give her hope he might have heard her—hope she wouldn't have another loss to mourn.

Chapter 13

*What Child is this who, laid to rest
On Mary's lap is sleeping?*

Nate felt moisture against his face, a drop that slowly rolled from his forehead to his temple. His closed eyelids twitched as he felt another strike, and he became aware of the music playing, music that had him clawing his way up to tell whoever was responsible to quit tormenting him with that noise.

As he recognized another sound, he completely forgot about the carol. It was April's voice—he was certain of it—and it was so much sweeter than the music that he was seized with the desire to drink down each syllable, to make a meal of every word.

"Just wake up. Wake up, please," she whispered, the weight of her hand atop his etching itself into awareness. "It's all I've ever wanted, all I'll ask, if only…"

He fought his way to comprehension, fought even harder to crack his eyes open to see her. Everything was a blur, a swirling smear of light and sound and color—until he disentangled her sharp intake of breath and her long-lashed brown eyes, her mascara smudged a little with the tears he'd felt on his skin.

"Nate," she whispered. "Can you hear me?"

Fighting his way past the fatigue threatening to overwhelm him, he managed the barest of nods.

"How are you feeling?" she asked him. "Do you need a nurse? Or what about some water? I have a fresh cup right here."

He shook his head, confusion trumping the dryness of his throat. He was in a small, green-walled room, in a hospital bed with an IV line trailing from his left arm. "What—what happened? Are you—did he hurt you?"

"Mueller? No, thank goodness. And the cavalry arrived just after you saved me."

He breathed a prayer of gratitude, relieved beyond measure that the dreams had been no more than fears stealing up out of the darkness. The nightmare of facing life without her, without the child she carried, was forced back into the shadows as he clawed his way back to the light.

"He's in jail now, just like Kevin," April added, "only Joe Mueller's going to stay locked up forever, if the governor has anything to say about what he's done."

"My—my father? Did he—"

Her smile warmed parts of Nate grown cold as dead flesh. "Alive and talking," she said. "He'll need a couple of months' recovery, but he's going to be fine. And he's going to be our state's next senator, now that you're finally back with us."

"But Mueller—what he said." Nate's mind swirled with

confusion, bits and pieces of the last thing he remembered rising from the muck. "About my father and the—something about a lawsuit and a deposition."

"Mueller got it wrong, it turned out. There was no shady backroom deal, no quid pro quo to fill that vacant seat in congress. All your father ever did was speak his conscience about how drastically Mueller slashed the budget after he bought the company, how he'd warned the man he was endangering both prisoner and guard lives. He won't support locking up kids like convicts, either, especially not for profit."

Nate struggled to make sense of it, figured there would be time later. What really mattered was that April was still here beside him, that the gunshot that was the last thing he remembered hearing hadn't taken her from him forever. "I'm—what happened to me?"

"Mueller's wife's a diabetic. He stole her insulin—enough of it to inject your father with a whopping dose. Only he ended up sticking you instead—and you're younger, bigger—still, if that syringe hadn't been found…" Her eyes glistened, and he raised a hand, then thumbed away the single tear that broke free.

"Don't cry. I'm here, April. And I swear to you, I'm not going anywhere again."

"You don't understand," she said, her voice hoarse with emotion. "It's taken three whole days for you to come around, and the doctors didn't know if—Nate, all our friends have gathered. Brady and Kara—he bought her an engagement ring for an early Christmas present, and the Rayford brothers—Zach's wife had two healthy little girls, but she told him he should be here, just in case. In case you didn't…"

"I've gotta—gotta quit—" Nate coughed, his dry throat

getting the better of him until April raised his bed enough so he could drink from the water she pressed to his cracked lips.

And all the while, the Christmas music continued playing in the background, undoubtedly his mother's doing. Only now, at last, Nate found he didn't mind it so much, focused as he was on the woman here beside him.

Once he'd recovered, he tried again. "I have to stop wrecking everybody's holidays. It's getting to be one hell of a bad habit."

"What if we gave them a happier reason to gather, since tomorrow's Christmas morning?" she asked. "I've been offered the chance to work from home on the computer for the Texas Justice Project, stay in Rusted Spur with you, no matter what Rory decides."

He blinked at her, comprehension dawning. "You aren't talking about that stupid ultimatum, are you? Because I was crazy, pushing you like that. Crazy not to tell you I'd be willing to wait a lifetime, if that's what it takes, to get this right with you. And not just sort of right, but absolutely perfect, April. Because that's what you are to me— the perfect woman, right there all those years waiting for me to quit being the perfect fool about it."

She let him pull her into his arms, her eyes shining. "Three days in a coma, and you—you finally—come up with a real proposal."

"So how about it, Geek Girl? Or are you going to run out on me again?"

"Not a chance, Bull Boy," she said, her lips so close to his that he could taste the promise of their sweetness. "This time you're stuck with me forever."

Unable to bear the space between them, he dragged her a few inches closer. Consumed by the kiss that sealed their union, neither looked up until much later, when they laughed to notice the sprig of mistletoe Nate's mother had hung earlier, with hope, above his bed.

* * * * *

COMING NEXT MONTH FROM

H HARLEQUIN®

ROMANTIC suspense

Available December 1, 2015

#1875 CONARD COUNTY WITNESS
Conard County: The Next Generation
by Rachel Lee
When his late wife's friend Lacy Devane discovers her bosses'
corrupt activity, recovering war veteran Jess McGregor insists
on protecting her from possible retribution. As life-threatening
danger crosses their paths, neither Jess nor Lacy is immune to
peril—and love...

#1876 HIS CHRISTMAS ASSIGNMENT
Bachelor Bodyguards
by Lisa Childs
Ex-cop Candace Baker has never understood other
women's weaknesses for bad boys...until she falls for
reformed criminal-turned-bodyguard Garek Kozminski. But
when Garek takes an undercover assignment to catch a
killer, he's risking not only his life, but also Candace's heart.

#1877 AGENT GEMINI
by Lilith Saintcrow
Amnesiac spy Trinity—aka Agent Three—is fleeing the
government agency that infected her with a virus. But before
she reaches freedom, she must dodge the agent on her tail.
Cal knows he and Trinity are two halves of a whole, and he
intends to make her realize it—if he can catch her.

#1878 RISK IT ALL
by Anna Perrin
When PI Brooke Rogers is targeted by the Russian mafia,
FBI agent Jared Nash rescues her. As the two embark on
a mission to search for Jared's missing brother, they fall
deeper and deeper into love—and into danger.

HRSCNM1115

Shock rippled through him, but not enough to completely
erase his desire for her. Man, she'd probably have nightmares if she saw the stump of his leg. It would inevitably
destroy the mood. Then there was Sara, a woman they
had both loved. He'd feel as if he was cheating on her, and
he suspected Lacy might as well, ridiculous as that might
be. Loyalties evidently didn't go to the grave.

Jess sighed and reached down with his free hand to
rub his stump, as if it could free him from the pain he had
never felt when he was hit, pain that his body evidently
refused to forget.

"Can I help?"

"Nah." Oh yeah, she could. With a few touches she
could probably carry him to a place where nothing but the
two of them could exist. But afterward... Hell, he feared
the guilt that might follow. He could ruin a perfectly good
friendship by getting out of line with this woman.

He and Sara had once had a serious discussion about
the possibility that he might not return from one of his

deployments. Just once, but he remembered telling her to move on with life, that he'd never forgive himself if she buried herself with him.

She'd cocked a brow in that humorous way of hers and asked, "Do you really think I'm the type to do that?"

"Just promise me," he'd said.

It was one of those rare occasions where she'd grown utterly serious. "I'll promise if you'll promise me the same thing."

Of course he'd promised. It had never occurred to him he might be the lone survivor. But that didn't mean he wouldn't feel guilty anyway. Maybe he had some more demons to get past.

He realized that Lacy had unexpectedly dozed off against him. Smiling into the empty night, he removed the mug from her loosening grip and put it on the side table. He guessed she felt safe with him, but he wasn't at all sure that was a good idea.

That note. It hung over him like a sword. What the hell did it mean? He stared into the fire, uneasiness joining the pain that crept along his nerve endings and the desire that wouldn't stop humming quietly.

Don't miss
CONARD COUNTY WITNESS
by New York Times *bestselling author Rachel Lee,*
available December 2015 wherever
Harlequin® Romantic Suspense
books and ebooks are sold.

www.Harlequin.com

THE WORLD IS BETTER WITH

Romance

Harlequin has everything from contemporary, passionate and heartwarming to suspenseful and inspirational stories.

Whatever your mood, we have a romance just for you!

Connect with us to find your next great read, special offers and more.

f /HarlequinBooks

🐦 @HarlequinBooks

www.HarlequinBlog.com

www.Harlequin.com/Newsletters

❤HARLEQUIN®

A *Romance* FOR EVERY MOOD™

www.Harlequin.com